A slice ~~~~~~~~~~~~~~~~~~~~~~~~ hone
through a ~~~~~~~~~~~~~~~~~~~ he go
in? Suddenly Jamaica felt unable to bear
the inky mustiness of the passageway for
another moment. She fell against the door
and staggered into the storage room.

The room was silent. Silent but not empty.
Perry Webb was slumped in a chair.
Jamaica thought he looked far less
disapproving than usual. His rounded chin,
rather than wagging about obscenity or
taxes, rested peacefully on his puffed,
white-shirted chest.

But the angle of his neck was frightening.
His head flopped against his shoulder
almost as if it were about to roll off his
body. And the blood! Blood splashed down
his white shirt front and pooled between his
thick, splayed legs. Blood also stained Mr.
Salinger's brand-new scissors. They bulged
out of the place where Mr. Webb's hard,
miserly heart had once beaten.

Also by Susan Steiner:

MURDER ON HER MIND

LIBRARY: NO MURDER ALOUD

Susan Steiner

FAWCETT GOLD MEDAL • NEW YORK

A Fawcett Gold Medal Book
Published by Ballantine Books
Copyright © 1993 by Susan Steiner

All rights reserved under International and Pan-American Copyright Conventions. Published in the United States by Ballantine Books, a division of Random House, Inc., New York, and simultaneously in Canada by Random House of Canada Limited, Toronto.

Library of Congress Catalog Card Number: 93-90086

ISBN 0-449-14822-X

Manufactured in the United States of America

First Edition: June 1993

Chapter 1

"I'M NOT A whore."

Detective Alexandra Winter stated those four little words to Barron Dysart III as he paced through her tiny living room, navigating an awkward path through flea market antiques and too many potted plants. She spoke with clear precision, but her client paid no attention.

"Alex!" Barron waved his arms and hit a potted orange tree in his enthusiasm. "I know that you're the perfect person to expose my dear, widowed mother to the truth about Luke Bishop—that damn gigolo. I've made reservations for you and Luke at a wonderful hotel in the resort town of Manzanita Springs. You'll adore the honeymoon suite overlooking the valley."

Alex smoothed back her always unruly curls, crossed her legs, and pulled her gray, mid-length skirt down toward her toes. Then she halted her client with a candy-laden platter placed directly in his path. "Please have a kirsch truffle," she offered in her best hostess manner. "They're from the Steenberg House in Belgium. I hear they're your favorites. And by the way," she repeated politely, "I am not a whore."

Barron accepted a truffle with a manicured hand and a manicured smile. "Alex," he cajoled. "Just seduce Luke away from Mother and into the honeymoon suite where there are hot tubs, vibrating beds. . . ."

Obviously politeness had failed, so Alex tried shouting.

1

"I don't care if there are mirrored ceilings, X-rated movies, or leather whips, Mr. Dysart. *I am* not *your damn whore!*"

"Of course not! Who suggested such a thing?" Barron Dysart III spun to face her. He was a tall, rugged man who'd spent a good part of his time working out and turning truffles into the muscles that filled out his Italian sport coat. With fierce energy he scowled around Alex's apartment, as though ready to do battle with any villain who would dare to sully her reputation.

Since he and Alex were alone, there was only Ms. Watson to take the brunt of Barron's anger. The black cat stared back, blinked her one, good, golden eye, then made a brave retreat under the sofa. Her plumed tail was a black flag of surrender.

"I'd never let anyone insult you," Barron declared to Alex.

Alex grabbed a truffle, then put it down remembering her diet. She always stuffed herself when she was upset, and Barron was infuriating. "*You're* the one who insulted me! I was hired to investigate. Not fornicate."

Barron's dark face reddened. "You're misjudging the situation."

"You've been telling me in ten different ways that you want me to have sex with Luke Bishop. Then you plan to have your mother discover us in the act so she'll leave him. Do you think the concept is beyond my mental grasp?"

"I'm trying to save Mother from a bastard who's less than half her age!"

"By putting *me* in the bastard's bed!"

Client and detective glared at each other.

Barron sighed and lowered himself precariously into Alex's ancient wicker rocking chair. "Let me explain," he said more calmly. "We both know that my mother makes a good living selling paintings created by movie stars."

"Pamela Dysart has made a great success of her Celebrity Art Gallery. You should be proud of her."

"She may be a success, but believe me, Mother can't afford Luke Bishop. He's stealing her money, and our future, and she's too much in love to realize it! Look, Alex, the Dysart estate and resort is part of my father's legacy. It's my sister's and mine by right, and Mother has always called the estate home. Right now, the property is heavily mortgaged to a man named Perry Webb, who'd love to foreclose. Our home is in danger, but instead of paying debts, Mother bought Luke a nice little yacht to go with the fishing tackle she gave him last summer! Now that greedy gigolo wants Mother to rent an Italian villa so he can research his new novel. Alex, we're going to lose everything!"

Barron leaned forward in an intimate manner. He seemed about to pat Alex on the knee, but at the last moment he moved his hand to the vicinity of her arm and gave her a gentle tap. "A gorgeous girl like you could get Luke to cooperate in photos that would kill Mother's infatuation. Your employer has told me about the sensual work you're capable of. My dear, money is no object."

Alex suddenly found herself chewing a mouthful of truffles. She hefted up her briefcase then slammed it down so hard that the coffee table wobbled dangerously on its patched Queen Anne legs. Candies tumbled from their silver dish.

"So that's where you got this idea. From my own boss—that imbecile!" Alex leapt to her feet and snatched the thick file out of the briefcase. Her red hair flamed out around her. Her green eyes were slitted in fury. "I'll bet George gave me a hell of a resumé! You must have thought you'd bought your very own nymphomaniac!" The heavy file thumped, none to gently, on a section of Barron's lap that made him gasp in pain.

3

"Read my report before you check me into your damn honeymoon suite! I've tailed Luke Bishop constantly for three weeks. I've practically lived in the Santa Linda Library where he writes his books and teaches. I didn't have to sleep with him to get the goods on him!"

She sank heavily into the old couch, eliciting a screech of protest from Ms. Watson, who crawled out from under the sagging springs. Alex barely noticed. Her temper had ended in exhaustion—the kind of weariness that attacks a person who suddenly becomes aware of all the work it will take to change her entire life.

Normally, Alex loved her work with Abromowitz and Stewart—the agency with a heart. But lately, the job was becoming impossible. Alex thought she'd made it crystal clear that she wanted no bimbo jobs. But George Stewart just didn't get it. Sometimes it seemed that her big, tough boss had a skull even thicker than his biceps.

She remembered their last argument. "George, I didn't become a detective to swish through some guy's room without my negligee," she'd told him.

"Since Sam left for Seattle business has been slow." George had taken on his mournful look—a look he used when he wanted to cut Alex's expense account. "Sweetheart, I know you want to go big time with larceny, or maybe a little murder. So why don't you and I bring in some action? A famous magazine wants to do an article on you ... take a few photos. We'll get great publicity, and you can have your pick of the new assignments!"

"That sounds good. What does Sam think of the idea?" Alex had great respect for Sam Abromowitz, the senior partner of the agency.

George placed his gigantic hand over his pacemaker. "I'm sure Sam will love my plan. Especially when he sees how tastefully *Playboy* can handle this." Picking up the

4

magazine, Geroge had waved it proudly. Like a Boy Scout with the flag.

"Playboy!" Alex snatched the magazine. "No! No bimbo jobs!"

"Woman, you are so *uptight*! Can't you take a compliment? The photographer just loves tall redheads. Be rational for once, Alex. This is a great opportunity. You could make centerfold!" George winced as the magazine hit his cauliflower nose. He pulled out a handkerchief to stop the bleeding. "Okay! No more bimbo jobs. Jesus, you don't have to get so pissed off!"

Now, sitting in her living room, remembering the scene with George, Alex realized that she was indeed "pissed off." She'd solved important cases, and she'd made enough money at the agency to help pay for Georgey's Porschey. Yet, he still believed that her only assets were in her jeans.

Shocked sounds from Barron interrupted Alex's brooding. "But Stacy's only seventeen!" Barron dropped Alex's report as if it burned.

"Your sister is nineteen." Alex corrected sullenly.

"You expect me to believe that Stacy is . . . is sleeping with Luke, too?"

Alex put her anger aside and regarded the man with sincere concern. "You understand now why I didn't leave the report with the agency, and why I wanted to see you privately. I didn't want to upset your family."

"Upset us? With this bunch of crap? It says that Stacy and Luke have sex in the library. Come on, Alex, the *library*?"

"Listen, they don't exactly do it on the magazine table. Luke has a book contract. He qualifies as a writer-in-residence, which allows him to rent a study in a tower room of the library. Whenever your mother is away, your sister Stacy seems to get an instant passion for library books, but I've discovered that her real passion is Luke.

5

Since it's photos you want, our agency's photographer could possibly climb the fire escape and get shots of the pair from the balcony outside the studio window." Alex hesitated at Barron's stricken look. She could almost sympathize with her handsome, well-heeled heel of a client. He was such a snob. How could he share his precious "Dysart legacy" with a mother and a sister who were both in bed with the same rogue?

"Would you like a drink?" Alex offered. These days she avoided alcohol, but this poor guy surely needed comfort stronger than truffles.

"The library!" Barron began to laugh. His wide shoulders shook. He laughed so hard that Ms. Watson (now seated at a safe distance in the potted begonias) stopped washing her face to stare at him. "That's Mom's pet charity. In fact that library building was built by my great-grandfather and donated to the county by my father! I'm almost sorry for Bishop. Just wait till my mother, Pamela Dysart, president of Friends of the Santa Linda Library, finds out that Luke Bishop is screwing her daughter in there." Barron's voice became hopeful, "Why, Mom might even castrate him!" He jumped to his feet clasping her hand. "You're a miracle!" he cried. "There'll be a bonus, and *you* will take the photos."

"Whoa, I'm no photographer!" Alex protested.

Barron ignored her. "On Monday, Mother flies to France to sell a Charlie Chaplin portrait painted by Picasso. So, Luke and my sister will probably be in his study where you'll be able to videotape them."

"You'd do better to hire a professional from the agency."

"Tsk, think of Stacy," Barron clucked. "She's young and vulnerable. I can *trust* you to be discreet." He smiled and took Alex's hand. He seemed to think the matter was settled. "I truly admire you, my dear."

Alex was astounded when her client raised her hand

6

gently to his lips. Before saying good-bye, the newly charming Barron even knelt to gingerly pet Ms. Watson.

When he was gone, the detective bent to retrieve candy from the carpet, where black velvet paws were batting truffles like catnip mice. "Imagine that, Watson. I'm a 'miracle'! Maybe George will shape up when he hears that the rich Mr. Dysart will deal only with me!"

Ms. Watson merely stuck out her tongue before she turned to wash her ebony back, and Alex sighed. Hopes that George would change were slim. And true, she was not a whore. But was it really so much better to be a paid pervert?

"Watson, I'm a lonely divorcée. The only man coming around my place is the meter reader. I've sunk into debt without much hope that I'll rise again. Worst of all, if my career has a future, it isn't the kind that I can tell my mother about—assuming I could even get back on speaking terms with her. I should go out on my own, but these are hard times. I've seen two investigative agencies fold in the past three months. I just may have to find a new profession to keep you in kitty litter."

Ms. Watson meowed and rolled her one, good eye. The black cat had heard it all before.

"But even though the Dysart case might be my last investigation, and even though it *is* sleazy, at least I've enjoyed my stakeouts at the Santa Linda Library." Alex's voice softened. "It's a lovely old building surrounded by beautiful gardens, and it's so grand that people call it the Castle."

Alex pulled another truffle from between Watson's paws. "Why don't you come with me to see the Castle while I finish the Dysart case? It may be sleazy, but at least it isn't dangerous. Hey, nobody's likely to be murdered in the public library!"

Chapter 2

PALE AND SHINING, the Castle soared out of the dull, suburban hills, like Venus rising from her shallow shell. Alex had heard that in spring thousands of unfolding petals twined round its walls to overhang the walkways. Golden, crimson, and even rare rainbow blossoms shimmered through the bright heat of summer and perfumed the early days of fall. But Alex came to the Castle in winter, one of the worst winters the county of Santa Linda had ever known. As she drove up the winding, misted road, dreams of summer contrasted with shriveled vines and leafless trees.

While Alex parked the van, Ms. Watson stared out the window, twitching her plumed tail. Alex followed the one-eyed, golden gaze. "I told you this was some classy joint. Look, Watson, no graffiti on the trees."

Chubby palms squatted around the edge of the parking lot. Beyond, inside a ring of evergreen shrubs, lay a wide, freshly mowed meadow, lush and oddly inviting under the hard winter sky. Stone steps rose from the lawn to a rounded, eccentric building, a stuccoed fantasy of towers and turrets, all crowned with a massive terra-cotta roof. Its entrance was guarded by stone lions with chipped wings.

"That's the Castle, Watson. It was built in the late twenties by the Dysart family, and it was their family home until they donated it to Santa Linda County Library, some forty years later. Come on, we'll put on your harness and you can take a look."

Up close it was obvious that the Santa Linda Library was in need of paint and repair. It had the worn look of a private residence suffering under heavy public use. Yet despite its deterioration and its architectural excesses, the building retained a shining grandeur and a soothing aura of timelessness.

"I'm glad we came a day early, Watson. We can do some sight-seeing before I check into the motel. You know this place has a wonderful history. Long before Barron's mother, Pamela Dysart, started selling 'celebrity art' at her gallery, the famous landscaper and horticulturist Kate Selby worked for the Dysart family developing 'celebrity flowers.' Selby lived on the Castle's estate grounds, and she named her flowers for the Hollywood stars who visited here. She developed beautiful Rainbow Irises for Judy Garland, and creamy blond roses that are named for Marilyn Monroe."

Taking their time, the odd little pair strolled past the Castle down a path of herringbone brick. The path eventually widened into gravel and sloped from the library grounds toward trees and parks. Here, the Santa Linda River slit a curve of silver through green hills. Farther north, visible through gaps in the thick clouds, rose Manzanita Mountain, dark with evergreen forests and mantled with gleaming snow.

Alex shivered. A heavy mist was closing in through the bare, drooping branches of willow trees, and the cutting edge of a late January wind had penetrated her heavy sweater. Reluctantly, she turned back toward the parking lot. She was already under the spell of the Castle. Even in bitter weather it was enchanting.

"In a few months, Kate Selby's famous Rainbow Irises will pop up right beside this arbor, Watson." Alex rever-

9

ently stomped the ground. "And in summer, petals from 'Marilyn's Rose' will form drifts like fragrant snow."

Watson had no patience with Alex's love for interesting flora. The lead of her harness was yanked from Alex's fingers as Watson chased after the local fauna, an indignant squirrel, who shrieked at the cat from the safety of a high oak branch. Watson pricked up her ears and started climbing.

"Come down," Alex ordered. "Barron Dysart's sleazy case is nearly over so don't make trouble now!"

"Do you always have conversations with your *cat*?" Sarcasm emanated from a figure in the swirling mist. Immersed in the Castle's gothic surroundings, Alex glanced up to see a strong, dark face and thought for one startled moment that she'd conjured up an apparition—a handsome Heathcliff with harsh features and eyes as gray as the fog. Then the mist cleared a bit, and she realized that the man was flesh and blood. She'd never heard of ghosts wearing designer jogging outfits complete with ankle weights.

Alex was impatient with herself. During the entire time that she'd tailed Luke Bishop, she'd remained anonymous. She'd even used disguises to avoid being recognized. It was Sam's staunch belief that good cover kept a detective safe, and Alex had never doubted him. But now, at the very end of the Dysart case and perhaps the end of her career, Alex had grown careless. She worried how much the jogger had overheard about "Barron Dysart's sleazy case," and she tried to distract him with nonsense.

"I always talk to my cat," she gushed. "People don't realize how wise felines are. They're masters at the art of communication. My cat is a *marvelous* listener, and so sensitive. . . ." Alex babbled on as if she had a brain full of kibble.

Meanwhile the squirrel was leaping to farther branches,

10

and Watson dashed after it. Alex called out, "Here kitty, kitty," But Ms. Watson didn't look back.

"I can see," Heathcliff said, "how *marvelously* your cat listens."

Alex rushed after Watson, glad to leave the sarcastic jogger behind. She chased the cat into a small clearing, only to slam to a horrified stop. She'd nearly tripped over a body.

A young man lay motionless, thin arms outstretched, palms toward the sky. His stubbled face, partially covered by greasy, shoulder length hair was bloodless and slack-jawed. It took a second look before Alex realized the man wasn't dead, just dead drunk. Sweet, alcoholic fumes rose from him, thick as smoke.

The irritating Heathcliff jogged up behind Alex. "Don't worry," he kicked aside a bottle of E&J. "This kid is no corpse."

No, the young man wasn't a corpse, but he *was* a bit of a mystery. Alcohol couldn't obliterate his strong smell of sweat. His clothes were Ivy League, but this button-down shirt had buttons missing, and his stained slacks seemed lived in rather than worn. Out of the corner of her eye, the detective had seen his tweed jacket lying some yards away, and she'd also seen a surprisingly large wad of bills spilling carelessly from his jacket pocket to the ground. Alex observed the young drunk with sympathy. She had experienced some bad benders herself after her husband Charlie had left her for one of his many thousands of girlfriends.

Obviously, the first thing she had to do was get rid of the jogger before Heathcliff saw all that money and decided to take some. She latched on to his arm: "It's fate that my cat found this poor man. She'll help him to drink buttermilk instead of brandy. Cats are experts at soothing troubled souls. Using her *amazing* advice and her calming powers, you and I will save this sad drunk!"

11

The gray eyes stared at her. "Now, just relax," the jogger ordered with the anxiety of someone who knows he is dealing with a lunatic. "I'll get help." He would have rushed off immediately, but he tripped over Watson, who'd abandoned squirrel hunting to rub affectionately against his ankles. She stared into his frigid gaze and began to purr. She even meowed lovingly when Heathcliff swore and jogged off into the fog.

"Ms. Watson, you must be the only female around who has worse taste in men than I do," Alex told her in disgust. "Someday I'll have to raise your feminine, feline consciousness. For now, behave yourself." Alex struggled to lift the drunk up, push his arms into his coat, and button his chunk of bills into an inside pocket she'd found in his lined jacket. At least this would make it less likely that he'd be robbed. The money totaled well over six hundred dollars, and the poor kid sure looked like he needed it. "Good luck," Alex whispered to the oblivious young man. "I can see Heathcliff bringing help, so it's time for me to get out of here."

The drunk replied with a deafening snore—a fog horn at close range. Alex had to pry Ms. Watson's startled claws from her shoulders before she hauled the cat back to the van.

The next afternoon, Alex climbed the Castle's fire escape clad in an oversize coat, a sausage curl wig, and a crocheted hat of dung brown and bile green. Near the rooftop, she paused to speak into a pocket-size tape recorder. "Monday, January fifth. One-ten P.M. I'm at Fifty-two Castle Drive, on the balcony of the Santa Linda Library. I'm observing Luke Bishop's writing studio, but rain may terminate this surveillance."

Switching off the tape, Alex leaned against a rough stucco wall to protect herself against the biting wind while she waited for the lovers to arrive. Kneeling on a curve of concrete that formed one of the balconies of the Castle tower, Alex might have surveyed a view of the river winding a rushing course past the dollhouses of the green Santa Linda valley. But when Alex looked down, she was preoccupied with how far away the ground was.

If looking down was unpleasant, staring up at the black skies was no better. "I hope Luke and Stacy get here and do their thing before it rains," Alex muttered. "Nothing is worse than water in your wig."

Carefully she eased Barron's expensive video camera out of its heavy, steel case and focused its high-powered zoom lens. She hadn't bothered to learn about the audio features, because the couple would likely keep their ecstatic cries to a mimimum. Loud sounds, as Alex had learned in her time at the library, traveled directly from tower rooms through exposed heating ducts to the main floor.

She pointed the camera at the studio window where, several minutes later, a light came on through the window, illuminating an all-white room that contrasted well with blazing art work and the colorful bindings of books. Apparently, the tasteful Pamela Dysart had approved the decor. Alex doubted she'd approve of much else in that studio.

Pam's daughter, Stacy Dysart, twirled before the bookcase. She was already nearly nude. Her waist-length hair was dyed to an electric blue-black, exaggerating her pale coloring and the sensuality of a slender, high-breasted body that was rapidly becoming even more exposed as Stacy performed a strip tease for her lover.

Fortunately, the pair ignored an arched, curtainless window that was too high to be easily viewed from outdoors. After all, who would be crouched on this freezing balcony, knees scraping on rough cement, just so she could videotape an amateur strip tease? Only an absolute moron, Alex decided.

13

Unaware of any nearby morons, Luke Bishop gave a slow, languorous stretch. His thick, sunny hair and large brown eyes made him look like a slightly bored lion. Luke was big, with muscled thighs, broad shoulders, and an all-over tan. Alex deduced this easily because he wore only mesh bikini briefs. Despite the chilly wind, the detective's face burned.

Stacy whirled closer to her seemingly indifferent lover. Suddenly Luke pulled her to him and put a rough hand on her breast. Stacy buckled into his arms, and they kissed until the man's face softened into a tender expression.

"That's right, Alex," the detective lectured herself as she adjusted the lens. "Concentrate on Luke's pretty face, which ain't what you're being paid for. Yep, think about his face because ... uh oh ... there goes his underwear." Light and thunder crashed around the library roof. Alex mentally swore at the weather as she inched forward toward the window to film this-all important moment. Luke had tumbled Stacy to the billowy, white couch.

Alex held the camera steady. Through the zoom lens she could see the thin film of perspiration forming on the girl's ecstatic face and the tiny beads of blood from the love bites on her upper lip. She could even film the dark red patterns Stacy's nails made on Luke's tanned, muscled back. Alex shivered inside her heavy coat. She found herself suffering from a hollow chill that had little to do with the weather and everything to do with her own loneliness.

She filmed the hard-working couple until, with an unexpected clatter, hail showered in all directions. Alex quickly covered the lens, packed the camera, and strapped the case's thick band of leather to her side. She hurried down the slick, metal fire escape while wind screamed and frozen water shot from the skies. Her boot immediately skidded on the treacherous steps, and Alex almost lost her footing.

14

After that, she forced herself to slow down despite the heavy pelting of the storm.

She'd almost reached the first story when the curlicued iron railing, decorative but none too strong, wobbled under her chilled and stiffened fingers. Tilting with the banister, Alex slipped and began sliding, fast. Fighting panic, she twisted and grasped at the step above her, but she caught only a fistful of freezing air. Banging and scraping her knee on the sharp metal edge of the steps, she hurtled toward the ice-speckled ground.

The fire escape ended inconviently near a thorny shrub, and the detective's posterior grazed a rose bush before it hit earth with a solid thump. A chunk of hail bounced off the bridge of her nose. "Damn!" Alex muttered with feeling.

Scrambling to her feet, she ran through a muddy picnic area, then around a redwood deck that was roped off because of rotten planking. She finally stopped under the shelter of an awning in the back of the Castle, rubbed her sore knee, adjusted her hat and wig (both of which were sliding over her left eye), then leaned her back against a Dumpster to catch her breath. A stinging pain propelled her quickly away from the trash bin, and she reached up under her coat and skirt to pull a thorn out of her panties. "Lord, there must be a better way to earn a living!"

Alex's equipment wasn't in much better shape than she was. Her watch was cracked and frozen at one thirty-six. And though Barron's precious camera seemed fine, the tape recorder had a disastrous looking crack in its plastic housing. "Maybe I should grow Marilyn's Roses for a living instead of falling on them," she muttered in disgust. Then somewhat startled, she realized that wasn't a bad idea. Could she sell "celebrity flowers"? There was certainly a world of information about them in this very library. The library . . . what in the world was going on in there? Alex craned her neck in the direction of the high window.

Even above the commotion of the hail, she could hear sobs and cries for help. Wincing at the pangs in her knee, and using a handle for leverage, she swung herself up to the strong steel top of the trash bin. Once again, she found herself peering into a lighted room of the Castle.

Located below the main floor of the building, the Children's Room was a large ground-floor space with high, arched windows on the north and east sides of the Castle, where the land sloped far enough from the foundation of the building to let in the light. Illuminated by harsh fluorescent bulbs, the Children's Room had a low ceiling whose old acoustical tiles sagged in too many places. Yet this was one of Santa Linda's most cheerful public rooms. Painted clouds camouflaged the ugly ceiling. Bright murals danced across the walls. Painted pigs with houndstooth caps and magnifying glasses, picnicking teddy bears, and crowned elephants in royal robes all smiled down on a fat candy-striped circus tent where the children sat during story hour.

Just now, most young Santa Lindans were in school, and the room was nearly empty. But Alex could see two children's faces peering out of the circus tent. Like the children, Alex's mouth made a little "O" of surprise and horror at the sight of a woman lying sprawled on the floor in a slowly expanding pool of blood. Nearby, two men fought in unlikely but deadly violence. The older man thrashed his opponent with fists and feet—like some overwound mechanical toy. The other man was the drunk that Alex had discovered in the clearing. Tears streamed down his grubby face even as he fought. He flailed a pair of large scissors that left terrible wounds whenever they connected with flesh.

Alex hurriedly unstrapped the camera. Haste made her awkward, and she lost precious seconds before she had it free. She had one brief moment of regret for Mr. Dysart's fancy camera before slinging it by its leather strap, and

16

swinging the camera, case and all, like a lasso, above her head. With all her force she crashed it into the window, smashing the glass, then smashing it again. At last she jumped through the newly created entry, ripping her coat, and dislodging her hat and wig. She prayed all the while that she was in time to stop a murder.

Chapter 3

AT EIGHT MINUTES past one on Media Day (about the time that Alex was climbing the Castle fire escape to spy on Luke and Stacy), Chief Librarian Mark Salinger was cutting out articles that praised the Santa Linda Library. His hands worked quickly and steadily, a fact that rather astounded him considering the stress he was under. The Castle was under siege and the burden of its defense seemed to have fallen on Mark Salinger's not so broad shoulders.

Perry Webb and his organization, Citizens Against Higher Taxes, were determined to eliminate public funding for the library. CAHT hoped to replace the Castle with a "privatized" book rental, and they were taking their case to the voters with Measure B. Today, Mark was fighting back against Webb, CAHT, and their Measure B with a tactic he'd never tried before. He'd invited a television crew from KPXX to come and film the Castle. Mark planned to use the library's "Media Day" to talk about the Castle's book collections, its flowering park grounds, and its value to the community. He was pushing hard to be ready for the library's first media event. Now if things would just go smoothly for the next couple of hours . . .

"This library is making dirty books available to children!" It was Lucy Bigelow, secretary of CAHT and friend of Perry Webb. She was waving a book in front of the chief librarian's prominent nose.

Startled, Salinger dropped his silver-plated European cutting shears on the library reference desk. He ran a distracted hand through his head of thinning hair and adjusted his slipping glasses. "We select our children's books very carefully," he said.

Ms. Bigelow lifted her pointed chin. She was a wispy, reed-thin woman with the delicacy of a jackhammer. "Careful? Your carelessness is a disgrace!"

"I'll be happy to read the book in question," Mark lied. He was never happy to deal with Lucy Bigelow. What was it this time? She'd objected to the "glorification of occultism" in a book explaining mysticism. She'd given the staff grief over "too much sex" in a teenage novel. She'd even recruited pickets to protest the pro-choice editorials in *Ms.* magazine.

Reluctantly, Mark Salinger took up his schedule book. Then he gave a silent, but heartfelt protest to God, fate and coincidence (Mark always covered all the bases) for sending Lucy Bigelow to the Santa Linda Library on Media Day.

"I can read the novel tomorrow after we're closed," he told her. "Then we can meet on Monday, at three o'clock."

Bigelow scowled. "By Monday, a child's mind might be polluted. I want immediate action!"

Mark wasn't exactly surprised. Thoughtful, planned action had never been Lucy's strong point.

"Mr. Salinger, this crisis can't wait," Lucy persisted. "What are you going to do?"

Mark launched into a variation of a speech he'd made hundreds of times in the past. "Lucy, if Measure B passes, there'll be no public funding for our library. We'll have to sell off the library's assets, including our famous collection of books, photos, and original documents on California history. We'll be forced to rent books instead of lend them and to charge for all services in order to survive—*if* we survive.

19

That's why I've asked Cindy Fayne of KPXX to come here today to televise a tour of the library. I'll agree to look over this book tonight, but today I'm concentrating on the Castle. I want the public to appreciate the fact that the Castle deserves to be preserved as one of the best libraries in the state!"

"Mr. Salinger, you know very well that Santa Linda County *is* heading toward financial ruin! Nobody wants to pay more taxes!" Lucy slammed her small fist down on Salinger's desk for emphasis. "You'll just have to stop leeching off the taxpayers and start being creative. We already rent out rooms in the Castle tower to writers. Why not raise money by renting out part of the second floor . . . say for aerobics?"

Lucy's idea left Mark temporarily speechless. He was used to fielding complaints about the library being too noisy. "You can practically hear heavy breathing through our outdated old heating system," his patrons told him. Salinger tried to imagine the bedlam of people doing jumping jacks above the reference room.

But Lucy appeared satisfied that she'd solved the library's financial woes, and she returned to her original grievance. "I'm glad you mentioned television! I should talk about this despicable book on television. Perry Webb was shocked when he discovered this book in the children's library! It's a good thing Perry told me about it!" To emphasize her point, she thrust the novel at Mark—a hardbound missile, aimed at eyeball level.

The librarian retreated behind the large reference desk. Damn that Perry Webb! Now he understood why Lucy Bigelow had showed up at such an inopportune moment. That cagey realtor had rushed Lucy "Book-Banning" Bigelow to the Castle on Media Day so she could do her act in front of the cameras. Mark's easy-going temper was beginning to feel strained.

Managing the Castle had never been easy. Mark had grappled with budget cuts, fought for grants, and recruited volunteers. But Perry Webb was something different, a dedicated enemy. Old Webb pounced on every problem in the library. He even invented some in order to prove that Mark mismanaged the taxpayers' money. And Webb's tactics were effective. Suddenly, a crotchety real estate tycoon who had never even managed to win a place on the board of supervisors was tasting political success with his Measure B. And suddenly, the future of the Castle was very much in doubt.

Even the weather wasn't helping. Through the heavy glass doors of the front entrance, Mark could see the wind tearing at the tree limbs. Flooding into the entrance were those ace weather predictors, a group of regulars who spent their day on the street and flocked to the library in storms. Mark recognized Scott Wilson who came in mumbling words to no one but himself. Wilson was followed by a young woman in a purple cloak, who supported another, older lady with a tattered dress and a glowing bruise under one eye. Mark didn't know the older woman's name, but he'd once caught the poor soul urinating in a wastebasket. Would she become the focus of the cameras on Media Day? Mark felt a twinge in his stomach.

"Now let's talk about important things, Salinger, like pornography!" Lucy waved her book again.

Mark grasped the book and looked it over. "Lucy, this is Luke Bishop's new novel. It's written for adults! Someone must have placed it in the Children's Room by mistake." *Perry Webb, no doubt.*

Mark looked around him. Despite the best efforts of its antiquated lighting system, the library grew darker as the weather worsened. In the shadows, the Castle's scuffed floors and shabby walls receded before the architectural grandeur of the old building. High-beamed ceilings soared up to arched, leaded transoms, where stained-glass swallows swooped against glittering glass fields and trees.

"Salinger," the librarian lectured himself, "it's time for this beautiful, if crumbling, old Castle to put her best pillars forward as a serene haven of learning and opportunity. You may be a balding, cowardly intellectual, but if you fail to help people connect with their Castle on Media Day, the demise of this great library is a certainty."

With a dramatic motion, Mark scooped up the articles he'd cut from newspapers and magazines. His long arm cleared a space on his desk, and he said with authority: "Put that novel next to my scissors, and I'll make sure it gets where it belongs." He paused a moment then added, "And Lucy, be wary of censorship. Curiosity is precious, and I've come to agree with Albert Einstein: 'What curiosity, that delicate little plant, needs more than anything is freedom.' " Flashing a farewell smile that felt as cracked as the Castle's aging plaster walls, Mark rushed away.

Some twenty-five minutes later, as streaks of lightening flared behind the Castle's windows, alchemizing the glass to gold, Chief Librarian Mark Salinger was furiously impaling magazine clippings to the cork board backing of the display cases. He wanted these articles that praised the Castle to be on exhibit, along with the Castle's plaques and awards, for the benefit of the television cameras.

At the same time, Mark was reconsidering his list of important facts for Media Day. Should he mention that the national library of the United States was open fewer hours than the national library of the former USSR? Nope. No one was scared of Russians anymore. Better to mention that the United States had a literacy rate of less than fifty percent while Japan had a literacy rate of one hundred percent. Then again, perhaps it was time to abandon facts and try show business. Why not bring in a coffin, lie down inside it, and moan about the death of America's free libraries? That might move the plight of the Castle on to prime time.

Preoccupied, Mark failed to notice Jamaica Polonsky running through the wide front aisle. Permed curls bouncing, the library page rushed up to Mark, making good time in high topped basketball shoes of neon pink. "Mr. Salinger! Mr. Salinger!" Jamaica called.

She was interrupted by a clatter from outside. The clatter became an overwhelming storm of sound, and the startled Mr. Salinger stabbed himself with a push pin. "Oh, hail!" he exclaimed in despair.

Jamaica's heavy, false eyelashes blinked rapidly, and her freckled cheeks turned as red as her oversize sweater dress. "Don't swear at me, Mr. Salinger."

"I didn't say 'hell', Jamaica, I said 'hail.' Hear that? It's the sound of ice striking the Castle. It hasn't hailed here since 1958, according to the *Farmer's Almanac*, so I hope this old roof holds up and—"

"Mr. Salinger," the library page interrupted, "the mumbler is back!"

Jamaica wailed this news in tragic tones, but Mark wasn't alarmed. In his experience, the teenager waxed dramatic about everything from grad night to glow-in-the-dark eyeliner.

"Take it easy, Jamaica. The mumbler, er, I mean Scott, is troubled, but he means no harm." Mark knew Scott Wilson by name, but even he thought of the young man as "the mumbler." This was a title the staff always used, even though "babbler" might have been more appropriate.

The mumbler, a young man in his twenties, talked to himself—or to visions inhabiting the air around him—in an often unintelligible monotone peppered with eclectic quotations from the Bible, classic literary works, or popular songs. Despite his mental instability, Scott was an artistically talented, peaceful soul, though lately his problems had been worsened by too much alcohol.

"But Mr. Salinger you don't understand! The mumbler is confused worse than ever. Instead of going to his usual place near the window, he's wandered into the Children's Room. He's sitting *under* Ms. Latham's desk." Jamaica raised her voice to be heard above a sudden shower of hail. "And you know how he mutters and grumbles. Mr. Salinger, what are we going to do?"

"Don't worry, Jamaica. As soon as I saw that the weather was bad, I made plans to show videos in the multipurpose room. Go to the front desk and have Ms. Ghiringhelli announce that our program will start in ten minutes. We'll run comedies and the cartoons that our special patrons enjoy."

"You can't use the multipurpose room for movies. Perry Webb reserved it for our meeting of Citizens Against High Taxes!" Lucy Bigelow had marched up behind Mark, her delicate jaw squared with determination. "And I've decided that Mr. Luke Bishop's dirty book shouldn't even be allowed in the adult section. I don't care what that Albert Feinstein says."

"Perry Webb is not yet king of our Castle." Mark replied sharply. "Movies are standard procedure on stormy days, and Webb will simply have to hold his campaign for Measure B elsewhere. It's odd, isn't it Lucy, that though he wants to close our library, Webb seems to need the Castle as much as the rest of the community?"

"Mr. Salinger," Jamaica stomped a foot in frustration, "What about the mumbler? Ms. Latham is alone with him, and she's frightened."

Mark paused as the second half of Jamaica's sentence sunk in. "You say that Ms. Latham is frightened?"

Jamaica nodded vigorously.

It was so unusual for Zoe Latham, the children's librarian, to be intimidated that Mark took off without another word.

Over a deafening shower of hail, Lucy Bigelow called out, "Mr. Salinger, this book promotes promiscuity and homosexuality!"

But when determined, the long-legged librarian could move even faster than the speed of complaint. And now, Mark was indeed determined.

He dashed into the poorly lit back room where the microfilm was stored. The room had an exit into a corridor connecting the first two floors of the building. The staff used this "inner sanctum" for wheeling book cars from one floor to another, and Mark zoomed into the sloping passage.

He raced down the narrow, cheerless corridor breathing in a stuffiness that always smelled of liquid pine cleanser. Younger staff called the hallway the "inner rectum" when they thought Mark wasn't paying attention.

Grace Ghiringhelli, who ran the library's front desk, had often complained in her booming voice, "The tunnel is the perfect place for a murder. No one would hear the screams of the victim."

Mark ran on, clutching his side to ease a stab of pain. He found to his horror that Grace was wrong. Echoing down the passage came a piercing scream. Oh God, it was Zoe! Dear, sweet Zoe! Mark wished to Christ, Allah, Apollo, and the Almighty that he'd paid more attention to all those new books and videos on physical fitness. Sweat dripped down his face. The stitch in his side expanded. The librarian ran faster.

Chapter 4

BREATHLESSLY CLUTCHING HIS side, Mark Salinger raced into the Children's Room just as a woman jumped through a shattered window, wrapped her arm around the neck of the mumbler, and wrenched him away from Perry Webb. The strange assailant wore a long coat, a bizarre crocheted hat, and a hideous wig that had been knocked askew. Her red hair flamed about her as she placed a choke hold on the mumbler, forcing him to drop the bloody scissors before she slowly pulled him to the floor.

The mumbler lay on the ground for several seconds before he crawled back under Zoe Latham's desk. He remained huddled in the dim cavelike space, sticking out a long arm that resembled a thin branch growing toward the light. Mark could hear him crying and babbling wild nonsense about "sin" and "Osiris" and never painting again.

"Mr. Salinger!" Mark was intercepted by two figures emerging from the striped circus tent. A dark-haired, wide-eyed little boy, who should have been in school, held the free hand of a plump toddler with her thumb in her mouth. Mark recognized Forest and Rosey Selby, who clung to his sleeve and deluged him with accounts of the tragedy.

Mark quickly comforted the children, but his attention and his heart were caught by the still, silent figure of Zoe Latham. "Zoe," Mark murmured. He rushed to kneel beside her. She was as lovely as a porcelain angel—and just as lifeless. Her hair fanned out about her in a golden halo, sticky with blood. Mark ripped off his coat to cover her, and then his shirt to compress against her shoulder wound. "Stay with me. Zoe, I love you." Had Mark said the words aloud or only groaned them out in his mind? His throat ached. His face was hot. If only he'd told Zoe how much she meant to him! He prayed it wasn't too late.

"Miss Latham is dead," whispered Forest Selby. He tugged at Mark's sleeve, his childish hand trembling with excitement as well as fear.

His sister removed a glistening thumb from her mouth. "That's Sleeping Beauty," Rosey announced. "Kiss her so she'll wake up."

"She's not Sleeping Beauty, dummy. She's dead." The boy confided to Mark, "That crazy long-haired guy held a pair of scissors. Then the old guy . . . he threw Miss Latham into those scissors and killed her. I saw it."

"Nonsense, no one has been killed." A soothing voice sounded near Mark's ear. It was the red-headed woman. She'd taken a pillow from inside the circus tent in the center of the room. Now she eased it under Zoe's head. Next she used the candy-striped tiebacks of the tent to keep Mark's dress shirt compressed tightly against Zoe's wound.

The woman's icy coat had been discarded. She'd rescued a video camera from the broken glass near the window, and it hung from her shoulder. Underneath the coat, she wore a normal, full-skirted dress that matched the intense green of her eyes and showed off a long-legged, curving figure. Her hat and wig had been stuffed into an oversize pocket. Without them, her fiery curls were revealed as well as delicate, cloisonne earrings shaped like irises.

"You'd better take care of these before they hurt anyone else." She had retrieved the bloody pair of scissors, and she laid them beside the librarian, who was startled to recognize his own European cutting shears.

"I'll call the paramedics and police," the woman offered.

The grateful librarian nodded quickly. "It might be best to go upstairs and have my staff make an official call. It's fastest if you go through the passageway on your left. There should be at least two of my staff at the library's front desk. Please send one of them down here to take the children upstairs."

Mark had little time to wonder why this strikingly lovely and seemingly normal woman dressed so oddly. She was barely out the door before Perry Webb had lunged to his feet. "You told that madman to attack me with those scissors, Salinger! I'll have you in court for this!" Webb's suit coat and white shirt were in tatters. His face was ashen, and his hair stood out in gray tufts. Horrible lines of red scored his broad chest and forearms. Blood oozed from the wounds on his hands.

Mark said tiredly, "Sit down and rest, Perry. You're hurt, and you're talking nonsense." The librarian's own anger and horror were banked down. His entire being was focused on Zoe's parchment pale face. He clutched her hand and willed her to open her eyes.

But Webb bellowed out more venom. "I know you gave the mumbler your scissors, Salinger! You wanted that lunatic to scare me away from the library, didn't you?" A bloody, frightening sight, Webb weaved drunkenly from side to side, raging like a gored and maddened bull.

Little Rose Selby began to wail, and her brother pulled her back toward the reading tent. Mark held tightly to Zoe's hand, but now his thoughts returned to Webb. He remembered the young boy's words: "The old guy threw her into those scissors and killed her."

Webb was staggering forward still shouting for revenge. When he nearly stepped on Zoe's ankle, all Mark's smoldering fury shot into flame. The ungainly librarian sprang to his feet, his thin rib cage heaving with passion. "You ass-holier-than-thou son of a bitch!" he screamed. "Sit down!"

Perry Webb hastily sat. Mark was clad in dress pants, an undershirt, and a tie. His glasses had slipped, and thin strands of hair fell in his eyes. But the furious librarian was no comic sight. "You pushed Zoe into these scissors, didn't you? You may have killed her!" Mark grabbed the bloody weapon that gleamed on the floor. He thrust it near Webb's startled face.

"You're crazy." For the first time, fear made Webb sound like an old man. "I've known Zoe since she was a child. I could never hurt someone so dear to me. She'd never have been harmed if it weren't for you and this library!"

"You old hypocrite. You'd even use Zoe's death to push your damn Measure B!" Mark burned with an emotion he'd never felt before. He'd always agreed with Napoleon Bonaparte that "a true man hates no one." But now, hatred for Webb overcame Mark. This old man cared for nothing but his own ambitions.

"You told that lunatic mumbler to kill me!" Webb shouted. "You tried to have me murdered!"

Mark brandished the scissors wildly. He ignored the blood that reddened his hands. "Stay away from Zoe!" he roared. "Stay away! Or, by heaven, I *will* murder you. And I'll take great pleasure in doing it myself!"

"Jesus!" Cindy Fayne gaped at the men from the doorway. "I hope you got all that on videotape, Ned. It's a damn good thing that KPXX is here early!"

"I've been talking with Sheriff Brody." It was some hours later when attorney Ross Coulter entered Mark's small, cluttered office. "Perry Webb gave the sheriff an earful. According to Webb, you dominated Scott Wilson—that young man they call the mumbler—to the point where you could control him. In fact, Webb claims you paid Scott to kill him, and the sheriff is inclined to agree!"

After dropping this bombshell, the lawyer took off his rain hat and overcoat, folding them neatly over the back of a wooden swivel chair. Coulter's dark face was set in harsh lines, and his gray eyes were searching. "Did you know that Scott carried almost six hundred dollars cash in his pocket tonight? Webb claims that the money is a payoff from you."

Mark's head hurt. His dress shirt was ruined, and he'd pulled on a sweatshirt from the library's lost and found. He felt tired, rumpled, and defensive. "I told the officers I knew nothing about Scott's money," Mark insisted wearily. "I did get him a job doing some work for Barron Dysart's resort. But he wasn't paid much, certainly not enough to fill his pockets with hundreds of dollars."

"According to Sheriff Brody, you admitted giving the mumbler money." Ross bent to move a pile of books from a chair before sitting down.

"Sure I helped Scott out. But it was just with my extra clothes and some money for food. And he was very grateful. He painted the Children's Room ceiling and created the murals, too. He wouldn't take a cent for his work."

Ross said with the sarcasm that made him formidable in court, "So Brody and Webb are right. You *do* have great influence over the mumbler."

"I've tried to be kind." Mark wondered why that phrase sounded so foolish. Maybe in these harsh times only fools attempted kindness. He tried to explain the relationship. "Scott is tragically ill, but he's always been peaceful and gentle—until today. And I've tried to encourage his considerable talent."

"Talent is beside the point, Mark. The point is that Webb claims you hired Scott to attack him. And Sheriff Ken Brody seems to agree with Webb. Brody's ready to ask the

D.A.'s office to press charges." Ross gave his friend a stern look, but his voice was puzzled. "Why is our sheriff backing Webb's accusations about you if there's nothing to them?"

"Underneath all his moral blustering and grandstanding, Perry Webb is damn shrewd," Mark answered bitterly. "He's made the sheriff an ally. Webb knows that Santa Linda is a big county full of small suburban towns, a county with no large commercial tax base. He also knows the sheriff's department and the libraries compete for 'leftover taxes.' That's the piddling amount of small change that remains after the state-mandated programs—everything from courts and welfare workers to dog catchers—eat a lion's share of county funds. If Measure B passes, we'll lose county taxes and the sheriff's department will have a lot more money."

"I see. The passage of Webb's Measure B could give Brody a raise."

"You've got it. Though I wouldn't mind if his department hired more staff. God knows they're needed. I've pushed for daily patrols and extra surveillance at the Castle, but Brody complains that county law enforcement is already stretched too thin. And we're just outside city limits, so Santa Linda City Police aren't in the picture."

Mark jumped from his chair and paced around the stacks of books that could find no room on his desk. "I battled for a security guard in the Children's Room, because it's isolated in the basement. But Webb convinced the Board of Supervisors to freeze all hiring, even though we've had two resignations and we're already woefully understaffed. The Castle roof is crumbling; the deck near the picnic area is rotting; and it's a damn good thing that the grounds are taken care of by Parks and Recreation, or our beautiful gardens would be a jungle. Ross, a library of this stature needs electronic surveillance, but we don't have any because

31

Webb led a revolt against capital expenditures!" The dramatic impact of Mark's complaints was almost ruined when he nearly tripped over a pile of outdated encyclopedias. "Webb would like everyone to believe that this stabbing was all my doing. But he's the one undermining the library's security. Damn it, Ross, I'm a librarian. Not a bouncer!"

Ross tried to imagine the lanky, bowed, and definitely unfit Mark Salinger lifting up stolid Perry Webb and the babbling mumbler to heft them out of the library. For the first time that afternoon, the attorney's severe features relaxed into a smile that almost warmed his gray eyes. "Maybe you're no bouncer, but you're tough, Mark. Brody couldn't have sided with Webb if you hadn't threatened to murder the old man right on television."

Mark didn't return the smile. "I never even knew I could swear like that, but I thought Webb had killed Zoe! The Selby children saw Webb shove her into the scissors." Suddenly, Mark was on his feet and swearing again. "Zoe's in the hospital, damn it! Brody should be hounding Webb instead of me!"

"Hey, take it easy! You don't have any proof Webb harmed Zoe. And children aren't the kind of witnesses we'd need to prove that he did."

"I wonder how much that woman saw ... the one who broke up the fight."

"But she didn't stay to talk to the police."

"No, she didn't," Mark admitted. "She was afraid of television cameras. She was in disguise."

"Oh, for Christ's sake." Ross was suddenly exasperated. "We're in the library here. Not a CIA movie!"

"Listen, Ross, that woman hid under an ancient wig, a hideous hat, and a moth-eaten coat."

"Maybe she's married and disguises herself to meet her boyfriend here." Ross dismissed her.

"Then why was she carrying a video camera? And without the costume, she was magnificent. Huge green eyes, curly red-orange hair that's as subtle as fire, and as for her figure . . ." Mark's hands traced an hourglass in the air.

"Did you say red hair?" The attorney tipped back his chair. "Red hair, green eyes, sexy figure . . ." Suddenly his chair crashed to earth. "Well, I'll be damned! I met her yesterday on the path behind the Castle."

"Could you find her? I know she'd help us." Mark was recovering his enthusiasm. "You should have seen her fly through the window. Poor Scott was totally unnerved. Believe me, that lady was *amazing*."

Ross winced at the word "amazing." It reminded him that his friend was relying on a probable fruitcake who followed the advice of her "amazing" cat. He put on his mantle of lawyerly authority: "We won't need your 'wigged woman' if you leave things to me. Webb may press charges, but that doesn't mean they'll come to court. Jenkins is a cautious D.A. who hates to lose. I'll ridicule the idea that you would hire the unstable mumbler to attack Perry Webb, and I'll remind Jenkins that he'd be martyring our most popular librarian to state and federal problems of homelessness and mental health."

Mark, about to tug at his hair in frustration, looked up in surprise instead. "Hold on, under all that jargon did I hear good news? I mean, are you actually predicting that Webb won't be able to frame me?"

Ross packed up his briefcase, put on his coat, and stepped over a stack of books that needed rebinding. "I'm no fortune teller, but here's the most likely scenario: Zoe's condition isn't critical, thank God, so if Webb intentionally, or unintentionally, harmed her, she'll be able to say so. Scott will be sent for observation to Santa Linda General. The court will designate him a 5150-class psychotic, 'dangerous to himself and others' and will recommend expensive psychiatric treatment that the kid will never receive. It's a shame, but the county hospital is so overcrowded with people just like him that Wilson will be out with a bag lunch in days."

The two men walked to the library entrance. "Perhaps our Castle will be able to return to its normal chaos." Mark shook Ross's hand. "I'm very grateful to you."

The attorney seemed uncomfortable with gratitude. He said harshly: "Webb will make all the trouble he can to keep Jenkins interested in prosecuting, so don't threaten Webb again, Mark. No matter what the old bastard does, keep your temper. Keep this place as quiet as . . . well, as quiet as a library."

Alone, Mark walked slowly back toward his lighted office, a beacon in an empty, darkened building, whose shadows seemed to creep into his heart. What had set Scott off like that? What would be Webb's next attempt to cause trouble? Above all, was Zoe truly out of danger?

Mark stared at the paneled wall of his office. Above his desk hung three framed renditions of the Castle in all her floral glory. Two were famous photographs, taken twenty years apart. The third was a painting, Scott Wilson's painting. Mark lost himself in it for a moment, as he often did when trying to lift his flagging spirits. This was a portrait of a Castle that might have welcomed the angels into paradise.

Brilliant sunlight danced off white plaster walls shining on an almost dizzying profusion of blossoms. There were spires of lilac, irises splashed with rainbows, clematis as delicate as tinted snowflakes, and of course, roses. Roses of garish pink, roses in shades of fire, roses that glowed like spun gold . . . "The splendor falls on Castle walls . . ." Mark was quoting Tennyson's calming poetry when he heard a familiar voice shouting and he hurried to open the staff door.

Outside in dim twilight wind battered the trees, and the

hail had turned to rain. Ross stood at the staff entrance, hatless, windblown and disheveled. The harsh lines of his face had sharpened. Raindrops coursed down his cheeks like tears.

The attorney pulled Mark outside. "There's a girl in a purple cloak in those bushes near the parking lot. I saw her in the headlights of my car."

The young woman lay in a thin patch of grass, her body partially hidden in boxwood shrubs. She had a full, almost chubby face, and she was curled on her side, her velvet cloak comforting her body like a blanket. Her plump left hand rested on her cheek as if in sleep, but vomit dribbled from her mouth, and her dark frozen eyes stared at nothing. A syringe lay between the inert fingers of her right hand. An open Bible lay nearby, sodden from the splashing rain.

Mark knelt on the wet ground. He knew her from the library, a dreamy, dark-haired girl wrapped in a purple cloak, carrying her well-thumbed Bible. He told Ross: "Her name was Claire Fraiser. I don't know much about her except that she was Scott's close friend, and a sweet girl who often asked me about books on religion. She hung out with street people and didn't seem to have a home." Mark spoke haltingly and used the past tense. It was obvious that Claire was dead.

Chapter 5

THREE WEEKS LATER, Media Day's explosive events were still sending aftershocks through the library.

"I'd like to get hold of that woman who saved Perry Webb's life and throttle her," raged Assistant Librarian Grace Ghiringhelli. "If that redhead hadn't meddled with the mumbler, maybe Webb would have been stabbed to death!"

Ghiringhelli's remarks were aimed at fellow librarian, Laurel Hanson, a small, pixieish woman with an elfin cap of brown hair and dark brown eyes behind her thick, round glasses. "Please don't talk like that, Grace." Laurel flashed a worried look to make sure that no one was near the front desk. "You know you don't mean it."

"Get real, Laurel. Don't you wish Webb had been found dead of a drug overdose in our parking lot instead of that poor Claire Fraiser? Come to think of it, Webb is always complaining about drug dealers. Maybe the library will get lucky and one of them will bump him off."

"Grace!"

But the assistant librarian was still fuming. Grace snatched a book from an untidy stack piling up on the return desk. "Webb has already damaged this library. Look how far behind we are! We need more staff, but the supervisors won't stand up to Webb and cancel that damn hiring freeze. And now that the mumbler has been released from the hospital, our volunteers have quit in droves. What will we do Monday night when all the classes and meetings are scheduled? We're going to be very shorthanded."

"Let's just concentrate on finishing these books." Laurel flipped back her heavy brown hair, adjusted her wire-rimmed glasses, and pointedly bent over the request slips she was filing, but her voice was mild. She knew that Grace was masking fear with all her angry words. It had startled Laurel when she discovered that this large, physically strong woman was approaching a state of terror. Grace was afraid of the mumbler, but she was far more panicked over Measure B. And Laurel didn't blame her; if Measure B passed, Grace would be approaching retirement age without her expected pension, and indeed, without a job.

Now Ghiringhelli was directing her anxiety toward the used-book table. She glared at it, her pale eyes round with shocked anger, her mouth pursed into a tight beak. Laurel felt like a mouse confronted with a large, glaring owl. "The used-book table has been tampered with!" Grace exclaimed. "Why aren't these books arranged the way Pamela Dysart left them? She's president of the Friends of the Library, and she's in charge of this table."

Laurel groaned inwardly. This was an old battle for which she had less understanding. As far as Laurel was concerned, ever since Ms. Dysart had begun lusting after that handsome Luke Bishop, her table had become a disgrace. Even Professor Clive Truesdell had noticed it. Sometimes on Monday nights, after teaching his art appreciation class in the multipurpose room, the professor and Laurel would discuss the rotten condition and high prices of the used volumes that Pamela offered for sale. Then Clive, the old dear, would charitably purchase the entire lot.

"*I* tampered with Pamela's sacred table," Laurel admitted with irritation. "I sold a lot of the junk in the back row. Perry Webb said he wanted to help the library, so I ripped him off with the most dilapidated, expensive books I could find."

"Perry Webb!" Anger brought spots of red to Ghiringhelli's square cheeks. "He's just buying books to get publicity for Measure B, which will destroy the Castle and our jobs. Laurel, if you believed Webb wanted to help the library, you'd believe this!" Grace shoved a picture book forward and pointed to a colorful illustration. Monkeys wearing business suits rode in a limousine driven by a bulldog dressed in a chauffeur's uniform. The dog's pug nose was in the air, and his canine sneer of superiority intimidated a motherly hippo in pink ruffles who was attempting to cross the road with her diapered skunk. Ghiringhelli slammed the book shut, lobbed it onto the Children's Room book cart, and nearly dislodged a rickety wheel. "Someone should murder Perry Webb," she hissed before exiting to the staff room.

Laurel shook her head and bent her head over her work. Those terrible events of Media Day: the stabbing of Zoe Latham, the bloody fight between Webb and the mumbler, the death of Claire Fraiser . . . they'd left everyone on edge. But today it seemed as though Grace had fallen over the edge.

"Is that what you think, Brown Eyes? Should someone *murder* Perry Webb?" Laurel nearly jumped when she heard the intense, eerie whisper. She looked up to see a tall, rumpled man at the front desk.

"Todd Hanson!" she exclaimed in relief and exasperation. "Don't scare me like that. And just where have you been?"

"Working on construction jobs days, sleeping in lumberyards nights, and haggling over valuable letters and a short manuscript that I'm sure is genuine Mark Twain."

The big man flashed the easy smile that had always stirred Laurel's heart. She forced herself to look critically at her ex-husband's work shirt with the pocket missing and his torn corduroy jacket. She took them as proof that his genius for scholarship was based, at least in part, on his stubborn disregard of practicality. If Todd was a drifter, it was because he spent all his money on antique letters and materials that supported his thesis on Mark Twain. There never seemed to be money left over for clothes or rent. Memories of why she'd divorced him came flooding back to Laurel.

"When can you come by for your junk mail?" she asked him shortly. "You know your boxes of notes are still in my garage. I can't get my headlights, let alone my car, in there. And you received a very official looking letter from Columbia University Press." Then she saw his expression, half hope, half fear. Impractical, he might be, but she couldn't delay the good news. "Damn you, Todd," she swore in a whisper. "If you had an address, I wouldn't have had to break a federal law against opening your mail to find out about your twelve-thousand-dollar advance!"

Todd grasped Laurel's hand as if she were pulling him out of quicksand. "It's true?" he gulped.

She nodded.

"You've brought me luck, Brown Eyes," he confided hoarsely. "Come on, honey. I'll take you out to celebrate. This will be good luck for both of us. I'll finish the book and authenticate the manuscript I've found. I'll get famous, but you'll get rich." He smiled down at her. "Now I have money to pay rent for your garage."

Laurel smiled back in spite of herself. She was trembling a little. But she shook her head. "Don't spend money on me. Rent an apartment to work in."

"I don't need one. Now that I have a book contract, I qualify for a writing studio in the tower—'a room with a view', as the great E.M. Forster might have said."

"I'll get you forms to fill out and a key," Laurel said grudgingly. "But remember you can't sleep in the library, and if Measure B passes, you'll have no writing studio either because the Castle will close." Laurel's fears tumbled out in a rush. "Todd, I don't know what we're going to do about Measure B. Salinger is trying to hold the library together, but where's his support? The whole staff is demoralized, and—"

"Webb won't succeed with his damn Measure B," Todd interrupted, scowling. "I won't let him!"

Laurel gaped at her ex-husband. The big face had gone red, and the veins stood out on his huge, clenched fists. She knew that Todd was slow to anger but never the first to back down in a fight. It was a side of him that she didn't like to think about. She stared down unhappily at the broad, book-littered counter.

"I've learned that Webb is going to use Measure B to buy and develop the Castle property!" Todd said harshly. "How will I finish my book if this place becomes an apartment building or a damned boutique? Besides, there's something awfully strange gong on in this library. And I believe it has something to do with Claire's murder."

"Murder? That's nonsense. That girl died of a drug overdose."

"Honey, I knew Claire. She was a sweet kid who lived for Jesus. The mumbler adored her, everyone did. She was one of those few people who practice religion out of love instead of fear."

"I don't understand. . . ."

"Because you don't want to understand. You know that old drunk Herbert Hamlisch, the one who went to jail for bigamy and comes to the library to write his memoirs? Hamlisch once made the mistake of jokingly offering Claire marijuana. She prayed for him and quoted the Bible in his ear until he threw the joint away in self-defense. Claire wasn't hooked on heroin. Drugs meant sin to her."

"But the police . . ." Laurel protested.

"The police," Todd echoed in disgust. "Claire associated with homeless people, so the police accepted the easy explanation that she used drugs. To paraphrase a quote from the great Mark Twain: 'First god invented idiots. That was just for practice.' Then he invented police."

"But what has Claire got to do with Measure B, or Perry Webb?"

"I've heard that she was trying to arrange a meeting between the mumbler and Perry Webb just before their fight in the Children's Room. Now Webb is trying to have Scott imprisoned, and Claire's been murdered."

Laurel gazed out at the shabby, beautiful library. Refracted light beamed through the stained glass to form a multicolored shimmer above the quiet people turning peaceful pages. She glanced at a beveled window remembering that Claire had often sat beneath it, wrapped in her purple cloak, reading her Bible. Laurel shivered and whispered in revulsion, "Murder . . ."

"Oh, murder!" Alex swore as she stubbed her toe on a potted iris plant while rushing to answer her ringing phone. "I'm coming, I'm coming." She maneuvered around another clay pot that sat beside her kitchen table.

By the time Alex made it to the cat-shaped telephone, there was no one on the line. She gently pushed aside the violet petals of yet another potted iris to discover that she'd forgotten to set the answering machine. "What a mess," she complained to Watson. "I never should have told Barron Dysart that irises are my favorite flower."

Barron had phoned just before he flew to France. "Mother just sold that portrait of Charles Chaplin painted by Picasso," he'd chuckled. "It's the biggest sale of her career, over five hundred thousand dollars! Once I meet Mother in Paris and she sees your steamy video, I'm sure she'll come rushing back to Santa Linda. Then that bastard

41

Luke will be out of a meal ticket, and I'll have help paying off our estate!" Barron sounded as if he were rubbing his hands in glee. "I'm very grateful to you, Alex. I'm sending you some flowers. . . . No, I insist. I tried to buy Rainbow Irises—the ones that Kate Selby developed and that my grandfather presented to Judy Garland—but these days even the bulbs are hard to find in nurseries."

Even as Barron said good-bye, a UPS truck had arrived along with too many pots of irises, a thank-you note dripping with flattery, and an invitation to dinner.

This morning, looking around at a kitchen full of plants, Alex sighed. "This is too much gratitude, Watson. But Barron is counting on getting hold of Pamela's latest Celebrity Art profits, over half a million dollars, so I guess I understand his gratitude, and I suppose I can accept his flowers. However, Watson, I'd prefer that you go to dinner with the man instead of me."

Ms. Watson, who had been trying to pick her way through pots of irises to reach her catnip toys, tossed her glossy black head and tail in disdain. But she watched with interest as Alex hurried by, jumping over flowers. The phone had rung again.

"Yes, George, I've looked at the photos," Alex said into the phone. "No, George, I won't pose for *Playboy*. Goodbye, George." She smashed down the receiver. Her boss was at it again.

At the kitchen table, Alex picked up the issue of *Playboy* that George had mailed to her along with a scrawled note that read: *"You could have been Miss February! Our phone could be ringing off the hook!"* Alex flipped to the pages where three women from rival agencies were featured in a photo spread. The investigators were undressed in gray fedoras and pin-striped suit coats. Their ample breasts and rounded buttocks peeked out from their short, unbuttoned jackets. (Apparently the women had never heard the rule that good investigating required good cover.) Each of the ladies pulled along a virile hunk in handcuffs.

Was nudity really the way for female detectives to succeed? George seemed to think so and obviously other agencies agreed. Alex frowned. Posing for *Playboy* wasn't what she'd had in mind when she became a detective.

But she had to face facts. Sure she had a deep respect for Sam Abromowitz, who had hired and trained her for his agency over George Stewart's objections. But Sam was rarely around. He'd started taking skip trace cases, searching for felons who'd jumped bail. Skip tracing took Sam far from L.A., leaving his junior partner George Stewart in charge of daily affairs. And George just wouldn't understand that Alex wasn't about to peel off her clothes or jump into bed for the sake of his pocketbook.

Alex stroked the catnip-befuddled Watson and made a decision: "I'll miss investigating, but I ought to consider gardening. If those Rainbow Irises are rare, I could grow and sell them along with the Marilyn's Roses, and Kate Selby's other movie-star flowers. Pamela Dysart makes a fortune selling celebrity artwork, and I might make a half-decent living selling celebrity flowers. Monday, we'll go up to the Santa Linda Library and do some research on Kate Selby and her famous blossoms. Think of a green, calm life, Ms. Watson. Honest manure just has to be an improvement over bimbo bullshit."

Chapter 6

"GRACE, I'M TAKING my dinner break early." Zoe wearily brushed her pale hair away from her face. "I should wait, but I have a headache. And, of course, now that we finally have our security guard in the Children's Room, I won't be leaving the Children's Room unattended. I'll be back at seven if anyone asks for me."

Grace Ghiringhelli was about to retort that Zoe had no business taking a break before Mark Salinger returned. With unaccustomed restraint, she held her tongue. Zoe spoke so softly that Grace strained to hear her. Zoe's brisk step had slowed, and she'd lost her cheerful smile. That woman is too quiet, Grace thought. Even for a librarian.

Zoe stepped away from the front desk, then returned. "Honestly, I don't know what's the matter with me. I forgot to tell you that we need an empty book cart downstairs as soon as possible. The one that Jamaica is using has a damaged wheel. It looks as if someone deliberately tampered with it."

"I'll send Laurel over when she comes back from her break," Grace promised. "Though heaven alone knows when that will be," she added under her breath. After a mysterious phone call, Laurel had deserted the front desk. She'd turned as gray as her cardigan sweater and had run from the Castle without consulting anyone. In fact, Grace had hoped that Jamaica could come up to the main floor to help out.

Grace watched Zoe leave the library and a frown creased her broad, square brow. "Salinger is on a dinner break. Zoe is gone. Jamaica is downstairs. Laurel is who knows where? I'm the only responsible person around here. So what else is new? I wouldn't worry so much, if the mumbler weren't out on the streets. Knowing my luck, he'll come back when I'm alone and all hell will break loose." Then Grace glared out over the first floor of the library, her anxiety turning to frustration.

A silver-haired man in his sixties, with the shape of a bottle distinctly visible under his frayed suit coat, had begun to sing bawdy songs in a loud and intoxicated fashion.

Grace yelled, "Mr. Hamlisch! Shh!" at the top of her lungs. When Mr. Hamlisch didn't shh, she escorted him out the door. She returned to the library only to find a weirdo in sunglasses awaiting her at the front desk. Honestly! What was this library coming to? The wierdo's face was hidden by a floppy purple hat and her dangling earrings featured a grocery basket's worth of papier-mâché fruit.

Not wishing to be recognized after her adventures in the Castle on Media Day, Alex had adjusted her purple hat low over her forehead before she said, "I've been searching for a book called *Famous Flowers for Famous Folks*."

The library assistant scanned the computer, then said sharply, "We don't own *Famous Flowers for Famous Folks*."

"But it's listed on the card catalogue."

"Our catalogue needs updating. It lists some books that have been lost or discarded. We're shorthanded, so perhaps *you'd* like to volunteer to do the updating."

Despite her caustic tone the woman was positively beaming. It took a moment for Alex to realize that the smile was aimed beyond her head at someone behind her.

The someone behind Alex said, "Hello, Grace."

"Pamela! Thank goodness you're back from France! Have you heard what's been going on?" Grace stomped out from behind the counter.

Alex swiveled and saw the library assistant plant her hefty frame in front of Pamela Dysart, who glanced first to the left and then to the right in search of escape routes. Finally Pamela exclaimed in whispered exasperation: "I can't chat now, Grace. I have to get upstairs."

Alex tried not to stare. After following Pam Dysart and Luke Bishop for weeks, she'd come to regard the woman as a high-society fashion plate. Pamela would change her dress for dinner, her hair color with each perm, and her face with every new crop of lines. Tonight, her hair was wild and snarled, and her face was puffy. Tears had ruined her careful makeup, leaving glittering smudges under her eyes and clownish patches of wet, caked blush on her cheeks.

"Is something the matter?" Grace finally seemed to recognize Pamela's obvious distress. She added in a confused, distracted manner: "Laurel shouldn't have tampered with the used books on your table. I warned her not to."

"Books!" Pamela lost all self-control. "There's more to life than all these fucking *books*! Everything's hopeless, Grace! Oh shit, just get out of my way!"

Alex was not the only one who was astonished to hear shouts and swearing burst from the normally poised and elegant Ms. Dysart. The murmured quiet of the library turned to a scandalized and absolutely enthralled silence. Feeling the attention, Pamela panicked, then bolted. She ran awkwardly, her spiked heels clicking on the linoleum. She nearly tripped over the first of the broad, oak steps that led to the upper floors and the study towers. But she rushed on,

46

stumbling once in her tight leather pants and high heels, nearly thrown off balance by her enormous snakeskin carry-all.

Some moments later, Pamela's high-pitched accusing screams and Luke's defensive masculine growls rang through the heat registers down to the main floor. Not long afterward, Stacy Dysart catapulted down the main stairs. She was barefoot, bare legged, and crying. She carried a rolled up ball of clothing and wore only an oversized man's shirt that was half unbuttoned. Stacy fled from the Castle and did not look back.

Down in the Children's Room, Jamaica Polonsky had grown tired of waiting for someone to bring a cart downstairs. With a rush of high energy, the library page had shelved all the books, and there was really nothing left to do . . . unless she wanted to baby-sit Eden Selby's kids. They were alone in the reading tent again, just as they had been on Media Day, though Zoe had repeatedly told their mother that the library couldn't be responsible for such young, unsupervised children. It was really a shame about those kids, especially since they were the great-grandchildren of the famous Kate Selby. Jamaica had done an extra-credit report on Kate Selby in social studies. She admired the creative woman who'd worked at the Castle when working as a woman had been unfashionable. Kate had even developed her own varieties of flowers.

But Jamaica was damned if she'd play nanny for Eden Selby when the Castle was so shorthanded. Eden Selby might be Kate Selby's granddaughter, but that didn't make her a decent mother.

She'd take the broken cart upstairs to the front desk herself, Jamaica decided. It did seem as though Ms. Latham had forgotten to send someone for it. Then Jamaica would find Eden and shame her into picking up her children.

Jamaica had seen Eden tonight in the library—you couldn't miss her. She always dressed like a pseudo Indian with her thick braids, beaded buckskin jacket, and long, cotton skirt.

The cart was awkward to manage. It limped and squeaked on three wheels, but Mr. Gilbert, the new security guard, pushed open the heavy door and helped Jamaica wheel it down the hall. He seemed glad of something to do. Alone, Jamaica navigated the cart into the dark hallway of the Inner Sanctum. Since the stabbing on Media Day, Mr. Salinger had installed deadbolts on the doors of this passageway that linked the Children's Room with the main floor. He'd kept the doors locked and issued pass keys to the staff. But someone had been careless. Jamaica found the door unlocked.

It was only when she'd locked the inside deadbolt after her and plodded ahead several yards with the gimpy book truck that the library page began to understand that something was very wrong. It had always been creepy in this hallway, but tonight it was also too dark. Some of the overhead lights weren't working. And what were those strange noises?

Alex was reading over the catalogue's subject listing of horticulture books when a shattering crash ricocheted through the library—a crash that sent Luke Bishop bolting down the stairs through the main floor of the library. He tried to stride to the front entrance with some dignity, but giggles and outright laughter trailed him out the door.

Pamela's sobs (mixed with some unlovely and unholy words aimed at Luke Bishop) filtered down to the first floor. Some moments later, a pounding and a deep voice poured through the registers along with the heat.

"Ms. Dysart!" The deep voice bellowed. "This is Clive Truesdell. I have a study right next door and I couldn't help overhearing you. Please let me in to speak with you! Now, now, Ms. Dysart, you needn't be so upset."

The first floor heard Professor Truesdell offering comfort, and for a bit, Pamela was quieted. Then gradually the sobs grew louder again, and Truesdell's dry voice grew impatient. "We've never admired one another, Ms. Dysart, but I wouldn't have expected you to howl like an overage rockstar!"

Pamela was distraught with jealousy. Soon the entire first floor could hear her: "I trusted that asshole. I gave him everything! How could he fuck my own daughter?"

Embarrassed laughter and knowing looks passed among the people on the main floor.

"This is too much!" In the eavesdropping silence, Grace's pained outburst sounded inordinately loud. She rushed out from the front desk and marched toward the staircase. But she was waylaid by three women in leotards and a portly man in spandex who claimed to have been notified that an aerobics class was starting in the multipurpose room. Grace retorted rather louder than necessary that there was no such class.

Alex watched it all in astonishment. Was the Castle going crazy?

Upstairs there were still loud remarks, but now it was Truesdell who was shouting. He was either cleverly distracting Pamela or matching her hysteria with pent-up emotions of his own. "I always said you shouldn't be head of Friends of the Library, Ms. Dysart. The Dysart family may have once owned the Castle, but that's no excuse for you treating this library like your little pet hobby. Our literate community depends upon you, Ms. Dysart, and more's the pity. I only hope you've come to your senses at last. Did you want to go on forever slicing your chins, dicing your nose, and tightening your boobs—all so you could totter after a writer with the morals of a worm? Good Christ, woman! Don't you care that this wonderful library is being destroyed by Perry Webb, a real estate buffoon who can barely read the Multiple Listings?"

"I've raised a great deal of money for this library!" Pamela defended herself.

"I don't see how, when even your used-book table is a mess!" the professor countered.

This argument was definitely duller than the one over Luke Bishop's sex life, and patrons on the main floor soon lost interest. Only Alex still strained to listen, feeling a concern for Pamela. She'd exposed this woman to the truth about Luke Bishop, and she knew how the truth must hurt. Maybe Truesdell had little understanding of Pamela's irrational behavior, but Alex had plenty to spare. She knew the unreasonable, overwhelming pain of loneliness and unrequited love . . . her ex-husband Charlie had branded that knowledge on her heart.

Jamaica was frightened. She shoved the book truck ahead of her, banging her knee on its lower shelf. In the Inner Sanctum's narrow, cavelike murkiness, horrible sounds brushed by her like bat wings. She heard an angry argument and some garbled yelling about something that sounded like a "beard virus." Strange crying filtered from somewhere up above. Down here in the blackness it was like someone moaning over your grave.

The library page pushed forward. She told her imagination to take a hike. "Pull yourself together, girl. You're in a library—not a morgue." She hurried on toward the first floor.

That was when she heard the groan. It was a horrible, liquid groan that choked off at the end. Footsteps sounded. Light spread into the corridor, and a figure came running through the doorway of the microfilm room. Jamaica froze. Then her shoulders relaxed. How childish she'd been, it was only Mr. Salinger. She was about to call out to him in relief.

And then, as suddenly as if a tape had been switched on, there began a familiar, only partially intelligible rambling that the girl recognized instantly. " 'An eye for an eye!' sayeth the Lord. Under my thumb, the girl who once had me down. It was the very best butter. . . ."

Jamaica's heart raced with unaccustomed terror. Her sturdy legs rocked like the unstable book truck. *Oh God, not the mumbler. Please God, not him.* At least it was dark in here. Maybe he wouldn't see her. Jamaica gripped the cart, keeping it rigid so it wouldn't squeak. If she let go of it to run, the cart would topple and crash. Hearing it, the mumbler might come after her. Even if she made it back to the door, what would happen while she struggled to unlock the deadbolt in the dark?

She stood motionless. As the seconds expanded into infinity, Jamaica was sure the mumbler hadn't seen her. If she could just stay silent and motionless, he would go out the staff exit without knowing she was in the passage. She began to shudder with the effort of keeping the cart immobile. Her hands trembled and perspired. The book truck's slick, metal handles nearly slid out of her grasp as she realized that his footsteps were growing closer. They were accompanied by mumbled phrases that made no sense at all. Too late, Jamaica dropped the cart to run. Strong hands wrenched at her shoulders and threw her to the ground. Everything went black.

Grace was finally confronted with the problem she'd been dreading all night. Just as Laurel returned to the library, and Grace prepared to go on her break, the mumbler appeared. Long hair flying and babbling wild nonsense, he shot out from the doorway of the staff corridor. "What were you doing in there?" Grace shouted at him. "Get out of this library before I call the police!"

The mumbler ran full tilt toward the door, bumping into the weirdo with the sunglasses and the goofy earrings. His exit knocked her flat.

It was Laurel who ran to help the woman up. The wierdo's floppy, purple hat tumbled to the floor and her long red hair tugged at Grace Ghiringhelli's memory. Wasn't this the redhead who'd broken up the fight on Media Day? Then Grace heard the words that the woman was saying, and her heart turned over.

"Did you see the man who knocked me down? He had blood on his coat. Look. It's smeared on my jacket." The woman thrust out her stained sleeve. "I'll go after him to see if he's all right. You'd better check the corridor in case he's hurt someone."

Grace Ghiringhelli tried to move, but her legs were suddenly shaking. What had that crazy mumbler done now?

Jamaica struggled to her feet. The library page stood swaying for a moment, trying to get her bearings despite her throbbing head. Then she moved gingerly around the overturned cart and made slow, halting progress along the corridor. She took a few stumbling steps before she leaned against the rough stucco walls for support. She had to rest. She had to clear the spots that danced before her eyes.

A slice of golden, welcome light shone through a partially open door. Should she go in? It was the door that the mumbler had come through. Still, he seemed to be gone, and this was the quickest way out of the Inner Sanctum. Suddenly Jamaica felt unable to bear the inky mustiness of the passageway for another moment. She fell against the door and staggered into the storage room.

The room was silent. Silent but not empty. Perry Webb was slumped in a chair. Jamaica thought he looked far less disapproving than usual. His rounded chin, rather than wagging about obscenity or taxes, rested peacefully on his puffed, white-shirted chest.

But the angle of his neck was frightening. His head flopped against his shoulder almost as if it were about to roll off his body. And the blood! Blood splashed down his white shirt front and pooled between his thick, splayed legs. Blood also stained Mr. Salinger's brand-new scissors. They bulged out of the place where, Jamaica surmised, Mr. Webb's hard, miserly heart had once beaten.

"He's dead," the library page whispered to no one in particular.

Chapter 7

MURDER IN THE lovely old Castle? Library patrons soon realized that the unthinkable had occurred.

Jamaica, the library page, had been rushed to the county hospital to be treated for shock. Mr. Gilbert, the new security guard, had slipped into a corner to sip a little alcoholic courage from a flask inside his shirt. Pam Dysart, coming down to the first floor, had gone hysterical and fainted, landing slap on top of Professor Clive Truesdell, who had flapped his thin arms in horror while his deep resonant voice hollered to the paramedics to help.

But the paramedics were already dealing with Mark Salinger who had a deep, bloody gash on his arm. Two teenagers had apparently waylaid the librarian as he returned to the library after his dinner break. "I'm sure it was more a prank than any attempt to rob me," Salinger had explained. "But I was rash enough to threaten to call the police and to try to push past them. That's when one of them knifed me—more by accident than design." When the boys fled, Chief Librarian Salinger had hurried through the staff entrance to the staff bathroom. He'd stayed there to clean his wounded arm, and he'd missed all the excitement in the main foyer of the library.

While Mark was being treated and Pamela was being revived, a harassed pair of deputies managed to keep everyone in the library while they took names and statements.

But the deputies weren't prepared for Todd Hanson. The big man had marched down from the writing tower bellowing that the sheriff's department was incompetent. Todd Hanson had proclaimed, right in front of the officers, that Claire had been murdered in the Castle parking lot, Perry Webb had been involved, and the sheriff's department had missed it all! The investigation of the death of Claire Fraiser was a gigantic farce that had led to this new tragedy!

But even Hanson calmed down when the back-up patrol arrived along with the medical examiner, his cameraman, and the forensic team, who immediately began to gather the evidence. A solemn hush greeted these technicians who measured and quantified the aftermath of murder.

Knowledgeable phrases were overheard, and they began to drift through the library in whispers. *"A contusion and two stab wounds, one piercing the lung and producing pneumothorax and the collapse of the lung, the other piercing the right ventricle of the heart. . . . That means that somebody hit Webb over the head and stabbed him through the lung with Salinger's scissors so he couldn't scream. Then they killed him by stabbing him through the heart. And did you hear that they're taking Webb to Eternal Life Mortuary? . . . Sure, this county hasn't had enough murders to justify the expense of having our own morgue. Maybe things are starting to change for the worse. . . . I'm more interested in the fact that Salinger admitted that those were his scissors in Webb's chest. We all know he wanted to see Webb dead."*

Slowly the novelty of the situation wore off. Curiosity gradually faded as the violent reality began to seep in. By the time Sheriff Ken Brody arrived, shock, resentment, and fright were the dominant emotions.

A whiskey nose, a six-pack belly, and a hung over disposition summed up Alex's take on the sheriff. She also figured he could crack a mean nightstick. Brody immediately detained the library staff. He also detained Alex along with several others who had been on the first floor and had seen the mumbler run through the library. "I don't like homicides in my county!" he'd declared. "And I'm going to handle this one personally." Commandeering Salinger's office, he'd herded his grumbling witnesses into the staff room, demanding that they wait while he reviewed statements.

"More questioning is ridiculous!" Grace Ghiringhelli marched up to challenge the sheriff with her hands on her broad hips. "The mumbler came running out of that corridor just after Webb was killed. Not only that, but the man had blood all over him! He's a fiend!" She stomped a heavy foot, just missing the county sheriff's boot. "Why are you questioning us instead of chasing him down? Are you inept?" A chorus from the others in the room echoed her question.

Even Mark Salinger, his long frame slouched uncomfortably over a small metal folding chair, mildly protested the sheriff's high-handedness: "This terrible tragedy is hardly a whodunit. We'll all cooperate as much as we can to help you find Scott, but the staff is exhausted." Mark shot a brief look at Zoe's strained, ashen face. "It's nearly ten. It's time they were allowed to go."

Strangely, it was Salinger's moderate words that lit an unexpected blaze. Brody leaned forward. His lips tightened, and his voice took on a fierce edge. "Make sure you *do* cooperate, Salinger. Make damned sure you tell me the truth about what happened here tonight!" Brody pointed a stubby finger at the librarian's bandaged arm, making it publicly clear that he didn't believe Mark's story about his knife wound. Having made a point of his suspicions of Salinger, the sheriff picked up his list. "Alexandra Winter!" he barked.

Alex stood up, slung her book bag over her shoulder, and told herself to expect trouble. There hadn't been much hope of hiding her identity or her profession in this murder investigation, and private detectives weren't exactly the darlings of law enforcement.

Brody sat down behind Mark's large, wooden desk, which was blanketed with books and papers. He ordered Alex into a seat across from him. "You and I should have met weeks ago. You witnessed the mumbler's first assault on Perry Webb, but you never stayed to talk to my men." He waggled a finger in front of Alex's nose. "You could lose your license, lady. I could damn well make sure of it."

Alex pushed his hand away from her face. "You could lose your job treating people the way you do. Maybe we could stand in the unemployment lines together."

The sheriff's face turned such a furious red that Alex wouldn't have been surprised to see smoke emerge from his freckled ears. Meanwhile, Alex had to force herself not to grin at him like an idiot. That painting of the Castle hanging on the wall behind Mark Salinger's desk—the one that hung just above and behind the bald spot on Sheriff Brody's head. That painting was such a gorgeous surprise! Alex felt a longing to step inside the frame and live in eternal summer. It would be heaven to be always among those bright, shimmering blossoms, especially the Rainbow Irises. My God, those flowers were splendid! No wonder they were famous, these lofty, elegant blooms with a ridge of golden fluffy "beards" across their centers. Cheerful rainbows splashed down their ruffled petals like multicolored waterfalls.

"Um, what was that? I didn't quite hear you." Alex crashed to earth. Brody was pounding the desk with a heavy fist.

57

"Jesus, lady, are you deaf? For the third time, when that mumbler attacked Perry Webb ... did he say anything about Salinger?"

"No, of course not." Alex took her mind off the irises immediately and turned troubled eyes on her questioner. Here it was again, this odd emphasis on the librarian.

Brody scratched at a broken vein on his nose. "And you're sure that the mumbler never once mentioned Salinger's name? Not even when Salinger came into the room?"

"Scott Wilson didn't speak to anyone, at least not anyone human. After the fight was over, he just crawled under the furniture and muttered to himself. I was too worried about the children's librarian to concentrate on what he was saying, even if I could have understood it. Ms. Latham was unconscious, and she'd lost a great deal of blood. Mr. Salinger never left her side."

Brody seemed disappointed. "Let's talk about tonight. What time was the mumbler running out of the library entrance?"

"Maybe seven forty-five. I was slammed backward and didn't check my watch."

"Your statement says you went outside to find him. Did you see where he went?"

"I was too late. By the time I followed him outside, he'd disappeared." Her hand restlessly moved to her pocket, and Alex forced herself to fold it in her lap. She wasn't about to confide to Brody that she doubted that the person who knocked her down was really the mumbler. The sheriff made her uneasy. He seemed determined to implicate the kindly, bookish librarian in Webb's death.

"When you were outside, Mr. Salinger should have been returning to the library from his dinner break. Did you see him?"

"No. And why all these questions about him? Is Mr.

Salinger on trial here?" Alex met Brody's hostile look with one of her own.

Surprisingly, the big man dropped his gaze. He busied himself with jotting down notes and, for the first time, spoke without aggression. "Does it seem to you that I'm persecuting the librarian, Miss Winter? What I'd rather do is clear him of suspicion. Even if I didn't know and respect Mark personally, I'd be stepping into a hornet's nest if I arrested Santa Linda's popular chief librarian. But Mark has publicly threatened Perry Webb, and he had a long association with the mumbler. Don't you think I'd be negligent if I refused to ask questions about what happened?"

It was a smooth comeback. But if Brody had meant to put Alex on the spot, he was thwarted by a rapping on the office door. A deputy stepped into the room. "Santa Linda City Police called. The captain of the watch received a dispatch you'll want to see."

"Bring it here." Brody glanced at the note, then swatted it away. "We're not taking over city's petty burglaries. Let them wipe their own asses; we've got a murder on our hands."

"But, sir, this robbery occurred just twenty minutes ago at 2682 Center Street, Suite 12. . . . That's the office of Perry Webb. Police patrols are fanning through the area now. And Lieutenant Drexler has a witness who saw Scott Wilson running from Webb's office building."

"Shit, why didn't you tell me that in the beginning? Tell Drexler to—" Brody bit off his words remembering Alex. "You can go now." He scribbled a note and handed it to her. "Show this to the officer at the exit. If we need you, we'll be in touch."

Outside the office, Alex met resentful stares from people still huddled in the staff room. They didn't give her any desire to stick around, and she was nearly at the door when

Mark Salinger caught up with her, "I never thanked you for your help on Media Day. I want to thank you now."

The detective looked into the librarian's gentle, dark eyes, unable to forget Sheriff Brody's pointed questioning. This man who worked so hard to bring the pleasures of reading and the gift of knowledge to people—could he be a party to murder? She said impulsively: "I should thank you. In your office I saw a lovely oil painting of the Castle in summer. I'm planning on coming back in a few months to see the real thing, the Castle in bloom. If the library is still open, I know it will be because of your good work."

Her praise brought a shy, lopsided smile to the librarian's tired face. "Scott Wilson did that painting. Have you seen the murals he painted for the children's room? He can copy an illustration so well you'd believe it was the original." Mark's smile faded. "You hear of it sometimes, someone who has mental problems yet possesses extraordinary talent, say in music or mathematics, or art. But I'd never have suspected that Scott, who creates such beauty, would be capable of killing."

Alex began rooting through her book bag for a white business card with only her name and work number. She penciled in the words "private investigator" on the top of the card before she handed it to Salinger. "If you find yourself with problems stemming from Brody's investigation," she murmured, "call and ask for me."

"You think Brody is out to give me trouble?"

"I believe he's out to prove you were an accessory in Webb's murder." Alex replied flatly.

"You're kind to be concerned, but Ken and I have tangled over one thing or another for years. There's monetary competition between our county departments, so the sheriff is no friend to the library. But he'll never be able to prove that I helped a troubled friend commit murder. It's simply not true."

Alex glanced at the librarian's bandaged arm. "Mr. Salinger, I'm giving you my card because I'm afraid that Wilson was nowhere near here when Webb died."

Nearly an hour later, Alex finally pulled to the side of a well-lit stretch of roadway. Reaching beside her, she opened a carpeted metal hump that covered the van's engine. That was the nice thing about these old Chevys, they had the engine compartment (or the oven) right in the middle of the cab. Alex removed and unwrapped two glittering, steaming foil packages. The package of chicken liver went into a pie tin to cheer Watson, who was miffed after her long evening in a cold van.

Once Watson was served, Alex bit into pesto lasagne and gave a murmur of pleasure. It was creamy, but not too rich. The pine nuts and touch of nutmeg lent the dish a subtle perfection. This was undoubtedly the best meal she'd created on the van since Salinger had showed her that terrific Santa Linda Library book, *Some Cars Really Cook*.

After a satisfying snack, Alex wiped her hands and reached into her pocket to pull out three long, thin strands of nylon filament that had been manufactured to resemble strands of hair. She held them between her fingers and tugged them harshly but they did not break. "A wig," Alex murmured.

When the murderer collided with her in the library, Alex felt sure she'd been overpowered by someone stronger and more muscular than Scott Wilson—that frantic man she'd tackled on Media Day. Then, while searching for Wilson outside the library, Alex had found long strands of fake hair stuck to the sharp thorns of a pyracantha bush near the library entrance.

She fingered a curl of her own bright red hair. It was the bane of her detective's existence, being too striking, too fiery, and far too memorable. To keep a low profile, Alex often wore wigs, and she recognized them on others. She also diverted attention from her face and hair with loud scarves, ugly hats, exotic earrings, or eccentric clothes that called attention to themselves rather than the woman wearing them. So Alex understood the purpose of a long "hippy" wig, a suit of tattered, blood-smeared clothes, and a tweed hat pulled down low over the face. In that attention-getting costume, an impostor could convince witnesses that they'd "seen" the mumbler.

But Alex hadn't told any of this to Brody. He'd seemed too eager to push the librarian into a cell. Alex turned to the cat who was busy cleaning liver from her whiskers. "I just can't imagine Mark Salinger as a murderer. . . . You don't need to squint at me in that cynical way! I've seen him move bugs off the library steps so they wouldn't get squashed. He's organized literacy programs, book deliveries to shut-ins, and even movies in the multipurpose room that cater to the homeless. He cares about people! When I was tailing Luke Bishop and spending hours in the library, Salinger was always kind and courteous no matter what crazy disguise I wore. And believe me, Watson, there were times when I looked damn weird. Salinger even told me about the book *How to Spoil Your Cat*. Aha! *Now* you're interested. . . . Yep, all those homemade catnip toys, and the battery-powered heating pad that you're sitting on right now, you owe them to Mr. Salinger."

Alex began devouring pasta again without really noticing what she was eating. If the mumbler were arrested, she'd have to step forward, of course, but until then she was free to ponder Webb's death on her own. A screech stabbed Alex's ears and drowned out her speculations. Ms. Watson detested pasta, but she'd finished her own meal and she didn't like to watch Alex eat without sharing.

Alex put her fingers in her ears in self-defense. "Damn it, Watson, who can be a great detective with such a noisy assistant? I can't even hear myself deduce!"

The Chevy van groaned to a start, and Alex headed home to Venice. Though she'd never admit it to her noisy associate, she was just as happy to postpone any more deliberations. Too many of her deductions led just where the obnoxious (but far from stupid) Sheriff Brody might have expected. They led to the good-hearted, intelligent man who owned the murder weapon and had a whopping grudge against Webb—not to mention a slashed arm, a thorough knowledge of the library, and the same lanky build as the mumbler. They led straight to the Castle's marvelous librarian.

Chapter 8

THE SHERIFF AND his merry men deserted the Castle for Perry Webb's office. By ten-thirty, the murder site was sealed off, and the Castle was shut down for the night.

There was nothing more for Mark to do, and no logical reason for him to stand in the parking lot in the January cold. He stood in the chilly air for one more moment to survey the Castle, shining like starfire against the dark hills. He remembered that he'd once asked Scott to paint this lovely night view of the old building. Would it take the murder of Perry Webb to finally bring Scott the psychiatric help he'd needed for years, help that might have prevented this tragedy?

Under a combination of early moonlight and outdoor lamplight, the white Castle glowed like an opal. But Mark gained no peace from the picturesque scene. He winced at the memory of Webb sprawled dead in the microfilm storage room, and he heard the ghostly echo of the rattling gurney carrying the corpse to the mortuary hearse. No, the Castle would never be the same, and neither, Mark thought, would its librarian. Like the evening when Mark's wife had demanded a divorce, or the moment when he'd looked into his son's eyes and seen an unhappy, preoccupied stranger, tonight's murder had changed Mark's perceptions and altered his life.

Mark turned on his heel and launched into his long-legged stride. He could not solve the county's dilemmas alone here tonight, any more than he could solve his personal dilemmas of divorce and alienation from his son. The librarian's wounded arm pained him; he was going home to a solitary dinner and a lonely bed. But at least, unlike Webb, he would not lie, indifferent, under a coroner's probing knife.

"Mark? Are you alright?"

He nearly jumped three feet. Pale and silent, she'd materialized like a ghost.

"I see I've startled you back to earth," she said.

"Zoe! I thought everyone had already gone."

"I wanted to tell you that a valuable book seems to be missing. About a week ago, Eden Selby asked to see that book her grandmother wrote, *A Child's Garden*. I realized it wasn't on the locked glassed shelf behind my desk. And it hasn't been placed in the adult reference section by mistake either."

Mark barely heard Zoe's words. He was too overwhelmed by her presence. They stood on the path between the lights of the library and those of the parking lot. In the semidarkness, stress and weariness were not as visible on her face, and she might have been the same lovely teenager he'd noticed years ago when he'd first begun working in the library. With her soft, romantic looks, Zoe had resembled a princess stepping out of a fairy tale illustration. It had taken months before Mark realized that the girl was not only mortal, but very troubled, coming to the Castle to escape problems at home.

For some odd reason, the young Zoe had admired him, approaching Mark for information, advice, or just for companionship. Over the years, she'd remained friendly while becoming his hard-working, practical colleague. But somewhere in those same years, Mark's concern for a lovely, unhappy teenager had transformed itself into this terrible,

65

overpowering feeling that made his hands shaky, his feet leaden, and his Adam's apple so swollen that he could barely breathe, let alone speak.

When he'd thought she was about to leave him forever, Mark had been determined to express his feelings to Zoe. But now, once again he was tongue-tied. Even if he did speak up about his feelings, what then? Zoe had a long string of besotted admirers. Some of them, lacking children of their own, borrowed the children of friends just so they could sit at her feet during the Saturday morning story hour. How could Mark compete with these younger, more suitable men? Tonight, alone with her in the dark, he felt the urge to get away before he made a fool of himself. "Don't worry about stolen books," he said rather brusquely. "This has been a tough night, and you're still not well. You shouldn't be out here. We've just had a murder, you know."

But Zoe seemed to have a need to talk. "It's a crime that Eden has received so little out of all her grandmother's work on the Dysart estate. Kate Selby developed the landscaping and the flowers that made the Castle so famous, but Eden's received nothing for it. She can't even afford to buy a first edition of her grandmother's book. You'd think the Dysarts would have given her a copy instead of donating all the first editions to the library."

"I understand," Mark said. Though he didn't really understand why Zoe was standing here in the dark, discussing old injustices. Not that he minded. He swallowed, trying to moisten his dry throat. She'd come closer to place her cool hand on his arm. Her perfume smelled of gardenias.

"And tonight Eden's kids were telling me that their mother was going to make a lot of money because of Perry Webb."

"That doesn't sound very plausible."

"No, but that woman has such rotten luck, doesn't she? I mean, whatever Webb intended to do for Eden, it will certainly never happen now . . . now that he's dead." Zoe shuddered.

"You mustn't trouble yourself," Mark urged. "You need to recuperate."

But she went on as if she hadn't heard him. "The book isn't the only reason I came back to the library. Brody wanted to know if I'd seen you with the mumbler in the staff parking lot. I told him I hadn't seen anything of the kind, because I didn't use the staff parking lot. The path from the lot to the staff door is an uphill walk. The steps up to the door are steep, and I was worn out. But Brody wasn't satisfied with my dull facts. He seemed sure that if Laurel and I didn't go into the library through the staff door, there had to be some sinister reason why you did. Brody is out to get you, Mark."

"I guess my alibi for my wounded arm isn't very convincing."

"No, it's not a convincing story." Her wide eyes observed him searchingly, and Mark found himself reddening under their gaze. He busied himself staring at his shoes.

"But you don't need an alibi," Zoe continued in her forthright way. "This is no mystery murder. We all know who killed Perry Webb."

"Do we? I'm not so sure. I went to see Scott at the county hospital just before he was released. He'd learned about Claire's death and couldn't stop crying. He'd torn out handfuls of his hair, and he hadn't eaten for two days. I was horrified. I gave him bus fare, and he promised to go to San Francisco. He has a brother there."

"But, Mark, that poor kid is an alcoholic and a mentally disturbed, artistic genius. He couldn't follow through on plans to meet someone for lunch. Obviously he didn't follow through on traveling to San Francisco and obviously he used your brand-new scissors to take out his grief on Perry Webb."

"And how did Scott get my scissors?" Mark tugged nervously at his own hair as he verbalized the question that had been bothering him for hours. "Since the stabbing on Media Day, I've kept them in the bottom drawer of my desk. Surely if Scott went into my office, someone would have seen him and tried to stop him."

"That place was a zoo while we were gone! Laurel got a crazy phone call. The wheel went out on Jamaica's book cart. And you heard Professor Truesdell's stories about the way Pamela Dysart carried on after she threw Luke out of the library. For once I'd indulge in one of Jamaica's California Cosmic Explanations—'the moon is full.' "

Mark thought of Alexandra Winter and her pointed message that someone other than Scott had committed the murder. "Zoe, what happened on Media Day between Scott and Perry Webb? What caused that terrible fight?"

"That's a long story, and I'm kind of beat."

"Oh, of course." He felt the sudden cold wind that whirled dead leaves over the asphalt. "I shouldn't be tiring you."

"But if you're playing detective, I'll tell you all about Media Day. Just take me somewhere with cheap, delicious food and decent liquor. Tomorrow we have a day off, thanks to the fact that the library will be closed until the forensic team is finished with the microfilm room. And you must know the best place to go, Mark. I've seen dozens of people at the reference desk asking you for summations of the local restaurant reviews." She began walking toward his battered Plymouth.

Mark hurried after her. He cursed himself for driving an old car whose broken trunk was held down by a bungee cord, but he was overjoyed that he'd bothered to vacuum the car for the first time in weeks. "I thought you never drank, Zoe, because . . . because of your father."

Zoe smiled and took Mark's arm, serenely unaware of

the electric jolt she sent right through him. "Even the children of alcoholics know that there are times when there's no substitute for a good, stiff drink. Murder is just one of those times."

"Did Webb consider Mark Salinger his enemy, Ms. Dean?" Sheriff Brody leaned back in Perry's well-padded executive chair to question Webb's secretary.

"Mr. Webb . . . always said . . . 'A man can't be effective without making enemies.' " Meg Dean sniffled up her tears and blew her nose on Brody's handkerchief. "Nothing stopped Mr. Webb when he felt he was helping people. He used to tell me, 'Meg, I'm on the side of the taxpayers, and the taxpayers are on the side of the angels.' He was so very brave." The secretary's thin shoulders began trembling with sobs. Meg Dean was a bony woman with an incongrously round, rosy face. Brody thought that crying made her look like a soggy apple.

The sheriff looked around the real estate tycoon's brokerage office. The burglary had left behind toppled chairs, scattered files, and rifled drawers. But Webb's place was still a class act. It was as gray as the old man's head, with pale gray walls, plush silver carpet, furniture of gray leather and even a desk of weathered, gray wood. The frames on those expensive paintings shone like silver. The sheriff sighed. Old man Webb had sure known how to make money. And if Webb had lived, Brody might have made some money, too. For one thing, Webb would have eliminated the county tax money going to that crappy Castle. Then a sheriff could earn a decent salary. For another, Webb had promised Brody a piece of the action when the Castle was developed into a hotel, golf course, and homes. Now the hope of real estate profits was dead, and Brody wanted to know why.

He asked aloud. "Did anyone ever threaten Webb?"

Meg nodded. "Salinger, of course, and drug dealers, too. They'd peddle their poison across the street at Center Street Park. Mr. Webb had several stores fronting the park, and he helped his tenants organize a neighborhood watch to drive the drug dealers out. One of the dealers, EZ they called him, broke those windows there on the street side of the office and used to phone us with horrible threats. But Mr. Webb never let threats stop him. He'd say: 'I'm determined to save Santa Linda from the stranglehold of tax-happy bureaucrats and the clutches of greedy drug dealers.' " The thought of Webb's heroism brought forth another gasping sob, and Meg blew more snot into the sheriff's handkerchief.

Brody fidgeted, a little annoyed. This had been his one quarrel with Webb. Those so-called drug dealers in the park were mostly high school kids who smoked weed when they got tired of playing basketball. Webb had made himself out to be a hero, cleaning up the town. To Brody, Webb was a bozo who screamed for cops when some punk gave him the finger.

Still, you had to hand it to the old bastard. He sure knew how to hire loyal secretaries. Brody's lazy secretary liked to be called a "managing assistant" and wouldn't walk across the room to make him a cup of coffee. Meg Dean had rushed out here late at night in a state of real grief for her boss. Thanks to Meg, Brody now had a list of the items stolen from Webb's office: petty cash, some papers, a radio, gold pens, a watercolor, and some discarded library books. The watercolor had been painted by Judy Garland, but far more valuable art items, including a Tiffany paperweight, had been left behind. This robbery had been pulled off by Scott Wilson, Brody guessed. It had "loony" stamped all over it.

There was a brief knock, and Lieutenant Karen Drexler's dark head popped in at the inner office door. "Sorry to interrupt you, but there's an important fax from San Francisco."

Brody was not unhappy to excuse himself and leave the sniffling Meg behind, along with his ruined handkerchief. He took the fax and read it over twice. "So the mumbler's been croaked all this time! He was shot to death last night in an alley behind a South San Francisco bus station. They've even caught the killer; the motive was robbery, the kid had plenty of money on him. Kind of makes you wonder about all our eyewitness reports from people who claim they saw him tonight."

Lieutenant Drexler's sleek head bobbed in assent. "So who killed Webb if Wilson was dead?" she asked.

Suddenly Brody grinned. "It was easy for Salinger to disguise himself, kill Webb, then dump his disguise and walk back into the library through the staff door. Just give me a day or two. I'll nail that librarian."

The evening that had begun as a nightmare was rapidly becoming a dream come true. Mark and Zoe had decided to drive to a Chinese deli for wine, lemon grass soup, and pot stickers before returning to Zoe's hillside cottage. Now, Mark relaxed in an overstuffed chair that faced a used-brick fireplace. Above the faint, intermittent sound of traffic came the rush of a swollen winter stream surging over rocks. Zoe sat on the raised hearth, holding a coffee mug filled with wine, telling Mark about Media Day.

The firelight picked up the flush on her high cheekbones and glittered on her golden hair. Stanzas of romantic poetry came to Mark's mind. "For she was beautiful/Her beauty made/The bright world dim" was one of the more fitting verses.

"Perry Webb was my father's second cousin," Zoe began. "He visited my mother often—too often. Mother was a good-looking woman, and even though I was small, it

71

was obvious to me that 'dear Uncle Perry' as she taught me to call him, was in love with her. Often, when Dad was working, 'Uncle Perry' would come and follow my mother into her room while I was sent out to play with a new toy he'd brought me."

Mark lifted his head in astonishment, but Zoe continued, her voice as gentle as if she were reading a fairy tale during story hour. "About a year after Mother died, Dad opened a bookstore. He rented a storefront from Perry—thank God I no longer had to call him 'dear uncle.' Dad and I scraped by for three years. Then, when my father tried to renew the lease, Perry Webb tripled the rent."

Zoe stared at the fire and sipped her wine. "Dad asked for just a small extension, and that horrible man told him no, but that he'd take a lien on our house for the increased rent. My father lost everything, of course, except visits from Perry, who came by to give us unwanted advice, and to try to win me over with presents and attention. That was also when my father began to drink. The whole town knows what happened after one of Webb's visits. Dad drove into the garage, closed the door behind him, and left the motor running while he finished a bottle of Cutty Sark."

Mark heard the pain in her voice and went to sit beside her.

But Zoe stood up, taking a log from an open tin trunk near the hearth. She shoved the log into the fire, rousing a fierce trail of sparks. "No one knew how much I hated Perry or how often I fantasized his murder. Funny, I never thought of scissors. My taste in poetic justice ran more to a lethal blow to the skull with a full bottle of Cutty Sark. But Webb began befriending me and helping me through school. I suppose he felt guilty, and though my hatred didn't die, I had no one else. I decided that success was the best revenge, so I kept my murder fantasies quiet."

"Until Media Day?" Mark guessed.

"Very clever, Sherlock. You can imagine that I was less than thrilled when Perry tried to enlist my help in some stupid campaign against 'crimes in the library.' I told Webb to fuck off, in bureaucratic terms, of course. Even if I hadn't had personal reasons to despise him, I had no patience for his nonsense, what with Media Day and the camera crews coming. Poor Jamaica had already gone running for you, because I didn't want KPXX's cameras focusing on Scott, who was mumbling like crazy from under the furniture."

"So Scott overheard your argument with Webb?"

"I don't know if he paid attention. It was odd, Mark. While Perry was haranguing me, Scott came out from under my desk and began apologizing to him."

"Apologizing? Why?"

"Who knows? Perry didn't. He stared at Scott as astounded as if an oversize insect had stood up and begun a conversation. Then, ignoring Scott, he told me in his pompous way that he was disappointed in my lack of concern for crime. He said, 'Of course, with that drunk Jon Latham raising you, I suppose I shouldn't be surprised.' When Webb insulted my father, those years of anger over his affair with my mother finally came out. I screamed the truth and my hatred at him."

"The wrath of angels," Mark murmured.

"Angels? Oh, I see. You mean me."

She smiled with such softness that Mark shivered in the warm room. "Zoe, I . . . I have to tell you something. . . ."

She wasn't listening. She stirred the fire, causing a bright leap of flame. "I hardly expected his response. He wrapped his flabby arms around me and said I was his child!" Zoe dropped the poker with a crash and nervously paced the room. Her delicate body was rigid. Fury blazed like the reflections of the fire in her angelic eyes. "I—I pushed him away, shouting that he was a liar. It frightened Scott, and he . . . well, he went after Perry to defend me. They battled

73

back and forth before Scott finally flashed the scissors." Zoe stopped and stood motionless, remembering: "I tried to push Perry out of harm's way. But he thought I was going to hurt him, and he shoved me. I slammed into the blades. Oh, Mark . . ." She collapsed beside him, her shining head bowed in her hands. "I can't help wondering if Scott killed Perry tonight in some crazy effort to protect me."

Mark enfolded Zoe in his arms, stroking her hair. He might be slow, but he was not oblivious. He understood now why she'd waited for him in the parking lot and invited him here. Murder had unleashed her terrible, repressed agony. Like the wine, the Chinese food, and the fire, Mark had been enlisted to bring her comfort. After tonight, she'd go back to her young crowd of followers, and he would suffer over her more than ever. But that was tomorrow. Tonight she needed him. When Zoe turned her lovely face toward him, Mark bent to kiss away the tears slowly welling in her clear, blue eyes.

Later, while the moon drifted in and out of the low, racing clouds, teasing the darkness and highlighting Zoe's gleaming body, Mark lay in her narrow bed. With the warmth of her limbs around him, Mark foolishly risked his temporary ecstasy. "Marry me, Zoe," he murmured.

To his astonishment she gave him a long, slow caress and breathed into his ear: "What took you so long? I've wanted to marry you for years."

The following day, cuddled with Zoe on the porch swing in a patch of rare January sunshine, Mark was less than prepared for the sight of Ken Brody puffing his way up Zoe's steep driveway. "A fine, good afternoon to you both." The sheriff seemed surprisingly cheerful. "I've had a hell of a time finding you, Mark. This was pure luck. I came here to tell Ms. Latham that she's prominently featured in Perry Webb's will." Brody gave Zoe a knowing wink. "She's a rich young lady."

The swing creaked as Zoe sat bolt upright in shock. Mark took one look at her startled expression before he hustled down the driveway to head Brody off. "Why look for me?" he asked.

"Your buddy, the mumbler, was in a Frisco morgue last night. So he couldn't have killed Webb. In the meantime, an informant called this morning saying you're the killer and the evidence is in your car trunk. Sorry, Mark. You know I don't believe a word of it, but I have to search your car. I have a warrant here."

Mark's love and sun-warmed body went cold. "Go ahead. You won't need a key. The lock on the trunk is broken so just unwrap the bungee cord." The librarian hurried down the crazy, vertical slope of the driveway, then stopped, stunned.

Brody was pulling bloody ribbons of clothing and a brown wig from the old car. The sounds of traffic and the rush of the hillside stream grew louder—roaring in Mark's ears. He could barely hear Ken informing him of his rights as an arrested man.

Chapter 9

WHAT A BUSINESS! Ross hit the brakes just as a ponytailed man careened off the curb. The pedestrian, with tattooed snakes slithering over his naked chest and a live, black King snake wrapped around his arm, bolted across the road and just missed being hit by the fender of Ross's Lincoln Town Car. The young man shook his fist at Ross, cursed, and sent a glob of saliva in the direction of the Lincoln's windshield.

Ross smiled and waved back. He was obviously in Venice, California. He drove slowly between the city's palm trees, listening to the call of the ducks in the canals. He never would have believed he'd be driving all the way from Santa Linda to Venice just to chase down that goofy Alexandra Winter.

Ross braked again, this time for a black-and-white dog wearing a red bandanna. He reminded himself that for Mark's sake he was going to "keep an open mind."

It had been on Friday afternoon, just before Mark's arraignment on charges of first-degree murder, that Salinger had asked Ross to find Alexandra Winter.

"Alex thought she could help me, and I'll never forget how brave she was on Media Day."

Ross knew he should have stated his feelings about the redhead right up front. But Mark had sounded so hopeful that Ross hated to disillusion him. Since the death of his own wife, Ross had learned to live with hopelessness, but he was not about to teach that bleak emotion to Mark. Besides, this had been one of the craziest weeks in Santa Linda's history. Perry Webb had been murdered in the peaceful heart of the book-filled Castle, and Mark Salinger, the kindest, most unlikely killer in the world, had been arrested for murder. Who knew what would happen next? Maybe even this nutty redhead who relied on a one-eyed black cat could be useful. Stranger things had already happened.

So Saturday morning, against his better judgement, Ross had called Ms. Winter's agency from the number on the card she'd given to Mark. The agency was closed, but an answering service had connected him with George Stewart whose praise of "our brilliant investigator, Alexandra Winter," might have reassured Ross if it weren't for Stewart's immediate follow-up mentioning "her extreme popularity and limited availability," with the consequent necessity of high fees. Still, Ross pressed to see the detective immediately and arranged to go out to her home that very afternoon.

It didn't take the attorney long to locate Ms. Winter's apartment on the second floor of a butter yellow Victorian near the boardwalk. The gingerbreaded house had a distinctive sign in the bottom bay window that read: Psychic Readings: Tarot Cards, Palmistry, Auras, or Crystals. By Appointment Only.

"Alex's landlady is a witch," George Stewart had explained to Ross, adding reassuringly, "but don't worry. Kerry's a good witch. She does a lot of work in missing persons."

Venice was a coastal town with milder weather than inland Santa Linda, and the Victorian contained a lush, beautiful yard. Ross didn't know what he'd expected, maybe a weedy jungle. Instead, he found cheerful whorls and vines of color that towered above the back fence in the alley where he parked. He went through a squeaky side gate and down a flagged path lined with patches of flowers, herbs, and the dark green of winter vegetables. Then he gingerly climbed the patched, wooden stairs at the back of the yard that led to the second floor. He tried to avoid kicking over the potted irises placed at the edge of each step. When he reached the porch landing, he found the back door closed and locked. A rapid knocking and shouted hello brought no response, and Ross cursed George Stewart who'd assured him that an appointment would be set up immediately, and that Ms. Winter would be available between four and five P.M.

Stopping at the front lower entrance of the Victorian, Ross decided to speak to the landlady about Ms. Winter's whereabouts. A glance through the front window revealed the "witch" to be a tall, heavily made-up woman wearing a dazzling, Day-Glo turban. Her flowing clothes were part coat, part cape, and maybe three-quarters satin nightgown. She sat on a fat purple sofa, arms outstretched, fingers splayed, her head bent over a crystal ball. A teenager, whose closely sheared hair was just a shade or two brighter than the couch, watched her intently and wrung his hands in nervous anticipation.

The sight sent Ross back to the car immediately. He felt a growing relief in the certainty that he wouldn't have to deal with Ms. Winter, the Great Cat Communicator. He'd tell Mark that it was too bad and a shame, but Alexandra Winter was just too flaky to be considered seriously.

So he was almost disappointed when, after heading his Lincoln back to the freeway, he passed the Safeway and saw a young woman clad in blue jeans and a bulky sweater, her arms filled with string bags of groceries. Her hair was a curly mass of fire. Silver hoops dangled from her ears, and her black cat jumped down from a nearby tree to trail the redhead's heels, as faithfully as any hound. Ross followed the pair from the store to the apartment, hanging about a half block back. He sat in the car awhile debating whether to go in. Then he remembered the sight of Mark in a prison jumpsuit. Ross sighed in resignation, returned to the Victorian, and once again climbed the back steps to her door.

The door at the landing was still closed, but through a high open window the attorney could hear Ms. Winter speaking. What he heard wasn't reassuring. She was playing her answering machine and discussing the messages with her silent cat.

"Ms. Watson," she was saying. "I've had it up to here! George just won't give up on his *Playboy* idea. After all the times I said I wouldn't pose, he sends a sleazy photographer over to talk to me. Just listen to the message that George left me this morning . . ."

Ross heard a beep, and then George Stewart rumbled on, telling Alex how much she'd like his "good buddy," a hell of a photographer who was coming that afternoon, "just to talk about a *Playboy* spread."

"Hear that?" the detective asked her cat. "I'll bet you a fishstick that the sleaze bag who tailed me from the grocery store in his big, expensive Lincoln Town Car (that scum, standing on our porch right this minute) is from *Playboy*!"

The back door swung open, and Ross found himself confronted by a redheaded fury pointing a weapon at his face. "Just who are you, and why have you been following and spying on me?" she demanded.

The attorney was not a man easily fazed by a squirt gun. He would have knocked the silly weapon out of her hand had the black cat not greeted him like a long lost friend and flung herself ecstatically at his knees. Ross staggered back, tripped over one of those damned terra-cotta pots of irises, and nearly toppled backward over the stair railing.

The redhead grabbed his arm with her free hand and

yanked him from danger with surprising strength. She pulled him toward her, and for a moment the two were nose to nose. Green eyes locked into icy gray ones. "I know you," Alex declared suddenly. "You're the jogger . . . Heathcliff! I saw you at the Castle in Santa Linda."

Ross wrenched his arm away straightening his sport coat. "George Stewart was supposed to make an appointment for me. I'm from—"

"Playboy!" She finished his sentence for him. "Damn that George! He hired you to photograph me even while I was working at the Castle! Well, you can just go right back down the steps, Heathcliff." She poked a harsh finger into his chest. "I'm not stripping for you today or any other day, no matter what George told you. Get out of here and don't come back! And Ms. Watson, you get away from that man and stop purring at him! Honestly, you have the morals of an alley cat."

Alex stomped back to her door and threw it open. The answering machine was still playing a long message from her landlady Kerry, who was complaining about Watson's behavior. Then the machine beeped again, and the next voice was George Stewart's: "Alex, I canceled the *Playboy* photographer because Ross Coulter, Mark Salinger's lawyer, is coming to see you between four and five about that murder up in Santa Linda."

"Oh, shit!" Alex said to George's voice as he went on with the details. She shot out the door and flew down the stairs.

There he was, tramping down her garden path, hampered by Ms. Watson who kept pouncing in front on him, trying to rub her body against his swiftly moving ankles. Jesus! How could she have thought that this arrogant, buttoned-down snob with his leather briefcase was one of George's low-life friends? She should have known at once he was an attorney. Hadn't she been married to Charlie, the liar lawyer? Alex chased after Heathcliff, fearful that she'd already lost the case of a lifetime.

She caught up to him at the gate. "I—I'm so sorry, Mr. Coulter," she panted. "I thought you were . . . I mean . . . well, you know who I thought you were, but I was wrong. Please come upstairs. I'd like to try to help you."

"You're too kooky to help your cat catch a flea! I'm sure a murder case is well beyond you." Ross turned his back to her and tugged at the reluctant gate.

Alex opened her mouth to argue, counted to ten speedily and forced herself to say politely, "Here, wait a minute . . . I'll help you with that." She pushed past him and twisted the catch up and to the right so that the gate opened easily. Then she gave the case a last try. "Please, Mr. Coulter, you've come all this way. Let's talk."

The attorney turned and faced her. He was just as she'd remembered him, his dark face set in tense, unsmiling lines, and his startling gray eyes as cutting as diamonds. "Just tell me one thing, Ms. Winter," he said with the sarcasm that she also remembered. "Do you attack all your clients with squirt guns?"

Alex stared at the orange, plastic toy she still brandished in her hand. "Oh, this," she said. "Some of George's so-called friends can be pretty rough, and this has a cayenne pepper mixture in it. I'm not legally allowed to carry a gun; California law makes it very tough for a detective to get a permit . . . even mace can get our agency sued these days. But cayenne is safe and very effective. Apparently a SWAT team in Colorado uses it. I learned about cayenne in *Organic Living*, a book that Mr. Salinger found for me, before . . . before he was arrested." Alex heard her voice rise with emotion. "Please reconsider, Mr. Coulter. Mr. Salinger deserves a chance to prove his innocence, and I'd be privileged to assist him."

Coulter hesitated. He gave Alex a long disapproving look

81

before he bent to push the purring Watson off his foot. "Let's go upstairs," he sighed.

Alex edged him through her small, herb-filled kitchen into the living room, and suddenly saw her living room through Coulter's unfavorable gaze. The comfortable furniture wasn't actually antique; it was secondhand. Her needlepoint rugs were sentimental, and she really should stop being softhearted about throwing out straggly house plants.

But she breathed a sigh of relief when the attorney deigned to sit down in her Queen Anne chair, the one facing a bay window that overlooked the sea. "Let me get you some coffee. It'll only take a minute," she urged. "Watson, get off the man's lap. I'm sorry, I'll throw her out. . . ."

But Coulter began petting the cat's sleek, velvet head, and Alex decided to leave well enough alone. She closed the kitchen door and took down the kettle to fill it with water. Then she put her hands on her knees and began to hyperventilate like a diver fighting the bends. This was it! All she had to do was be a decent hostess and convince this Coulter jerk that she was somewhat eccentric but not deranged. Then she'd be working for that nice Mark Salinger, and it would be good-bye Sleazy Street, hello murder! But what should she serve a sarcastic, son-of-a-bitch attorney who held the key to her future?

Alex settled on bringing in coffee laced with amaretto and (since Heathcliff was a jogger) low-fat golden squash muffins. She'd copied the recipe from a book in the Castle, naturally. The muffins sounded horrible, but they tasted better than pumpkin pie. In the living room, she set down a tray in front of Mr. Sarcastic Son of a Bitch, who still had Watson on his lap. He was staring out through the window, where sunlight struggled through gray clouds. A worried frown touched his full, dark brows.

"What kind of case do they have against Mr. Salinger?"

Alex asked as the attorney took coffee and, at her urging, reluctantly picked up a muffin.

"An anonymous call came into the county," he told her. "The caller claimed he'd seen Mark Salinger running out of the bushes near the picnic area behind the library. Mark supposedly carried a wig and a bundle of slashed, bloody clothing in his arms." Coulter sipped his coffee and flicked a muffin crumb off of Watson's head. "The caller said he'd followed Mark. He saw Mark take the clothes into the parking lot and stuff them into the trunk of his car."

"That story is full of holes," Alex protested. "No one could have recognized the mumbler *or* Mark Salinger. I know the picnic area very well." She didn't add that it was the place where she'd tumbled off the fire escape and fallen into the rose bushes. "The only light comes from the arched windows in the Children's Room, and those of the upper floors. Those lights barely illuminate the old picnic deck or the bushes." She put down the coffee. Her wicker rocker creaked as Alex thought things over. "And why would Mr. Salinger risk hauling bloody clothes around the side of the Castle to the brightly lit staff parking lot where anyone might see him?"

To Alex's surprise, Ross nodded approvingly at her logic, and without disturbing the purring Ms. Watson, reached over the cat's head for a second muffin. "The accusation has even more problems. Although bloody clothes and the wig were found in the trunk of Mark's old car, anyone could have put them there. The Plymouth's trunk doesn't even lock. The damn thing's held down by a bungee cord, and Mark's been meaning to fix it for months. If it wasn't for the physical evidence that was established late Friday afternoon, I wouldn't be so worried." Ross put the muffin down as if his appetite were suddenly gone. "But that evidence is damning. The clothes were slashed to pieces, and the cotton fibers of the shirt fabric held traces of two unmistakable blood types, O and A. The material was rushed to a serology lab in Los Angeles for DNA analysis, and traces of both Mark's blood and Webb's blood were identified on the fabric." Ross stared out at the water and shook his head in dismay. "And that's what worries me, Ms. Winter."

"Mark's blood and Perry Webb's blood on the same shirt . . ." Alex stared at her guest wonderingly. "That means Mark was nearby when Webb was stabbed."

"I have to agree," Ross admitted. "If I were prosecuting, I'd have a forensic expert on the stand testifying that the blood must have splattered on Mark's shirt when he stabbed Parry Webb. Then I'd explain how Mark ran through the library in the bloody shirt pretending to be the mumbler. I'd point out that the two were approximately the same height and build. Of course, since I'm on defense, I'll attack the credibility of D.N.A. analysis, but frankly that's an uphill battle."

Outside the clouds parted, and the sun lit up the gray ocean with cheery flecks of gold. Alex had rarely felt so depressed. "What's Mark's explanation?" she asked.

Ross removed the protesting Watson from his lap and stood up. He strode angrily to the window, and Alex saw that the lawyer's fists were clenched. "He has none, but there has to be an explanation! I've known Mark for eleven years. He couldn't murder anyone. Not even that bastard Webb!"

Alex shook her head in dismay. "For Mark's own sake, make him explain his vague story that some unknown teenagers threatened him and wounded him with a knife. . . ."

Ross spun around. "It's that knife story that I want you to investigate. I've talked to police, and I've learned about a young man in his twenties named Earnest Zachary Moore. He's called 'EZ,' and police tell me he hangs out at Center Street Park in the downtown area of Santa Linda.

He's known for flashing a knife around, and for his threats against Webb." The attorney returned to his chair and took an envelope from his briefcase. "In addition, there are two people who seem to have disappeared since Webb's death, Eden Selby and Luke Bishop. No one's seen them anywhere. I have a mug shot of EZ when he was arrested for possession of pot two years ago. I have photos of Selby and Bishop, and I also have a list of items from the robbery in Webb's office. Police feel the break-in was coincidental to the murder and that one of the addicts in the area was responsible. I'm not so sure of that, though the stolen items make an odd list. Some of Webb's mortgage files may have been taken, along with a watercolor, two gold pens, a radio, and, of all things, some discarded library books that Webb bought at the Castle."

Alex gladly appropriated the envelope and a card with Ross's home and office numbers and addresses. "Do you mind if I kibitz with witnesses about some of the mysteries surrounding this murder?" she asked.

"Kibitz?" Ross asked incredulously.

"That's what my boss calls it. I want to chat ... you know ... chew the fat. My boss, Sam, taught me that good detectives flex their jaws before they flex their muscles or reach for weapons. He's often said that even with a doctorate in forensic science, you're not a good investigator if you can't shmooze." Ross's face was returning to its usual harsh lines, and Alex added quickly: "I know that there's value in having tough detectives bully people into cooperation. Brody was damn good at that, but there were also people in that library who were scared, upset, or just plain relieved that Webb was dead. Brody could have used those emotions to draw his witnesses out, and, for example, he might have found out why the library was in such chaos. Instead—"

Alex stopped her explanation as a willowy, turbaned figure entered the living room, tripping over her flowing robes. "Damn this dratted costume!" the landlady complained. "Clients these days are so demanding. I don't know what's the matter with this new generation. It's not enough if you solve their problems and straighten out their lives. You've got to dress up like some sort of circus gypsy while you do it. Take the accountant I saw just yesterday. I'm telling him to slow down that BMW of his or he'll be in a tragic accident. And he's looking around my place complaining about its 'ambiance.' "

Alex clutched her envelope. From the look on Coulter's face he was about to snatch it back, fire her, and make this the shortest investigation on record.

"That reminds me, Alex," the landlady shook her finger at her surprised tenant before she could be interrupted. "When you go away to solve this latest tragedy in Santa Linda, you're going to have to take Ms. Watson with you. Whenever you leave that cat behind, she gets lonely and comes down to talk to my clients. The group I have coming over this next couple of days will just collapse and foam at the mouth if a one-eyed, black cat strolls through their reading."

Kerry turned to Alex's stiff-backed, frowning client. After smoothing her flowing clothing and pushing wayward strands of gray hair back under her turban, she held out her hand. "Hello. Mr. Ross Coulter, isn't it? I'm Kerry. I've known Alex for years. She'll do a great job. Don't you worry. You wouldn't know it to look at her, but she has good, old-fashioned common sense."

"Kerry!" Alex demanded in embarrassment. "How do you know Mr. Coulter's name? And how did you know I was going to Santa Linda?"

"Just a moment." Her landlady waved Alex's question aside with a vague flap of her heavily jeweled hand. "You just wouldn't believe how *superstitious* my clients are, Mr.

Coulter. Lately, it's not enough to tell their future; they don't believe anything unless it's accompanied by fifteenth-century tarot cards or Himalayan Crystal, or some other faddish nonsense." She shook her turbaned head and sighed. "Honestly, Mr. Coulter, when you're able to *see* you just *see*, that's all. It could be while you're mopping the floor or sitting on the can. . . ."

"Kerry!" Alex warned.

"Or it could be when you're looking into someone's eyes." The landlady peered nearsightedly upward into Ross Coulter's cold gray eyes, caught her breath, and took a step backward. "Oh, my," she said suddenly, sounding old and confused. "Oh, dear, I'm so sorry about your wife."

Alex nearly fainted. This ice cube of a man was probably a bachelor. Well, it was nice to be part of a murder investigation for five minutes, anyway. She tried quickly to change the subject: "How did you know that I'm going to work in Santa Linda, Kerry? Don't tell me you saw it in a crystal!"

"I know about your job interview, darling, because you don't answer your phone. That rude George Stewart was pestering me to make sure that you kept your appointment with Mr. Coulter."

"Ah, so George browbeat you into coming up to check things out. I'm sorry, Kerry. Why don't you sit down and have a muffin while I escort Mr. Coulter out." The sooner she got Coulter out the door, the better. By now he was gaping at Kerry in shock, and Alex couldn't blame him.

"George didn't send me here," Kerry snapped. "I wouldn't let that bully push me around. I'm here because of the emergency call from that poor Barron Dysart." Kerry pulled her robes around her indignantly. "He needs you very badly, Alex. His sister Stacy has almost died. . . . Mr. Dysart found her in the bathtub with her wrists slit!"

Chapter 10

A BRIEF STORM washed muddy cat prints off the roof of the Chevy van as it rattled over the interstate, through a narrow mountain pass, and into the wide lanes of Santa Linda County. Alex's vehicle lumbered through rain, on into shrouded floating puffs of mountain fog, and at last into cool, intermittent sunshine.

Santa Linda was a large, mountainous county made up of small towns and miles of county unincorporated lands. Alex drove north though Minersville, Arboles, and Greenwood. She watched the road, enjoyed the scenery, and ate the blueberry turnovers that she'd heated for breakfast on the van's motor. The Chevy rolled along under the shadow of Manzanita Mountain before Alex reached the city that the county was named for. In Santa Linda City, Alex checked herself into a motel-apartment complex called the Blue Flamingo.

She'd stayed there before. Santa Linda was well over three hours northeast of L.A., and there'd been times during the Dysart investigation when it was impractical to make the long commute back to Venice. At those times, the Blue Flamingo had been Alex's home away from home. The apartment had several advantages, not the least of which was its tolerant owner, Mr. Rudnick. Rudnick left his tenants strictly alone once they'd paid well and heard the story of the Blue Flamingo. "This used to be a failing hotel," Rudnick loved to explain. "The minute I saw that pink flamingo on the roof, I hired an artist to cover the bird with blue paint." Rudnick puffed on his cigarette and grinned. "People started coming in from the highway complaining that flamingos are pink. While they were spouting off, I'd talk them into taking a room. That blue bird of happiness turned my business right around!"

Like the azure bird on the roof, the apartments were colorful. Alex turned the key into her mauve door and put her suitcases into room thirteen. She packed the pink refrigerator freezer full of vegetarian meals, precooked at home, and brought in the box of catnip toys and the stereo radio that would keep Watson company. She did a quick bath and changed into a suit with a flared skirt before pinning up her hair, making up her face, and replacing her dangling, black cat earrings with pearl studs. Natural Apple Blossom perfume went behind her ears and touched her throat.

At last Alex patted the cat farewell. "Keep your claws crossed, Watson. I'm off to begin the case of a lifetime."

The Chevy bounced on old, badly worn shocks past commercial buildings, some of ivy-smothered brick, others trimmed in styles that ran the gamut from gingerbread to wedding cake. Santa Linda City's famous "charm" flashed by the van's windows almost unnoticed as Alex pondered her new situation. In her shoulder bag was the envelope Ross had given her as well as a note signed by Mark Salinger, asking people to cooperate with her investigation. There was also a cellular phone, a symbol of her new status.

"Don't use the damn thing too much. It's expensive," George had growled.

But Barron Dysart had already called her twice on that phone—just to make sure she was really on her way. "Mother is hysterical," he told her. "We found Stacy sprawled out in the Jacuzzi water. She . . . she was just lying there while the jets pumped her own blood around her."

"Are you sure you want *me* to visit Stacy? I'm probably the last person that she'd want to see."

"She asked for you. Not by name, of course, but she knows I hired a detective to prove to my mother that Luke Bishop was a scheming, lying—"

"Why does Stacy want a detective?" Alex interrupted Barron's familiar diatribe against his mother's lover.

"Luke has disappeared. He's left Santa Linda. Maybe he's left the country. Who the hell knows? Stacy is afraid he's gone off with some woman. She's desperate to have you find him!" Barron's voice caught and choked. "Stacy's not a strong girl, Alex. Thank God the doctors saved her. When she opened her eyes in the hospital, the first thing she told me was that Luke alone could make her want to live."

Alex reassured Barron with the explanation that she was working for Mark Salinger, and that she'd been assigned the task of finding Luke Bishop so that she could question him in regard to Webb's murder. Her explanation seemed to satisfy Barron, and he'd relaxed enough to recover his own brand of humor.

"Is Luke Bishop a suspect, Alex? Terrific! I'm going to insist that Mother quit giving money to the American Civil Liberties Union. If Bishop is the murderer, I wouldn't want the A.C.L.U. to abolish capital punishment!"

In contrast to the quaint architecture of downtown Santa Linda, the hospital was an ugly, squat, square stucco whose unadorned boxiness was almost a relief to the eye. Alex parked her car near Barron's black Cadillac and headed to the entrance where heavy glass doors closed behind her on a dark and hushed interior. She crossed over gleaming, high-gloss floors to a waiting area of thick carpeting and heavy furniture. Barron was there in slacks and a sweater, engrossed in a low-pitched conversation with his mother.

Pamela extended neither her hand nor any greeting, but Barron enfolded Alex in a smothering hug. "You'll see," he told his mother. "Alex will fix everything."

"Terrific," Pamela answered dryly. "You stay here, Barron. I'll talk with Miss Fixit outside. I need some air."

"But, Mother—" The large rugged man was stopped in midprotest by a quelling stare. He backed up and collapsed into his chair, saying weakly, "Don't be long. Visiting hours start at twelve o'clock. I want to take Alex to Stacy's room on the dot."

Alex followed Pamela out through a side door leading to a glassed-in building. "That's the cafeteria, and there's a small patio outside. Take a table at the far end where we can talk," Pamela ordered. "The patio is the only place in this hellhole where a person can smoke. That's one reason I didn't want Barron with us. I'm dying for a cigarette, and I just can't take another one of my son's pious lectures."

Alex found a table still wet with the morning's brief rain. She stepped back in the cafeteria a moment and collected some napkins to dry it and the chairs. Someone, for the sake of privacy, had pushed the table to the edge of the flagged tiles near a hedge of oleanders. Alex brushed away poisonous oleander leaves that the February wind had scattered across the tabletop.

Pamela came out of the cafeteria with a tray bearing two danish pastries and two glasses of orange juice. In the sunlight, Pamela's platinum hair glowed with the same chemical luster as the polished hospital floors. Her slender figure carried clothes well, like today's sapphire suit of pure silk. But the fine lines around the older woman's mouth and eyes were clearly visible beneath her makeup, and she held her body stiffly, as if too much movement pained her.

Pamela set the tray down and sank into her chair. "The

91

coffee here is made from water they wash the bedpans in, but the orange juice is freshly squeezed. Well, Alex, if I may call you that. Your videotape has ruined my life, and you've caused my daughter to try to kill herself. Tell me, are you satisfied now?"

"I'm sorry for your pain, but the videotape just told the truth."

Pamela stared out at the sword-shaped leaves of the oleander bushes. "Are you a truth seeker, Alex? Santa Linda is full of them, but usually they choose harmless spiritual activities like standing on their heads, sitting on their meditative asses, or traipsing off to drool at the feet of some guru with flowers around his neck and millions in his pockets. Next time you go looking for truth, stay away from my family and my love life! To me you're just a thief who stole my happiness!"

Alex fiddled with her heavy inedible pastry. She suddenly felt as though she were sitting across from her mother. The two women didn't look alike, of course. Mother's rayon knits, unlike Pamela's designer silks, were bought on sale. Her hairstyles were formed from rollers and hairspray rather than expensive scissoring, and Mom usually liked a drink that had more of a kick than orange juice. But Pamela's failure to accept responsibility for her own muddles, and Pamela's laments over Alex's behavior—these were Mother's forte.

"You've stolen my happiness, Alex," her mother would say. Then she'd list the *"if only's."* "If only I didn't have to worry about you every minute. If only you'd go back to dear Charlie. If only you'd find a decent job I could tell my friends about. If only you'd get rid of that hideous one-eyed cat!"

Alex spoke to Pamela with the same overly reasonable tone of voice she used with her mother: "You're welcome to blame me for Luke's unfaithfulness if it makes you feel better. I can't stop you. But why not give up on blame and just get on with your life?"

"I see you're full of advice. You're a real 'Dear Alex,' aren't you?"

"I'm only speaking from experience, Ms. Dysart. My ex-husband Charlie makes your Luke seem like a eunuch."

"Oh, Alex, I wish I were dead!" The words burst suddenly from the elegant painted mouth. "I can't live without Luke!" Pamela's cool expression collapsed and she opened her black Chanel bag, fishing feverishly in it for cigarettes while she blinked back tears. After a few moments, she said more calmly, "There was talk about the age difference, between Luke and myself, but he always managed to convince me that he was content with his 'older woman.' " Pamela lit and puffed the cigarette greedily, "Oh, I guess deep down I knew better. Luke's novels weren't commercial, and he enjoyed the good life that I was happy to pay for." Her voice faltered. "But he was so attentive . . . so loving . . . he was even writing a novel about me based on my youthful career as an actress."

A growing, chilly wind swirled the smoke from Pamela's cigarette. Several oleander leaves drifted onto the table. Pamela stared out at the cloudy skies, her voice taking on a note of despair, "But it was all lies. Everything he told me was a goddamned lie!" She threw her cigarette stub down, grinding it under the toe of her suede pump. Then, with a feverish motion, Pamela gathered up the leaves, crushed them, and dropped them into her juice. Snatching up the glass, she put it hastily to her lips.

Alex's hand flashed across the table catching Pamela's wrist. "I wouldn't do that if I were you. Three leaves from that bush could kill a horse."

"But that's the idea!" Pamela struggled with surprising strength. "I can't live without Luke! If he doesn't love me I want to die!"

93

"Not from oleander poisoning." Alex wrested the glass away and tossed the orange juice in the bushes and spoke bluntly. "Unless you don't mind hours of vomiting, not to mention bloody diarrhea, before you even lose consciousness. Besides, if you really want to kill yourself, you've picked a lousy place for it. The hospital will have a tube down your throat in minutes. Is that what you're after? Having your stomach pumped?"

Pamela's powdered chin was quivering. "Last week I sold a portrait of Charles Chaplin painted by Picasso in 1954. I sold it to a French executive for over five hundred thousand dollars! My success is something that a person like you could never understand. But despite success and money, I have nothing to live for. And that's something you can't understand either!"

"Your daughter needs you alive, Ms. Dysart. She's just been found soaking in her own blood."

"Are you kidding? Stacy has always wanted to spend Mama's money and play with Mama's toys, including Mama's boyfriend. If I'm gone she'll have it all. As for Barron, he'd have my money to pour into his precious estate. Every once in a while he'd feel guilty and put too many flowers on my grave."

Alex heard true bitterness. Those Dysarts were some family. She sought to turn Pam's thoughts from suicide. "I may need your help. I'm trying to help Mark Salinger prove his innocence."

Pamela straightened up, and brushed at her tears. "Mark is a wonderful man . . . a saint. He couldn't kill anyone! But—"

"Ms. Dysart, please help Mark! I'm not only looking for Luke Bishop, I'm also looking for Eden Selby, who apparently has left town. You must know her fairly well. Where would she have gone?"

Alex appeared to have at last deflected Pamela's thoughts

94

from herself. She dabbed at her eyes and began repairing her makeup. "Naturally, I want to help Mark, but Eden and I don't communicate. She's never grown up. Eden made Kate Selby's old age miserable because she refused to finish college or take up a profession. Eden seems to think she has the right to live off Dysart money."

"Pammy!" The cheerful voice sailed over the patio. An athletic, dark-haired woman—who must have been freezing in a short, white tennis outfit—waved and smiled.

"Oh, God, Francine Jenkins of all people." Pamela rolled her eyes at Alex, signifying that she was trapped. She muttered in a quick aside, "I don't want that bitch to know about Stacy. Though she's so self-centered she probably won't even wonder why I'm here at the hospital." Then Pamela was smiling and cooing as if she hadn't a problem in the world, "Come and sit down, Francie! Are you enjoying the Gary Cooper abstract?"

"Heavens yes, it's lovely. All that man's good taste simply shines in his color choices and muted edgings. I've hung the canvas in our entryway just above the Bombay chest. We get so many lovely compliments, and of course when people learn that Gary Cooper painted the abstract while he was filming *High Noon* . . . well, they're just flabbergasted. We tell everyone about your fabulous gallery."

"How nice of you! You know I appreciate it."

The woman called Francie flashed a self-satisfied smile as she sat down next to Pamela. "Robert and I are the ones who should talk about appreciation. Our painting has doubled in value already. Professor Truesdell re-assessed it for us three weeks ago."

"Francie! I don't want to hear about that professorial fraud!"

"Are you calling me a fraud these days, Pamela?" Clive Truesdell emerged from behind her with a tray.

"My God, it's Scarecrow," Pamela murmured under her

breath, but Alex heard her and understood. Truesdell wore ragged blue jeans and a faded Henley shirt. With his long, gangling body and untidy thatch of hair, he did look more like a scarecrow than a scholar.

Francie, seeing the hostile glares exchanged between Clive and Pamela, rushed to smooth things over. "Clive, don't be so touchy. Everyone knows that you're the academic expert on modern California art history, including Hollywood's celebrity art. Robert says so, and he studies such things exhaustively. That is, when he can . . . these days Robert's not up to much."

"Francie, darling!" Pamela pointedly ignored Truesdell, who was seating himself beside her and putting his tray on the table. "Are you here because Robert is ill? I'm so sorry!"

"Oh, he's just having moles removed, but he's terrified of doctors. Clive came with me to keep his spirits up."

"I've been entertaining Fran and Rob with information on the theft of the Judy Garland watercolor," Truesdell said.

Pamela gasped. "But Perry Webb owned that watercolor! Who stole it?"

"That's what the sheriff's office would like to know." Clive said, reaching for his coffee. "After I talked to them, they began to suspect a drug dealer. They respect me, even if you don't, Pamela."

Francis nervously squeezed a lemon on her salad. "I wish you two wouldn't bicker. Pamela, it's time you forgave Clive for the way he appraised our Fatty Arbuckle!"

"Francie, some people may think that Clive is an art-appraising genius." Pamela was her cool, snobbish self again. "But that Arbuckle work was worth more than five hundred, and Clive knows it!"

Clive snorted. "It was a finger painting, for Christ's sake!"

Francie rushed in again. "Just tell us about the Judy Garland!"

Clive shrugged. "The sheriff asked me if the watercolor was as valuable as the other paintings hanging in the office. But the Clark Gable sketches of Marilyn Monroe that the burglar left behind were worth far more than Garland's watercolor of the Rainbow Irises. I ventured the opinion that whoever took that painting knew nothing about art. They stole it only because it was small enough to fit in a knapsack."

"If they don't know its value, the painting may be destroyed by now." Pamela tut-tutted in distress.

Alex, who wanted to hear more, exclaimed: "You mean Judy Garland painted those glorious Rainbow Irises that grow near the Castle?"

Truesdell really looked at Alex for the first time, squinting appraisingly as if trying to remember where he'd seen her. Francine pulled her chair close to Alex, delighted to talk about her hobby. "*I* think Judy painted as exquisitely as she sang! To collectors of celebrity art that watercolor is precious! It has a dated signature of 1939, which was the year that Judy filmed *The Wizard of Oz*. Not only that, but she wrote a note on the back of it. The note was dedicated to Pamela's father-in-law and it read: 'I'll think of your irises whenever I sing about rainbows!' "

"The note is worth more than the painting," Clive muttered. "The flowers are executed in a childish, amateur manner at best."

"And how much is the painting worth?" Alex asked.

"Oh, perhaps seven thousand," Truesdell replied.

"Don't be stupid. It's worth at least fifteen," Pamela snapped immediately.

Francine ignored their bickering and turned to Alex. "If you're interested, hon, you should go to Clive's seminars on Hollywood's Contributions to the Arts on Monday nights in the Castle."

"If there *is* a library after all that's happened," Truesdell pointed out. His deep, rolling voice turned peevish. "Though I'm sure *dear Pammy* is working day and night as president of Friends of the Library to save our beloved Castle from closure. Ha!"

Pamela had no trouble giving as good as she got. She patted Alex's hand. "Alex is investigating Webb's murder on behalf of Mark. I plan to keep abreast of all the details, and I'm sure we'll bring our beloved librarian back to his Castle soon." She smiled sweetly at Truesdell. "Of course, helping our librarian will take a lot of money. Why don't you contribute right now to the Friends of the Library . . . say a few hundred? It will show your faith in Mark's innocence."

Clive gave a quick look around, as if searching for escape, before he reluctantly pulled out his checkbook. But as he wrote he said slyly, "Of course Mark is innocent. There are plenty of people with more of a motive to murder Webb . . . like Pamela's son. How many thousands did Barron borrow from Webb to improve the old Dysart homestead?"

Pamela flushed and grabbed Clive's check. She stood up abruptly, pulling Alex along. "I'm sorry, Francie. We must go."

"I understand. Clive is being very naughty. But you'll come and visit me soon, won't you, Pammy? I'd so like you to see where we've hung Gary Cooper!"

Chapter 11

AT TWELVE NOON Alex entered Stacy's private room, trying not to knock over the vases of roses that were crowded onto every available surface. The room resounded with heavy metal rock music, and Alex wasn't sure Stacy heard her come in. The girl wore a red, lace negligee, and her thick blue-black hair fanned out over her pillow, contrasting with a face that was even whiter than Alex remembered. Stacy's wrists were thickly bandaged, and her thin lips were colorless.

But her bed had been raised to a sitting position, and Stacy had a *Victoria's Secret* catalogue in her hand. Just now, Stacy wasn't reading but was watching a screaming, gyrating group of guitar players on MTV. Close by Stacy's side was a T.V. remote and a half-eaten doughnut. She was clearly nowhere near as close to death's door as Barron had implied, and when she looked up at Alex, there were no tears of grief to be seen on her dark-eyed, pale face. If Stacy's jaw was trembling, it was from the exertion of cracking her gum.

"Hello, Stacy," Alex shouted over the clamor of the television.

Stacy turned a page in her catalogue and pushed the mute button on her remote, so that silent bodies continued to writhe across the television screen. She said, "Welcome to the rose garden. I hope you aren't allergic to roses. They're all from my dear brother, Barron Dysart Esquire. Whenever Bear does something particularly despicable ... like filming fuck movies of me to show to Mom ... he'll try to make up for it by sending me a flower shop. The head nurse is taking most of them to the maternity ward, thank God."

Alex, who was still tripping over Barron's potted irises, made sincere sounds of compassion and began to introduce herself.

"Oh, I know who you are," Stacy waved aside formalities with a languid hand. "Come on over and sit in this chair, Alex. Just throw all those movie magazines on the floor. You know you're not as tough-looking as I expected." She tilted her head appraisingly. "You'd look great in this slinky green thing." Stacy turned the catalogue toward Alex and pointed to a silken teddy. "Why don't you ask my brother to buy this for you? He's totally hot for you. Has he humped you yet? I know he's dying to."

Alex asked calmly, "Is that why you had me come up here? To learn about my sex life?"

Stacy gave Alex a sharp look. "Why shouldn't I learn about your sex life? You know all about mine. You filmed it!"

"Fair is fair," Alex admitted. "Here's my sex life summed up: Nonexistent."

"Shit, isn't celibacy the pits?" Stacy commiserated. She put down her catalogue and blew a bubble that popped on the tip of her nose. "Luke is such a stud. He really turns me on before he turns me out. Yum! Last night I thought I couldn't stand to live without him another minute." She pulled gum off her nose, popped it in her mouth, and chewed some more. "Mom was going on one of her rampages about suicide ... which she does only to torment Barron. I was so horny and depressed that I stole the razor

100

she'd left on the sink for Barron's benefit. I decided to end it all."

"No man is worth that, Stacy."

"Luke is!" The pale lips set in a stubborn pout. "He's going to write a book about me."

"He told your mother that he was writing about her."

"So what? He was *lying* to Mom. Luke wouldn't lie to me. He was even going to have me star in a movie, but that miserable Perry Webb ruined everything."

Alex could feel the conversation moving faster than expected, "Just a minute, how did Perry Webb harm your chances to be a star?"

"Luke's agent was negotiating a movie deal for his book. It would have brought Luke enough money to marry me and leave Mom. Then the publicity broke over Webb's campaign to remove Luke's 'pornographic, homosexual novel' from the library. Webb is such a troublemaker that the producer got cold feet." She puckered her thin face, trying to recall the right words. " 'It's a stunning book, and I'd love to produce it, but the biz is so-o-o tight, I just can't offend the average ticket buyer with a movie that would appeal only to a limited audience' . . . that's the line the shmuck gave us."

"Luke must have been very angry at Perry Webb," Alex volunteered.

"Oh, he wanted to kill him and so did I," Stacy admitted casually after she popped another bubble. "But Webb's gone now . . . the old fart, and I'm going to get Luke back and have him try to do that movie after all. Unfortunately, I decided that in the bathtub after I'd already slashed my wrists. So I started screaming for help. Why should I just give up and let Eden Selby keep Luke? He may be with her now, but unless I'm in the morgue she won't have him long."

Once again, Alex felt that Stacy's logic had taken a leap

that required some catching up. "Are you saying that Luke went off with Eden Selby?" Alex asked.

"Yes, and she's nothing! Although she thinks she's some pure sole because she tries to act like an Indian. She fasts, and sweats in muddy lodges, and hits herself with branches and stuff." Stacy rolled her eyes up in disgust. "She hates our whole family, too. Eden lived with us when her parents died. Well, not us exactly. Eden's grandma Kate did the landscaping work for my father and my grandfather. Eden lived with Kate in a little house on our property. Anyway, when the Castle was donated to Santa Linda County, Kate's house was donated too, and . . . it's a long story, but Kate and Eden decided they were cheated."

"And Eden is still bitter?"

"God, yes! She even tried to write a book about how her brilliant grandmother had been robbed by the evil Dysart family. She was always hounding Luke to help her with the manuscript. He thought she was a pain in the ass." Stacy raised her head, her jaw working the gum frantically, her pallid face strained with indignation. "That's why I couldn't believe it when I saw Eden in Luke's car on Monday night!"

"The night of Webb's murder?"

"Yep. When Mom threw me out of Luke's study in the Castle, I drove to the Polar Bar on Center Street, near the park. I didn't want to go home, and Luke goes to the Polar a lot. I waited for him, but he was a no-show. So I went outside to hang out in the park, 'cause, well . . . that's where I can get drugs, to tell you the truth."

"Do you know someone named EZ Moore?" Alex interrupted quickly, remembering Ross's story about the knife-happy teenager from Center Street Park.

Stacy shook her head. She cracked her gum, pulled a rose from its vase, plucked its petals, and continued, "I saw Eden, the thrift-store Indian, in her usual braids and buckskins. She was running out of some bushes in Center Street Park with this bulging backpack, and she was peering behind her shoulder like she was afraid of cowboys. God, it was a hoot! I would have laughed myself sick if I hadn't suddenly seen Luke's Mercedes pull up with Eden's kids in it. Eden jumped inside and kissed *my* Luke! Then they drove away."

Alex was beginning to feel a tingling sensation. (The last time that had happened was when she'd cleaned her husband's golf bag and discovered his love notes from her best friend.) Tingling was a sign that she was onto something. "When you saw Eden at the park, what time was it?"

"I dunno, I guess it was between nine thirty and ten."

"And Luke left town after that?"

"Damn straight. None of his friends have seen him, and he's even left his clothes and things at the house without coming back for them. He's disappeared, probably to poke Pocohantas!" With this anguished statement, Stacy fell back on the pillows. "So I want you to find him, at once!"

Alex heard the imperious tone that was so like Pamela's, but she paid little attention to the words. Her mind was off in Center Street Park across the street from Webb's office. And Webb's real estate brokerage office had been robbed just before Eden Selby appeared in the park with a bulging backpack. There was a good chance that Eden Selby had robbed Webb's office. Had she also killed him?

Barron seemed delighted with Alex when he came out of Stacy's room. "You've already done her a world of good," he said. "She's certain she'll see her true love again."

"I never gave her any guarantees," Alex cautioned. "Your sister has no idea where Luke Bishop is."

"You'll find him, I have every faith in you," said Barron comfortably. "Will you drive me home, Alex? Mother took the Eldorado and left early. You put a bug in her ear about helping Salinger, and she's eager to begin."

Alex climbed behind the steering wheel and cleared the passenger seat of catnip toys to make room for her client. "Luke has caused a lot of pain. Are you sure you want him back in your mother's and your sister's life?"

Barron stood outside the van peering in with an expression of distaste. "Mother is tougher than she pretends, and to be honest, I hope that by the time you find Luke, Stacy will have forgotten him. But even if Stacy insists on taking him back, I'll deal with that slime. Luke can be ruthless, but he's desperate for money. He always needs someone to support him while he writes his oh-so-sensitive, rebellious novels. This time I'll wield the purse strings, and I won't give that rat the long leash that Mother did."

Alex drummed her fingers on the wheel impatiently. She wanted to get going, but Barron was fastidiously removing cat hair from the seat. Ah, well, at least Watson was settled in the motel. The Chevy had been aired out, and for once there was no fragrant cat box in the back.

As Barron cleaned, he also grumbled: "Your agency is wasting time on Mark Salinger. Believe me, he's guilty or our politically minded D.A. wouldn't go after him. And another thing, you don't carry a weapon. A murder case might be dangerous!"

Alex wasn't surprised that Barron disliked sharing her services with Mark, and she ignored his comments, until at last, the man deigned to put his designer-clad buttocks in the passenger seat. Then Alex pointed her unwieldy, unreliable vehicle up the winding back road that would take them from the hospital to the Dysart estate.

They drove through rounded hills and towering groves of eucalyptus. In the northern distance, the rugged, snow-touched slopes of Manzanita Mountain rose into a slate-hard sky. A hawk circled far above them, riding the current

104

of the wind. Almost reluctantly, Alex turned her mind back to scandal and gigolos. "According to your sister, Luke took off with Eden Selby. Have you any idea where the two of them might have gone?"

"Stacy must be mistaken. Plenty of rich women in Santa Linda would pay for the privilege of diving 'between the covers' with our local, famous writer. Why would Luke shack up with Eden? She has two children by some guy who disappeared on her. She supports her family with odd jobs. She's not his typical rich victim."

"Stacy also told me that Eden feels your family cheated her grandmother."

Barron shifted uncomfortably, "That's true. Eden's grandmother, Kate Selby, was a brilliant landscaper, but she didn't understand business. She and my grandfather did everything by handshake, so there were problems when Kate claimed she'd been promised the ownership of her cottage. My father found no record of any such promises and simply didn't believe Kate. Then a chimney fire burned her cottage down. Creosote fires in chimneys are common enough, but Kate tried to have my father arrested for arson."

Alex gave a soft whistle. That was quite a grudge. She asked, "Webb's office was robbed the same night he was murdered. Apparently a valuable artwork was taken."

"You mean the Judy Garland? Mother told me about it."

"Would Eden feel a claim to the painting as part of her grandmother's estate?"

"Sure. Eden is obsessed with her 'legacy,' everything connected with her grandmother's celebrity flowers. She even identifies with the local Indians because she feels their land was stolen just as her grandmother's property was stolen."

By now the Chevy van had reached the broad drive of the Dysart estate. The view of the grounds was hidden by double rows of mature acacia trees, their green boughs glistening with fat rain drops from the mourning storm. A speckled doe grazing near a scrub oak, lifted her head to stare at the van with soft, round eyes.

Alex felt as if the Chevy were bouncing her into heaven. They'd come down the wide drive under spreading evergreens that emerged into a cloud banked meadow. A swarm of tiny gray birds with dark caps of brown, flitted in the twisted branches of buckeye trees. As Alex pulled into the drive she could view the Santa Linda River tumbling in foaming spills toward the deep, clear shine of the Dysart lake. Presiding over it all was Barron's massive house of river rock and redwood. This was the 'new' Dysart mansion, built to look fashionably old. Alex had heard that Barron's father had moved into it when he'd donated the Castle property to Santa Linda County. He apparently had little desire for the Hollywood glamor that Barron's grandfather had loved. From the looks of his lavish log cabin, Daddy's taste must have run to "Fashionably Frontier."

"Beautiful, isn't it?" Barron looked around with obvious pride. "I've been making improvements, remodeling old buildings and putting in new cabins to make the estate turn a profit as a resort. That lodge," he pointed to a two-story log building, "is brand-new. Come and see it."

The lodge had the requisite large gathering room with pine walls and a high stone fireplace. On one long, unbroken wall, there was a mural. In bold strokes of color, it told Santa Linda's history, with depictions of Indians, Spaniards, and ranching pioneers. Barron was eager to walk Alex past the painting and upstairs to view the lodge bedrooms, but the detective held him back.

"Did Scott Wilson paint this fabulous mural?" she demanded.

Barron nodded. "Say what you will about the mumbler, he paints like an angel, or in this case like Diego Rivera.

The kid was erratic but generally contented when he was painting. I didn't have much ready cash what with Mother spending all of her money on her damn gigolo, and Scott was all I could afford."

"The first time I saw Scott he had a lot of money in his pockets."

"Not from this mural job. I paid him every working day, and I gave him forty dollars for five hours. The system was easier for Scott to handle."

"You must have been sorry when your great artist went to San Francisco."

Barron coughed and changed the subject. "Hey, I bet you'd like to come upstairs and see photos of Kate Selby's orange-flame orchids. My grandfather named them after Rita Hayworth, and the Aga Kahn grew the orchids for Rita in his gardens."

Alex fought back her fascination with flowers and persisted, "We were talking about Scott."

Barron sighed. "I suppose you'll find out sooner or later. I fired the mumbler after Media Day, because Webb insisted on it." Barron sounded embarrassed. Was it because he felt bad about Scott Wilson? Or was he angry because he'd been forced to let his creditor, Webb, give him orders? What if Barron had killed Webb to get out from under the old man's thumb? Or to avoid paying up on his financial obligations?

Alex's latest murder suspect grabbed her hand and hustled her out the door and down a wide trail bordered with blackberry vines. "At least come see the new beach cabins. With Mother's financial help, this place will be a famous resort, and it's because of you, Alex, that Mother's finally come to her senses."

Alex did not find the suicidal Pamela particularly sensible, but she let that pass. She pulled her hand free. "I can't stay long. I want to get to Center Street Park. I'm looking for Earnest Zachary Moore. Ever heard of him?"

"Don't tell me they've sent you after that dangerous kid! Damn it, Alex, your boss must be crazy!" Barron stomped a shortcut through a bramble patch, and Alex followed him, pulling thorns from her skirt.

"How do you know EZ?" she asked, panting after Barron's rapid strides.

"He did roofing work for me, but I fired him after he came to work stoned. I think EZ was selling drugs to the crew."

"Do you know where he is now?"

"No!" Barron skidded to an angry halt. "Jesus! Give your job a rest for five damn minutes! Why the hell should we talk about that creep? I've been looking forward to seeing you for days. I've been longing to bring you here."

They'd reached a thin stretch of sand, where a sprinkling of tree-shrouded cabins circled the lake. Barron's angry expression relaxed as he looked out over the breeze-rippled water. He leaned close to Alex and lightly touched her shoulder. "Finding a murderer is a job for Sheriff Brody, or for the police, or for that brick-wall-sized boss of yours, George Stewart," he said gently. "It's not for someone like you."

Annoyed, Alex stepped away from him. "What do you mean 'someone like me'? Do you mean that the job is too much because I'm a woman?"

"I mean that EZ Moore is no one for you to fool with! He's strong, stoned, and stupid. He's also obsessed with knives. He'd be quick to hurt you, Alex." Barron gripped her this time, bruising her skin. His face was mottled, his voice filled with intensity. "For God's sake. Leave this murder investigation alone!"

"Let go of me. Now!" Alex's voice was cold, but her imagination was heated. She could see herself using the force of Barron's hold on her arm to yank him off balance. Then it would only take an upward thrust from her leg to topple him facedown into the sand. The image was so pleasing that Alex was almost sorry when Barron released her immediately.

"You don't understand," he said sadly.

"No, *you* don't understand!" countered Alex. "You may be a client, but you have no right to manhandle me!"

"*Manhandle* you? Darling, I don't want you hurt because I'm *crazy* about you!" This time the big man moved like lightening. His arms enfolded Alex in a crushing hug as his lips came down on hers, and his hand moved to hike up her skirt.

"Barron, for heaven's sake!" Pamela's shocked voice rang out from behind them.

Barron released Alex. "Why are you out here spying on us, Mother?" His voice and face were sullen as a child's.

Alex supposed Pamela was the last person Barron wanted to see just now. Not that she gave a damn. She stepped away from him, straightening her disheveled clothing. Looking up she saw a pair of disapproving eyes, and her heart fell to her shoes. Next to Pamela stood the last person that *Alex* wanted to see at that moment—Ross Coulter.

Chapter 12

JAIL STANK OF sweat, urine, chlorine, and above all, fear. Even here, in the relatively clean and spacious prison library, Mark could still smell the county lockup. This morning he'd opened his eyes from a strange dream of whirling Zoe through the Children's Room to the strains of a Strauss waltz. When he awoke, he lay on his cot disoriented and confused. It took the lumps in his mattress and the stench that permeated the thick stuffy air to bring his situation screaming back to him.

Now, Mark removed a book from the library shelf. He ran his finger over the cloth spine of a science-fiction novel to focus his attention on the tired, inadequate prison library that he'd asked to help reorganize.

He'd hoped the work would keep his mind off his troubles, particularly the arraignment. Mark preferred to forget the sharp-faced prosecutor and the drowsy, multichinned judge who'd only seemed to open his hooded, sleepy eyes when he'd pronounced charges of first-degree murder. Instead, the librarian tried to remember the perfume of flowers and the spice of evergreens that surrounded the Castle in the summer, or the bite of wind that stirred the oaks on the Santa Linda hills. Fresh air never seemed to penetrate this old stucco building, a building knowing unaffectionately to its inmates as the Adobe Inn.

An Isaac Asimov novel went into a section already set

aside for futuristic fantasy. Mark continued to organize the fiction, shaking his head when he found *Video's Lusty Ladies*, a biography of video porn queens that came complete with "intimate photos." The book was well hidden behind the poetry collection.

It was a world of its own, this Adobe Inn. In return for cigarettes, Mark's new acquaintances were quite eager to explain how mellow the Inn could be. It had, they insisted, all the advantages of nearly edible food, decent television reception, and a relative lack of hassle from the guards. For the most part he'd been treated well. Mark knew he was something of a celebrity among these car thieves, petty burglars, and small-time dope dealers. His face, pale and bewildered as he walked handcuffed, into the courtroom for his arraignment, kept reappearing on the local news along with a rerun of the film where he'd threatened Perry Webb.

And those close-ups of Zoe at the courthouse during the arraignment, her hair soft and golden, her dress white and flowing, had really impressed Mark's friendly felons, especially after Cindy Fayne did an "exclusive" story on KPXX. "Drop-dead gorgeous Zoe Latham will inherit over two million dollars in assets from the dead man! And she had plans to spend it all on Mark Salinger, her long-time lover!"

But what really contributed to Mark's notoriety was his status as a doomed man. Most of the Adobe Inn shook their heads and agreed that it was a shame the librarian had taken a fall and might wind up being sent to San Quentin, "the Country Club," where a man waited for his "one night stand" in the gas chamber. Mark had heard that bets were being placed as to whether he'd pull down a death penalty. He hadn't cared to ask how the odds were running.

After all, what did it matter what was said to him or whispered about him? Even in Mark's brief experience of the lockup, certain things had become obvious. Boredom

111

and forced companionship led to much conversation in the Adobe Inn, and none of that conversation affected the jail's permeating, soul-destroying loneliness.

Mark carefully replaced *Lusty Ladies* in its hiding place and pulled a Zane Grey western out of his new science-fiction section. Usually the orderly action of sorting books had a calming effect on his thoughts, but today thoughts wouldn't stop chasing around his brain. The bail hearing was on Monday. Ross was optimistic, saying: "Judge Lipton was always a big fan of that literacy program you started at the library. According to courthouse scuttlebutt, it helped his brother-in-law get a job and saved the judge a fistful of money. Lipton may not give you a release on your own recognizance, but he won't allow prosecutors to hold you without bail, either. Whatever bail is, we'll raise it, and you'll be out of here the day after tomorrow. And once you're out, Mark, I'll keep you out."

Mark reached for a nonfiction book that had somehow found its way into the fiction and knew he wasn't looking forward to Monday or to freedom. The pain of facing the people whose lives had been shattered by this arrest was far worse than the food, the smell, or even the loneliness of the Adobe Inn. Mark had a string of people he felt he'd harmed. First on the list was the dead Scott Wilson, who'd gone to San Francisco on Mark's suggestion. Then there was Mark's ex-wife, Trish, who had already sent a message that she'd received "terrifying" threats and was sending their son to her parents in Boston. His ex–in-laws had never cared for Mark, and his arrest certainly wouldn't raise his status. The librarian didn't imagine that he would be allowed much access to his son, Virgil. Yet he had to talk to the boy immediately. He had to apologize for past misunderstandings as well as for this horrible disruption of his son's life. This was Virgil's senior year in high school, an important year when he hoped to be accepted at Stanford. Mark's murder trial would hardly help Virgil's ambitions.

The librarian checked the Dewey decimal numbers, 635.944, on the back of a nonfiction book that belonged in a horticultural section. Mark opened the book absently, his mind on Zoe. Zoe belonged in this hideous murder scandal the way a swan belongs in a cesspool. Somehow he'd work up the courage to tell Zoe to forget about him. After all, she was young, lovely, and about to become very wealthy. If she chose to marry, it should be to someone suitable, someone, say, who combined the poetic abilities of Shakespeare, the wit of Oscar Wilde, and the looks and sexual abilities of Byron.

Mark stared at the open book in his hands, actually noticing it for the first time. There was a thump as it hit the floor.

"You okay?" snapped Branson, the guard in charge of the library.

Mark nodded and picked up the book that had dropped from his suddenly nerveless fingers. He opened it, stared at it, adjusted his glasses, then stared at it again. It was written by Kate Selby and entitled, *A Child's Garden*. The book bore the same title as the stolen first edition Zoe had told him about. This volume wasn't that same valuable first edition, though it was still remarkable. Even the end papers were ornate, pale lavender in color with stylized roses drifting across them in diagonal patterns. As he studied them, Mark's intelligence suddenly revved up, cutting through the confusing tangle of his emotions.

These stylized roses, he'd seen them recently. Grace had been holding a book just like this, looking it over before she returned it carefully to the used-book table. But Mark also recalled that the book had been enclosed in a different cover. Mark had an acute memory for titles of books, and

113

it took him only moments to remember that the bold red title on the jacket of the book that Grace had been examining had something to do with agricultural diseases and nothing to do with *A Child's Garden*.

Why had Kate Selby's book been hidden in the wrong book jacket and then placed on the used-book table? Who'd want to get rid of it? It was hardly controversial. Even "Book-Banning" Bigelow wouldn't find anything objectionable in a volume of instructions to children on how to raise vegetables and flowers, along with a brief biography of Kate Selby, and details on her "celebrity flowers."

He thought back to the robbery of Webb's office, remembering that discarded library books had been taken. Mark had barely paid attention at the time, but now he found the idea preposterous. He chose the discards that left his library. The Castle was no small cramped building, and Mark had been free to limit discards to those books that hadn't been checked out for years and were readily available at other nearby branches. He was careful to check the *Catalogue of Fiction* and the *Library Catalogue*, and he preferred to keep any books that were of value historically or financially. So what crazy burglar stole the Castle's discards? Unless they weren't discards after all. Had valuable first editions like *A Child's Garden* made their way into Webb's office via the Castle's used-book table?

Crimes in the library. Webb had told Zoe that he'd discovered crimes in the library. Had the old man discovered book thefts?

Mark nearly slammed the book into the wall. *Damn, what a fool I've been! Accepting imprisonment, thinking only of apologies instead of how I could defend myself and the people I love.* He'd left the fight to Ross and Alex, when all the time, he knew more about the Castle than either of them. He'd been Shakespeare's definition of a coward, "Letting, 'I dare not' wait upon 'I would.' " If Mark wanted his life back, he'd have to exonerate himself by finding Webb's murderer.

Chapter 13

"YOU'RE SUPPOSED TO be investigating Webb's murder, Alex, not playing sex games with my son!" Pamela's voice was high, shrill, and as unstable as her emotional state.

Barron turned red. "Please forgive my mother. She was an actress before she married my father, and she likes to make a scene whenever she can."

Pam and her son both stared at Alex, waiting for a response. But the detective was far more aware of Ross Coulter, who was eyeing her with all the happy pride of a husband who'd found his naked wife beneath a traveling salesman. Was that disapproving frown permanently etched between his black brows?

Alex smiled at the group of jolly folks and began to edge away. "I'll be in touch, Barron, as soon as I have information on Luke's whereabouts. In the meantime, Ms. Dysart, you're right about one thing. I have a big job and some urgent business waiting, so if you'll excuse me . . ."

She'd gotten all of three feet before Pamela clutched her hand. "Oh, dear, I've been melodramatic, haven't I? Since Luke's been gone, I . . . I haven't been myself." Pamela gave a deep, husky sigh as she led them back toward the Dysart mansion. "But I want us all to be working for Mark every moment! Alex, you were right. Our librarian needs help, and *I'm* going to make sure he gets it."

Pamela flitted to Ross and draped herself on his arm.

116

"Monday is Mark's hearing. I've called this brilliant attorney here to discuss raising money to meet bail." Pamela gave Ross's arm a squeeze and a glance that dripped with affection. "I also wanted him to know that my son and I are ready to help fund Alex's investigation. Aren't we, Barron, dear?"

"Barron, dear" said he thought that was a fine idea. Alex thought it was a lousy idea, though no one asked her. For Barron, money meant control, and with control he could try to send Alex packing. Alex stole a glance at Ross, who still had not spoken. Ross glared back at her. Obviously he'd be no help. Alex was impatient to leave and get on with her case. Between Ross's dirty looks and Barron's money, she could be facing an early retirement.

Pamela turned hospitable as the uncomfortable little troop came in sight of the log house. "Perhaps we can have a late lunch and plan the investigation together."

"What a shame that I have to leave," Alex lied quickly. "Several people promised to see me."

"I'll walk you to your van. I have something to discuss with you." Ross moved purposefully beside her, and Alex's heart sank. Was the "something" severance pay?

He didn't waste time getting to the point. "I hired you to prove Mark's innocence. Not how sexy you are. Just what was going on by the lake?"

"I don't kiss and tell," Alex quipped.

"I'm not in the mood for jokes!"

"And I'm not in the mood for interrogations. Especially since I've been working my tail off." She blushed at Ross's arched eyebrow. "Not *that* way. Look, I've helped Barron in the past, and he's a bit too grateful, but it's nothing I can't handle."

Ross made a skeptical grunt. "I don't want you to 'handle' it. I want you to *end* it. You represent Salinger, and I expect a decent level of morality."

Alex's temper had already been sorely tried. "Don't preach to me about morality," she sizzled. "Especially since you're traipsing right back to Pamela Dysart, who seems eager to lay out a lot more than lunch for you!"

Alex pulled open the van door, jumped in, and turned the key in the starter. Somewhere in heaven was a goddess who protected unjustly accused detectives, because the old van fired up immediately, belched at Ross Coulter, and allowed Alex to exit on the last word.

She mentally cursed the arrogant attorney as she drove away. The trees and shrubs and then the buildings streamed by in a blur while she swore all the way to the downtown section of Santa Linda City. That uptight son-of-a-bitch had put himself in charge of her sex life! She was still furious when she pulled into the parking lot. And how like a man to blame her for Barron's overactive hormones!

It was Sunday in the business and office district. The weather was overcast, and there were few people on the streets. Alex crossed the road to Center Street Park, a patch of green in the center of the downtown's concrete thoroughfare. Suddenly she began to smile. In the middle of the intersection she began to laugh. She laughed her way across the street and into the park. At long last she was working for a man who urged her to stay out of bed instead of jumping into it, and she didn't even appreciate him! Then she stepped onto the grass of the park and frowned again. Even a client who encouraged a detective to keep her clothes on could be a bastard in his own miserable way.

Center Street Park was sliced in half by a tree-and-bramble-sheltered creek. To the right was a playground, but there were no children kicking their legs up on the swings, riding down the slides, or scampering along the creek that ran through the far side of the playground. The swings were hiked out of reach, up over the top of the poles. The climbing structure had been gouged with knife marks and vandalized with spray paint. Even as she neared the fence, Alex could smell the urine that formed a small pool at the bottom of the slide.

She recalled that this park had been Santa Linda's chief scandal until the Castle stole center stage. Like many parks, it was the site of choice for alcoholics and drug dealers, some of them the community's own children. It had been Perry Webb who'd forced police to deal with the drinking and drug use that blighted the area. He'd organized citizen patrols and badgered the town into passing an ordinance that outlawed drinking. He'd raised money for perimeter lights and urged officials to have the curbs around the park painted red, so that vehicles wouldn't block the view of the playground from patrol cars. Looking around, Alex realized why many people mourned the loss of the sometimes misguided, but also fearless, Mr. Webb.

She tramped through the grass to a knife-carved redwood bench that faced the creek. Her heels made dents in the soft earth that was still wet from the morning rain. Two teenagers in black pants, ripped T-shirts, and leather jackets sat on the bench listening to a boom box and passing back and forth a hand-rolled smoke that gave off the pungent tang of marijuana. The joint disappeared when Alex came in sight.

"Hi," she yelled.

No one answered. The wailing on the boom box sounded like Watson's feline friends on an amorous night. Alex took a deep breath and hollered out, 'I'm looking for EZ Moore. Have you seen him?'

The taller boy looked up and squinted. He had a partially shaved head with a top ruff of brown hair. A silver skull and crossbones hung from his right, pierced ear. "Skull" asked a question of his own. "Have you got any spare change for a beer?"

Alex looked in her purse and fished out two fives, giving one to each teenager. She ignored the tugs of conscience telling her that the last thing these kids needed was beer money. As the surprised boys put the cash in their pockets, Alex said urgently, "I've got to find EZ."

Under the influence of ten dollars, her listeners were much more sympathetic. The shorter kid, who possessed a good set of features and a bad case of acne, even made the effort to turn down the boom box. "I know EZ," he said. "He's an asshole."

Skull agreed. "EZ's always getting high and showing off—throwing his knife into the trees even when there's kids in the park. Then the cops run everybody out of here. But EZ's not around now. He split after he cut that librarian ... ow!" A cry of pain cut off Skull's speech when his friend jabbed him in the ribs.

The short, spotted-faced boy stared meaningfully at Alex's purse.

Alex took two more fives from her wallet. "Where'd EZ go?"

"He's roughing it, in the hot tubs of Manzanita Springs," Skull said.

"Manzanita? You mean the resort town at the top of Manzanita Mountain?"

The shorter boy turned up the boom box after pocketing the two fives. He sang to Alex along with the disjointed music. "Where, oh, where did EZ go? Gee, lady, I dunno. Maybe down to Mexico?"

Skull laughed hysterically at his companion's doubtful wit until he was yanked from the bench and tugged along by his friend. The two disappeared, along with Alex's money, into a labyrinth of tangled underbrush beside the creek.

But Alex had something to chew on as she left the park. Mark's story about being wounded in front of the library had just been verified by these kids. But how could Mark have been outside the library fighting with EZ Moore if the blood on his shirt said he was close by when Webb was stabbed through the heart? Alex was preoccupied with her questions until she reached the curb of Center Street.

Well, look at that . . . here came luck, as glorious as a budding iris! Luck was the elderly man walking slowly along the street, his posture proud and upright, his shabby wool suit hanging neatly on his jaunty frame. Alex rushed after him.

A station wagon, plastered with bumper stickers calling for world peace and global meditation, zoomed toward Alex, nearly running her down. The peaceful driver gave her the finger as she retreated back to the curb, trying to remember the old man's name. . . . Hamlet, Hamil, Hamlisch! That was it! On the night of the murder, while Alex had been searching through the card catalogue, Grace at the front desk had called out, "Shh! Mr. Hamlisch." Grace had good reason to quiet Hamlisch. He'd been very drunk and disorderly. Had someone paid Hamlisch to cause trouble? Someone who wanted the Castle in chaos so that he or she could commit murder? Alex looked both ways this time before she raced across the street and followed the footsteps of the ill-behaved Mr. Hamlisch, who'd turned into Mickey's Corner Grocery and Liquor.

The store was dark and cluttered. Alex searched through the crammed, narrow aisles before she heard a familiar voice.

"Writing a masterpiece is hungry work, Mickey!" Hamlisch was standing near the register. He rattled a bag of potato chips at the store owner. "The muse is demanding. Mental muscles need sustenance. Feed me, and I will dedicate my book to you, Mickey! You'll be immortalized . . . if I don't die of starvation before the damn thing's finished." Hamlisch hummed a funeral dirge.

The slender man behind the counter shook his dark head, "How many times I gotta tell you, Herbie? I can't sell you groceries on credit unless Eden comes in here and gives me an okay. She's the one who pays the tab, and it's already high."

Mr. Hamlisch was taking milk and eggs from a nearby refrigerator. He put them down on the counter, straightened his crumpled tie, adjusted his carnation, and harrumphed, "I've bought here on credit before. Your memory is getting short, old friend. It's all that Loopsang Tea you Asian Americans drink instead of booze. Tea rots the old cerebral cortex."

Mickey smiled, flashing a gold tooth as he bagged the small pile of groceries. "Send Eden down here to give me the go-ahead, and I'll deliver personally. Then you can mention my name when your book wins a Pulitzer. Tell everyone how Mickey's rum-raisin ice cream fed your starving muse."

Hamlisch sighed. "By the time you deliver the groceries, my ice cream will be nothing but a puddle. I'm in need of something to ease my mental pain, Mickey. It's not just the trials of being an author; Eden has deserted me. She's broken our deal. I cared for her children during the day so she could work. She helped me with rent and groceries, but now that's over. She's gone off with a good writer who's a terrible bounder. And she's taken her darling children with her."

"Sorry to hear that buddy," Mickey said. "Where'd Eden go?"

In a shadowed corner near the pickle jars, Alex caught her breath. Yes, where did Eden go? If she found Eden she might find the connection between the office robbery and Webb's murder. But when Hamlisch's answer came, it only confused her.

"Eden's fled to the home of Injun Joe, my good man." Hamlisch filtered the information through a mouthful of potato chips. "She's gone into the bowels of the earth in order to enter the mouth of hell. And she's left me with barely enough money to pay for the rum-raisin ice cream." Reluctantly he put a pile of coins on the counter and pulled a carton from the freezer.

Alex rushed up to the register just as Hamlisch was turning to leave. "I'll buy your groceries." She put a twenty down, avoiding Mickey's curious gaze. "I believe in helping writers. I love to read," she gushed.

Hamlisch gave her a thorough stare that began at her heels and moved slowly upward over her body. "I thank you, my dear. My name is Herbert Hamlisch. Beautiful redheads like you are entitled to call me Herbie." He winked at Mickey.

Alex and her quarry left the store together, Hamlisch still staring at her. "Let me guess. Your last name is Hepburn and you're an actress just like your mother, Katharine, correct?"

Alex smiled. "My name is Alex Winter, and I guess I do some acting now and then, though I'm not in Hepburn's class. Can I talk to you a bit?"

"Please do." Herbie bent from the waist with a graceful florid bow that was ruined when potato chips fell out of the tipped grocery bag. He hastily straightened up and led Alex around the corner to an alley behind the market. "I live above this store." He pointed to a graffiti-covered door in the side of the building.

"Tell me about your book, Mr. Hamlisch," Alex encouraged as they entered a dim foyer.

The older man went ahead of Alex up a steep staircase, chatting all the way. "I'm writing my memoirs. I knew a great many film stars. In my day the word Hollywood meant something. If my tendency to marry too many ladies at once hadn't sent me to prison, I'd have become quite famous. By the way my dear, perhaps you remind me more of Ginger Rogers than Hepburn. . . . Do you dance?"

"No. At least not professionally."

"You should dance. Movement is crucial to an actress. I used to coach dancers in the great MGM studios. I still have contacts there. . . . I might be able to help you with your career, Alex." Herbie turned a moment to stare at her, his weak eyes moving once again over her body. Under the layers of time and alcohol were the remains of flashy good looks. Herbie could have easily been the Luke Bishop of his day.

Alex calculated how to begin her questioning. If she asked the old man immediately about his friend Eden Selby, she might scare him off. She'd test the waters first, by asking about EZ.

The carpeted stairwell was dark and musty. Hamlisch paused at the top and Alex dove in: "I'm trying to find EZ Moore. Do you know him?"

Hamlisch stiffened, "A nice girl like you should stay away from Moore. He is a drug dealer . . . very small-time and very stupid. But under the influence of too much nose candy, he waves a large knife."

"I have to find him. Some teenagers said he'd gone to Manzanita."

The old man nearly dropped the groceries. "Manzanita. That's a very big mountain, isn't it?" The hands carrying the bag began to shake. He glanced around as if there might be spies lingering in the tiny landing, though there were only the dust motes dancing in a lonely shaft of light from a cracked window.

"Farewell, my dear." Hamlisch unlocked a deadbolt on the one apartment door facing the landing. He slammed it behind him, shutting Alex out.

Terrific. Now what? She shouted at the blank door, "Mr. Hamlisch, I have to find EZ. Otherwise Mark Salinger might be convicted of murder!"

No answer. Alex sighed and wrote down her motel name

and room number on one of her cards and slipped it under the door. "On the night Perry Webb was killed, I saw you on the main floor of the library. You were very drunk. Did Eden Selby buy you drinks that night, Mr. Hamlisch?" she yelled. "Can you help me talk to Eden?" She waited, but she was only yelling at herself.

Alex gave up, rushing down the stairs, sneezing from the clots of dust that her feet had pounded from the carpet. Kibitzing was not as easy as it appeared. What had frightened Mr. Hamlisch? Why wouldn't he talk?

Depressed, she opened the door to the alleyway. The sun had temporarily pushed through the clouds, and it blinded her for a moment after the darkness of the building. A sudden overwhelming burst of sound came from behind, rattling her eardrums and adding to her disorientation. Even as she turned toward the sound, she saw a blur of black. A crack to her head sent the daylight splintering.

Chapter 14

ALEX SLUMPED AGAINST the rough siding of the store. She was conscious, but she was almost sorry about it. Pain shot through her skull as she tried to stand. Through dazed eyes, she saw one of the teenagers from the park bolting down the alley. Discordant noises trailed from the heavy boom box that he'd used to stun her.

Rotten little bastard! Alex willed herself to chase him, but her legs didn't get the message. She gave a groan, and her eyes began to close against her will.

Then she knew that the other boy was still near her. She inhaled the smell of his sweat and heard his breath, harsh and ragged. Its sound knifed through her head. Alex was still mentally encouraging her legs to stand, when she felt a tug on her shoulder bag.

Her purse. So that was what they wanted. Damn little sneak thieves! Enraged, she half turned and made a weak kick that would hardly have been effective if it weren't directed straight to a blue-jeaned groin.

"Awww!" It was Skull, groveling to the asphalt. Alex, still functioning on the adrenaline surge that had dropped him to the ground, half climbed, half collapsed atop him. She twisted his arms behind him and sat on him. This wasn't an easy job, considering that Skull was writhing beneath her like a newly branded steer, and his every movement caused a protesting throb of pain behind her forehead.

Fumbling in her bag for something useful, Alex grabbed a silver-plated perfume bottle. She twisted off the ridged cap and put cold metal to the back of her attacker's head.

The boy quieted instantly.

"Don't try anything, or I'll blow you away," Alex snarled. She glanced quickly down the deserted alley, praying that no came up to see her straddled atop a kid and sticking a perfume cap into his neck. It wasn't a trick to try on anyone with a high I.Q., but Alex figured that with Skull that wouldn't be a problem. When the boy started wailing in a high nasal voice, she was pretty sure she was right.

"It wasn't my idea to rob you!" Skull sniffed up tears. "It was Tony's. He thought if you were looking for EZ, you might have speed or blow in your purse."

"Tell me where EZ is now."

"Tony told you. EZ's in Mexico."

Alex let the knob of her trembling knee sink into the teenager's ribs. "Quit screwing around. Tell me where he is." *Or I'll puke all over you.* Alex's stomach didn't care for the pain in her bashed head, and she couldn't play the intimidation game for long.

The boy groaned and blurted, "EZ's in Manzanita Springs. He's staying in an old cabin near town. He goes into the Bluebeard Bar at night and gets his messages and stuff."

"Why'd he go to Manzanita?"

"Tony and I figure it was the murder at the library that sent him out of town. EZ bragged about killing Perry Webb lots of times. And there are plenty of caves up in Manzanita Springs if he has to hide out."

"But why was EZ after Webb?"

"Because the old man was always phoning the cops to chase us out of the park. EZ had to leave and do his deals down behind the library. You aren't the only person who's

127

looking for that damn dork. His brother Doug is ready to kill him because EZ took his '77 Porsche. My sister is mad at him 'cause he stood her up, and Tony and I are after him cause he's never paid us back for—"

Alex wondered if she was about to hear EZ's misdeeds starting from diaper rash. Once he got going, Skull really knew how to confess. "Did EZ know Eden Selby or Luke Bishop?" Alex demanded.

"Who?" the kid asked, and a knee in his spine didn't improve his memory.

Alex fished in Skull's back pocket and pulled out one of the two fives she'd given him earlier. It would pay for the pain pills she was going to buy. Retrieving her money from the would-be thief gave her a childish but undoubted satisfaction and the courage to try to stand on her buckling legs. "I'm going to keep this gun trained on you until I'm out of the alley. So you just lie there and count to one hundred," she commanded while removing her pumps.

"Count loud!" she ordered. Then she was running, holding her shoes, ignoring the pain behind her eyes and the protest of her stocking feet as they pounded against the asphalt. At last she was on the sidewalk of Center Street where the heads of startled Sunday strollers turned as she raced, shoes in hand, through the quiet business district to an old and ugly van.

"I'll just take a brief break in my investigation," Alex told the wide-eyed Watson. The cat seemed to take great interest in the way Alex staggered out of the bathroom and collapsed on the sofa bed.

"What a day, kittyo. Who'd have thought kibitzing could be so dangerous?" The detective groaned before she turned on the bed and reached down to the floor to fish in her bag for her tape recorder. "Since I'm not capable of much else, I'll talk into this tape and try to keep my suspects straight.

There are plenty of 'em, Watson. Too many, in fact. Believe me, old Webb attracted enemies the way Kerry's roses attract aphids." Alex puffed up the pillow and eased her head down onto it with a soft moan. She reached into her shoulder bag and took out the envelope Ross had given her, studying a photo before showing it to Ms. Watson. Somewhere Ross had obtained this fading Polaroid of a beautiful, if somber little family. Eden and her two children were wide-browed and dark-haired, with bleak eyes and delicate unsmiling mouths.

Alex switched on the tape. "Eden Selby is suspect number one. Today my informant, Stacy Dysart"—Alex broke off for a whispered aside—"Stacy's a kick, Watson, she's elevated bubble-gum chewing to an art form."

Alex spoke into the recorder again. "Said informant saw Eden in the vicinity of Webb's office just after that office was robbed. Stacy also claims that Eden drove off from the scene with Luke Bishop. Luke supposedly lives off rich women, and Eden is a single mother with barely any money at all. Has Eden become newly wealthy? If she has, does this money have something to do with Webb's death?" After asking these questions Alex turned restlessly in the bed. The pain pills didn't seem to work fast enough.

"Suspect number two is Stacy herself, who admitted that she hated Perry Webb, because she feels he ruined her chances to marry Luke Bishop." Alex pushed herself up out of bed, and headed to the kitchen, recorder in hand. In the narrow corner of the motel room that formed the kitchenette, Alex wrapped a frozen dinner into a dish towel and held it to her aching head. It was too bad the motel's old fridge didn't have an ice maker.

"Ugh," she said to Watson who'd padded behind her. "I feel the way Herbie Hamlisch must feel after one of his benders. Unfortunately I don't know much about Hamlisch—aside from the fact that he's a bigamist—which is too bad because he's my best hope for finding Eden Selby. And come to think of it," she added to the recorder, "Herbert Hamlisch is suspect number three. He might have only pretended to be drunk on the night of the murder. Maybe, after making a scene and being thrown out of the library, he snuck back into the Castle through the staff entrance to kill Webb."

Alex returned to the sofa bed with a frozen dinner held to her head. She continued her list. "Suspect four is Luke Bishop, lover extraordinaire. He was thrown out of his writing studio before the murder took place, and no one knows where he is now." Alex gave another quick aside. "You'd love Luke Bishop, Watson. He's just your type—tall, handsome, and despicable. Mr. Despicable may have been angry at Perry Webb because the old man soured a movie deal for Luke's book."

"There's Zoe Latham, the children's librarian, who has the brains to carry out the murder as well as, according to the media, the important motive of a large inheritance from Perry Webb."

Alex wrapped herself in a quilt, while the cat sat on the bottom of the bed, ears pricked forward, as if she were curious to hear more gossip. "And speaking of wealth, you should see the Dysart estate, Ms. Cat. It has a mansion overlooking the river, a private lake, and a view all the way to heaven. So what would suspect six, Barron Dysart, do to protect his muy splendid house and his beaucoup gorgeous acres? Plenty, I'd bet. Perry Webb held a second that was coming due on the Dysart property. Now Webb is dead, and—surprise—mortgage files may have been stolen. If his file is missing, Barron's second mortgage could be delayed for months, maybe even years. That will give Barron time to wring money out of the cabins and lodge on his lakefront to pay off his debts. And who could have masterminded Webb's murder better than Barron Dysart? He's the one who knew that his mother would be screaming homicidal threats at Luke Bishop up in the tower of the library on Monday night. For a start, what about all those seemingly random events that had created such confusion in the Castle? He could have conspired to create more confusion in the Castle, and then hired someone with the mumbler's build to complete the dirty deed. I'd go straight to Ross Coulter with my theory, but he's involved up to his gorgeous eyes with the Dysart family, which, I guess, makes Mark's attorney suspect seven." Alex sighed.

Ms. Watson sighed, too, and began to thoughtfully flick her tail.

"Those are the major players, Watson, though I shouldn't rule out suspects eight and nine and ten. Would art lovers Francine, Professor Truesdell, and Pamela Dysart conspire to kill Webb so that they could get hold of his Judy Garland watercolor? It's pretty far-fetched, but it's possible, no? Of course it's also possible that Salinger is actually as guilty as the forensic evidence suggests."

Watson began to scratch her ear as if she'd heard enough.

"However, first things first. Tonight I'm off to Manzanita Springs to find suspect twelve, the knife happy EZ Moore. Alex pulled out the mug shot and stared at a skinny, pinch-faced kid with a pouting mouth, and brown-blond hair pulled back in a ponytail.

Alex switched off the recorder and put the photo away. She rolled over, taking her frozen dinner and half the covers with her. For a while, Alex lay on her back, eyes closed, the frozen dinner propped against her skull. Watson came closer to knead her claws into the fluffy blanket, those claws precariously close to Alex's feet. "Damn," Alex muttered. "I got more than a hit on the head today. I got a blow to my self-confidence. It's one thing to be set upon by the Mafia with semiautomatics, but imagine the headlines for this ambush, DETECTIVE BEANED BY BOOM BOX! Jeez, I feel stupid, Watson."

Since her cat was always independent, generally unruffled, and never self-doubting, Alex didn't expect much sympathy. Watson rarely overexerted herself, and she certainly never stuck her beautiful neck out. After reciting her troubles, Alex expected a look of disdain from Watson's one, good eye. So the depressed detective was surprised when the cat moved silently toward her on soft paws. Ms. Watson hesitated only a moment before she curled protectively against Alex's chest. Stretching her dark head forward, she purred soothingly into the detective's ear until, despite pain and the thoughts playing tag in her brain, Alex drifted off to sleep.

Grace Ghiringhelli stood in the small living room staring at two books from the library. One was entitled, *A Child's Garden* and the other *Famous Flowers for Famous Folks*. They were both stamped, "not for circulation." But Grace had taken them home anyway. She hadn't stolen them exactly, she'd borrowed them.

And wasn't she entitled? Hadn't she worked for the library full-time for sixteen years? Hadn't she taken a lower salary then she deserved, worked overtime without pay, and accepted more and more responsibilities as the county had become strapped for funds and cut back on higher paid staff? Low salary, big responsibilities, unpaid overtime . . . those were her lot. But had she ever complained?

Damned right she had! Not that it had done any good. The memory of Webb's speeches about "privatizing the Castle so that the people who use the library also pay for it" had left Grace with a residue of fury that hadn't cooled. Despite Webb's death, the future of the Castle was more precarious than ever. Let others in the Castle worry about how public information and education would be threatened if there were no free library. Grace knew that her job was in jeopardy and that her right to a retirement with a full pension was about to be demolished. So if she borrowed a couple of books without permission, who could blame her?

She turned and scanned her small condominium. It was too cluttered, too boxy, and too small, but it was home, and she'd lose it if she didn't take some action. If she didn't use her knowledge to her own advantage, she'd be out on the street like that poor kid Claire, who'd died in the Castle parking lot.

Grace walked to her phone. The word "blackmail" entered her mind, but she pushed it firmly away. She hadn't stolen the books, and she wasn't about to enter into blackmail. It was only that things were bad at the Castle and she couldn't afford to lose her job without securing another income. She was networking.

But her thick hands trembled as she picked up the receiver. She mustn't fool herself. She had stolen the books, and this wasn't networking. It was blackmail. And it was dangerous.

The road to Manzanita Springs was steep and white under the shining of the highway lamps. Another rainstorm had battered the valley, bringing in an icy slush, which, at the higher altitudes, became delicate drifting snow. The highway skirted the mountain, following the curves of the plunging Santa Linda River. Once, Alex opened the window to hear the rush of water that made its way down from the mountains and through the town of Santa Linda, but the blast of cold air from outside quickly overwhelmed her van's inadequate heater. Alex rolled the window up, shivering a little and wishing that, back in mild, temperate Venice, she'd had the foresight to pack long underwear for her murder investigation.

The mountain road seemed to zig and zag along forever.

She'd been late getting out of bed and getting started, and it was already nine o'clock. There'd been so much to do before leaving. Alex had brought food along to heat up on the motor, and a thermos of hot coffee. She'd packed emergency paraphernalia as well as quilts and pillows to store in the van in case snow or fatigue forced her to pull to the side of the road.

And there'd been all those agonizing fashion decisions to make. Of all the many useful books in the library, it was a shame that there was no published dress guide for detectives. Perhaps Alex should write one herself: *The fashionable operative prefers the layered look when kibitzing with suspects in the snow. In addition, an overly made-up look along with black-widow-spider earrings are bound to make any slime ball, drug-dealing interviewee extremely comfortable.*

Speaking of accessories, Alex should probably mention the squirt gun of cayenne tucked in her waistband and the pendant watch Sam had given her for Christmas. The watch kept terrible time, but the mike inside it was terrific. In Alex's oversize black canvas shoulder bag was also a cigarette case that held a microcassete. *Yes, a bugged pendant watch and a cigarette case equipped for an eavesdropping nonsmoker neatly complete the well-dressed detective's ensemble.* Well, no, it wasn't quite complete. . . . Alex had stopped at the automatic teller to pull out some cash. *Fashion is fine, but money is de rigeur for kibitzing with a drug dealer.*

Alex wondered if EZ might be expecting her. His friends had certainly had time to warn him she was coming. The idea made her nervous, and she tried to concentrate on the comforting smell of the garlic bread and broccoli soup that heated atop the motor beside her.

Some miles along, Alex reached for the bread. It was delicious. Soft and buttery, fragrant with garlic, the bread was one more reason to bless the Castle and its remarkable selection of books. Alex munched her way toward the outskirts of the old gold-rush town of Manzanita. She searched through the snow-filmed darkness, driving slowly toward the center of town. The downtown wasn't much, and it looked small and dowdy in the bright streetlights, just a cluster of bars, coffee shops and tourist boutiques popping out of a clean expanse of snow.

Alex was about to pull into the small parking area of the Bluebeard Bar next to a red Porsche when a voice distracted her. The voice whined and complained in a way that was both aggravating and familiar.

"Watson! You rat of a cat! Did you sneak in here while I was packing? What am I supposed to do with you now? And this interview might be dangerous."

Ms. Watson seemed unconcerned with danger. She came bounding up from the back of the van. She also put her claws in Alex's legs as the Chevy executed a sharp turn. Then she demanded in no uncertain terms to be let out.

A block past the bar, Alex pulled the van over beside a small vacant lot. She opened the van door. "All right, get out then. I didn't bring a cat box, so maybe the weather will teach you a lesson."

Ms. Watson bounced out, momentarily startled when she landed in a soft pocket of snow. The black cat shook white powder from her fur and dashed off to the shrubbery making indignant noises at the cold.

Meanwhile, that tantalizing fragrance of butter and garlic was still wafting out of the Chevy van. Alex, who'd followed Watson, was shivering and couldn't resist returning to the Chevy to serve herself some delicious, scalding soup. She leaned against the van and let the steam from the mug warm her face and hands. Then she saw that Watson, having apparently obeyed the call of nature, was now busy playing, hopping through the drifts and batting at the few snowflakes that continued to straggle down from the sky.

Alex moved impatiently across the lot. She'd never found Ms. Watson more irritating. This was no time to have to chase a playful cat, and what was she going to do with her when she went to the Bluebeard Bar? No. This was no time to be bothered with a cat that was stubborn, uncooperative and . . . and suddenly a rough arm jammed against Alex's throat, pulling her back against an unknown body. Her lungs burned as she fought for breath. Vicious threats were whispered in her ear. A knife blade flicked cold against her neck.

Chapter 15

THIS WAS THE second time today she'd been attacked, and Alex was furious. As soon as she felt the prick of the blade, she ground a boot heel into her assailant's toe. At the same time she jammed her left elbow back into her attacker's chest. When she heard the grunt of pain and felt the sting of the knife into her skin, she did a right-handed flip of the scalding broccoli soup back over her shoulder, and she was rewarded to feel the painful hold loosen. Alex blew her breath out in relief just as the man behind her screamed in pain.

She whirled to find a young man on all fours, with soup and pieces of broccoli clinging to his scalded face. The mug had landed near his feet, and Alex snatched up the bone-handled hunting knife that had fallen beside it.

It was EZ, swearing and moaning. His light, lank hair was, at present, tinged with green. His lips trembled childishly, and he seemed about to cry. "You didn't have to torch me!" he whined. "Shit, lady, you're fucked up. You need downers!"

"I get upset about knives stuck in my throat." Alex touched the shallow cut on her neck. "I've come a long way to buy good cocaine. You should treat your customers better."

"Tony says you're a mama bear." EZ was still on the

137

ground pushing snow against his burned face and staring at Alex with real fear.

"Tony is an idiot. If I were a police officer, you'd be in big trouble for pulling a stunt like that. Then again, if I were a cop, I'd make sure I had a better partner," Alex frowned as Ms. Watson frolicked toward them, sniffing with curiosity at green, soupy patches of snow. Approaching EZ on delicate, snow-powdered paws, she stopped to take a whiff of his strong, marijuana fragrance.

EZ gazed at the cat with eyes that had such black, dilated pupils it was difficult to guess their color. Ms. Watson opened her rosy-roofed mouth and gaped back at him. Alex supposed the cat had never seen anyone that stoned before. EZ began to make odd bursts of noise at the cat. It took a few moments before Alex realized that he was giggling.

"Come inside the van," she suggested. "We'll clean you up, and I've got stuff to make your face feel better." She picked up her mug and helped the sputtering boy to his feet. She held on to his knife, and as he climbed into the van she pulled another from his back pocket. EZ entered the van unsteadily, his giggles becoming hiccups.

"You're right. Tony's a no brainer," EZ confided to Alex when his hiccups died down. "What kind of Charlie's Angel wears black spider earrings and travels with a one-eyed cat?"

"Hmm," replied Alex. She was busy using a snow-dampened cloth to clean EZ's face. She took aloe vera gel from her herbal first aid kit and dabbed it gently on the scalded patches of skin. "Do you want to sell me some coke and see some money?" she asked.

EZ made no answer. He pulled away from Alex, reached down to a lever, and reclined the passenger seat. Alex offered him garlic bread and he lay back and chewed slowly, while the black holes of his eyes stared at nothing. Alex hoped EZ was doing his own version of thinking. If he was slipping into a catatonic state, she wasn't going to get much information from him. She was straining for a way to jump start some sort of conversation when Ms. Watson, who'd been sitting on the futon in the back of the van, came forward to lick a residue of soup from the very bottom of the mug on the engine cover. Watching Watson, EZ's puffy lips turned upward in a grin. He asked: "Who told you I sold nose candy, lady?"

"Herbert Hamlisch for one."

"You listened to that old alkie? Man, he's full of shit. Sometimes I'll snort a few lines or toke a few meatballs. I've even been a duster once or twice, but that's strictly personal. It's uppers and muscle puffers that I sell to high school yuppies. The nerds buy the uppers, and the jocks pig out on muscle puffers."

Alex translated his words in her mind. EZ used cocaine and sometimes he smoked crack. He also used PCP, known as angel dust. But his business was selling amphetamines and steroids to ambitious high school kids. Amphetamines went to the kids studying all night for college, while the ones training for athletics bought steroids. In an upper-middle-class town like Santa Linda, kids were under a lot of pressure to perform and succeed. Very likely business had been good for EZ. Alex regarded him with nearly as much curiosity as Watson had shown. This zonked young man, with his pouting mouth and empty eyes, was actually quite an entrepreneur.

Ms. Watson was not a fan of broccoli. After dipping her face in the mug, she emerged both green and disgusted. A small stalk formed a vegetative mustache and made EZ smile. Alex smiled with him, and in the good will of the moment, took five twenties from under her jersey. "Why don't I just give you something in advance so you can find

139

some good blow for me? I've brought some vino, too. Would you like some?"

"You're one cool lady," EZ said as he pocketed the money, though he was looking at Watson, not Alex as he spoke. "I guess I don't mind getting high with you." He took a plastic bag out of his pocket, and a pipe. He filled the pipe with slivers of gray-white crystal, lit up, and passed the crack pipe to Alex. She made an elaborate show of pretending to smoke before she passed him a paper cup of wine.

"I really must be getting paranoid," EZ confided. "But I was sure the cops would come after me. I won't be safe till they put Virgil's dad away." He broke off, distracted, as Watson unhappily cleaned her green whiskers. "I used to have a black cat, but my brother ran over it with his damn car. Black cats are the smartest animals in the world. That's why people are scared of 'em and think they're bad luck."

Alex ignored the unsubstantiated animal lore. She put on an ecstatic expression as she pretended to puff the pipe. She also casually asked: "Who's Virgil?" Then she slid her hand to her chest and pressed the mechanism of the pendant watch praying that Virgil was someone connected with the murder of Perry Webb.

EZ hesitated a moment before answering, but when Watson looked at him inquiringly and batted a tiny bud of broccoli from her nose, he laughed and said: "Virge is that damn librarian's son. Who else would name their poor kid after some candy ass Roman poet? Virgil Salinger is my connection to the students at the high school. Those nerdy scholarship types really trust him. He knows where their heads are at, and he sells a lot of speed for me." Even as Alex digested the information that Mark's son was involved with drug dealing, she was also gazing at Watson in fascination. The animal seemed able to draw EZ out and get him to talk. This cat had true investigative talent.

Watching Ms. Watson clean her green face, EZ smiled even as he complained, "It's tough to make a living these days. When Perry Webb threw us out of the park, the library seemed perfect for doing a few deals. Virge and his clients were always studying in the Castle anyway. Who'd guess they were also doing business?" He puffed on the pipe, forgetting to pass it on to Alex. "Everything was cool until Virgil's father found us out. He waylaid us in the parking lot and threatened to bust us all, even his own son! Damn, I wish I'd sliced that librarian's throat 'stead of his arm!"

Alex nearly dropped the wine bottle. She was glad that EZ was distracted by Watson, who was sitting on the engine cover licking butter off his slice of garlic bread. It was difficult to keep her face devoid of excitement. It took all her self-control not to clap a hand to her head, and exclaim, "Aha! Watson! No wonder Mark was so vague about that knife wound to his arm! He was protecting his drug-dealing son from prosecution!" She calmed herself and poured EZ some more wine.

"It's not like we were doin' anything heavy," EZ complained. He still seemed to be talking to Watson, who gazed back at him with much more sympathy than she usually showed to Alex. "We were just helping kids study for their SAT exams or make varsity football or whatever. But that fuckin' Salinger knew all my dealers. They were his son's friends, and he threatened he'd put them all away, even Virgil. That asshole! He was just like Perry Webb. Don't the assholes remember what it was like to be young and have nowhere to go and nothing to do?"

"Some people don't give kids a break," Alex said mournfully.

"But I got 'em both," EZ proudly explained to Watson. "Webb's dead, and I put Salinger in prison."

Alex felt her mouth grow dry with the longing to know

141

more. How had EZ put Salinger in prison? By knifing Webb? Was she about to hear a confession of murder? She hoped the thrilled pounding of her heart didn't disturb the bug in her pendant watch. She waited, saying nothing, as calmly as she could. When EZ didn't follow up on his statement, she remarked offhandedly, "I thought only police sent people to prison."

EZ didn't seem to hear her. He drank more wine and stared vacantly into space. Alex looked at Watson in desperation, and the cat settled into EZ's lap. That seemed to rouse the boy, and he bent over to scratch her ear. "Cops are stupid, aren't they, Blackie? They'd still be looking for that loco mumbler if I hadn't called and set them straight." EZ tickled Watson's chin as she gazed up at him and purred. "You see, Blackie, the night of the murder, I cut the librarian, then ran to hide and clean my knife up behind the dumpsters. That's when I saw someone go into the bushes, carrying a bundle of clothes. I made some noise, and the crazy got scared, dropped that load in the bushes, and bolted up the fire escape back into the library." EZ stroked the cat who was rubbing her face against his arm with a low, throaty purr.

What a little flirt you are, Watson, Alex thought. George should send you out on bimbo cases. You're the lady with the gift for it. Maybe you could model for *Playboy* on the side.

EZ's stoned ego was still blooming under Watson's admiration: "Blackie, I'm the guy who pulled those clothes and that wig out of the bushes," he bragged. "I checked them out in the bit of light that came from the library windows. . . . I saw the blood on the clothes, heard the screams from the building and the sirens coming up the hill. I knew that whoever had stashed those clothes was someone in trouble, and since Salinger had given me shit I gave him some back. I cleaned my bloody knife on those clothes while I slashed them up in ribbons." EZ made the horrible wheeze that was his drugged attempt at a laugh. "Virge had already told me that his dad . . . that loser . . . drove a junker with a trunk that was kept closed with a bungee cord! So I ran to the staff parking lot and hid all that bloody stuff in Salinger's car trunk!" EZ wheezed out laughter again, and Watson turned on her back, waving her legs in the air with mirth.

Alex stared at her cat with a dropped jaw. With this undignified creature Watson? Alex contemplated the upside-down feline, and her mouth snapped shut. Had Watson winked at her? Alex wondered if she was suffering from a contact high. She shook her head to clear it and got back to business. "Did you see the murderer? You could blackmail lots of meatball money out of him if you did."

EZ was disgusted at Alex's ignorance, "Naw, it was too dark. Who knows if the killer was a man or a woman?"

Having dismissed Alex, EZ continued his private conversation with Watson telling her of all the great deals he would do in Santa Linda once the heat was off and he was back in his own territory at the park. His voice began to fade with fatigue and long pauses occurred between his words. Alex was tired, too. The excitement of the night was wearing off, leaving her dull, sleepy, and wondering how she was going to get rid of her guest and accomplish the long ride home.

It was Watson who seemed to solve the problem . . . again. The cat curled up near EZ's shoulder and purred a lullaby of sweet nothings into his ear. Alex did her own small part by keeping him plied with wine.

At last, on a faint stain of bravado: "I may never go back to civilization. There are caves near the river where a guy could hide out forever. . . ." EZ nodded off.

Alex drove him back to the Bluebeard Bar. She removed his car keys from his pocket so she could unlock the

Porsche and bundled him into it. She also removed his license from his wallet. Back in the van again, she downed an entire thermos of coffee and could barely remember how she made it back to the sofa bed in apartment thirteen of the Blue Flamingo.

Chapter 16

BUT ONCE SHE was finally lying down, Alex couldn't sleep. Whether it was too much coffee, too much driving, too many lumps in the sofa bed or simply all the noise that Watson was making as she slurped up some well-deserved shrimp, Alex couldn't relax. Her success in Manzanita stimulated her mind, and weighed on it, too.

What if EZ woke up, remembered his confessions, and then decided to run or hide out in some cave? Alex ought to play this tape for Coulter and have him deal with EZ right away. She called Coulter's number but could only reach his answering machine. Well, considering the hour, that wasn't surprising. Alex decided to bring the cassette to the attorney in person. It was late at night. He'd be angry, and he would yell at her. So what else was new?

She left her bed to pull on clean slacks and a bulky sweater. At the last minute, she remembered to remove her black widow spider earrings and replace them with a more conservative pair. Then she was on her way.

Just as she was going out the door, she hesitated. Did she entirely trust Ross Coulter? Alex delayed her departure to copy her tape of EZ's exploits and to place the second tape beneath Watson's litter box, a temporary hiding place. Now, if Ross failed to do his part for Mark, Alex would have a copy of the tape to personally deliver to the librarian—even if she had to enter the prison to do it.

Alex wasn't surprised that in Santa Linda, a town filled with old fashioned cottages and gardens, Ross's town house was spare and modern and standing at the end of a gravel path that featured very little greenery. She knocked on the heavy black door and leaned on the bell awhile before Ross opened the door. He was barefoot, clad in a brown velour robe and probably nothing else. Alex tried to ignore his broad, bare chest and to hide her surprise at the fact that Ross wasn't alone. A large, gray, lively dog had also come to the door. With his fat, shaggy body and thin, elongated nose he reminded Alex of a leggy, hairy anteater.

The dog looked at Alex, wagged his disreputable tail, and stuck out a long friendly tongue. Ross looked at Alex and seemed disturbed. With one hand on the dog's collar he ushered her to a chair in the living room: "Are you all right? You're not in trouble or hurt?"

"I'm okay." Alex was a bit startled. She'd expected his usual sarcasm and impatience. Instead Ross acted embarrassed, perhaps because when Alex sat down in the large reclining chair, the big dog immediately jumped in her lap and drooled.

"Come on out, Cyrano," Ross ordered. "Come on!" he repeated in a voice that was suspiciously like a plea.

Several minutes and a few hefty tugs later, the unwilling dog was sliding on his back end, staring with large, longing eyes in Alex's direction. Alex heard him being pulled somewhere to the back of the house. That was a slow process, accompanied by the sounds of cajoling and then swearing, and it gave her a chance to look around.

She thought that the living room suited Ross Coulter because it was richly furnished with leather, brass, and glass. But it didn't fit in with her perception of the attorney to find dog hairs on the Bakhara rug. And though the mantelpiece of the marble fireplace was cluttered with photos of

146

a gorgeous, slinky brunette, the woman shared her poses with a younger, puppyish version of Cyrano.

"Who'd have thought the man would tolerate animals?" Alex wondered if Ross had other virtues that she hadn't suspected—like being human. She glanced at the large glass coffee table where papers regarding Mark's case were spread out. When she saw the underlined note on a legal pad—"investigate Barron's mortgage"—she sighed with relief. It would be helpful if she could remove Ross from her suspect list sometime soon. That list definitely needed pruning.

A crash echoed into the living room. Ross was yelling at the dog to get his feet off the kitchen counter. Alex leaned back into the soft leather chair, put her feet up, and relaxed. Somehow she wasn't as intimidated by Heathcliff anymore. With a hound like Cyrano, he certainly had no right to be so superior about her problems with Watson. She closed her tired eyes, just for a moment.

She awakened to find herself staring into a strangely concerned gaze. Ross had changed into slacks and a flannel shirt. A fire blazed in the fireplace, and the papers had been stashed to the side of the coffee table to make room for a tray of food. Alex knew what had awakened her, the smell of fresh brewed coffee, eggs, and whole-grain toast.

"You shouldn't have let me sleep," she said in agitation.

"You've only been sleeping for forty minutes or so, and you looked terrible." He stood up to pour orange juice from a pitcher into her glass and added, "I didn't want a dead detective on my conscience."

When he spoke in that caustic manner it was easy for Alex to recall how little she liked him. Still, it had been a long time since a man had bothered to cook her a decent meal.

"Somehow I felt that my usual fare of stale doughnuts and instant coffee wouldn't do for someone who reads *Or-*

ganic Living." Ross looked at the table with pride. "I just managed not to burn the eggs."

"This is great," Alex said with surprised gratitude. "Now, I want you to listen to this tape. I think you're going to like it."

She brought out the cigarette case and pressed the play back on the microcassette. Ross looked startled as EZ's thick, groggy voice began its story. Alex ate her delicious eggs and watched the man who normally seemed to have such strict control of his emotions. He was leaning forward, listening intently. As the tape went on, his stern face began to relax, his taut, severe mouth actually turned up at the corners, and he grinned at her.

Alex couldn't help smiling back. She was no attorney, but she knew this evening had been a minor triumph. EZ's rambling had explained away the forensic evidence that was so damning for Mark. Now it was clear why the clothes in the trunk were stained with both Salinger's and Webb's blood. . . . EZ had gashed Mark's arm with his knife. Then, with a knife covered in Mark's blood, he'd cut up the murderer's clothes, clothing already stained with the blood from Webb's stabbing.

Alex hefted up her large overnight bag and found the knives she'd taken from EZ. She'd wrapped them in tissues. "One of these knives was very likely used to slash up the killer's clothing before EZ threw it in Mark's trunk," she explained. "I don't know if a lab could find fibers on one of them now, but just in case, I brought the weapons to you." Fishing again in the handbag she handed Ross a laminated card with a sheepish shrug. "You know, a funny thing happened. Mr. Moore dropped his license on the ground. I happened to pick it up and stick it in my purse . . . um, without knowing what it was, of course."

"Oh, of course," her client's attorney said with a grin. "I'm sure you didn't steal that license from his wallet. But since you've found it, we might as well run a check on his I.D. and see what we come up with."

Who'd have believed that Ross could be so attractive when he smiled? That harsh face could look responsive . . . even affectionate. And those cold gray eyes could warm you with a friendly gaze that was almost embarrassing in its intensity. Alex dropped her own eyes, feeling oddly nervous. She began to concentrate on buttering an already buttered piece of toast.

"It's a pity I can't use this tape in court," Ross murmured thoughtfully.

"I know. California law makes it a crime to use electronic devices to record any confidential communication without the consent of all parties." Alex quoted a law she'd learned early in her career. "And EZ never consented to having our conversation recorded." She hesitated, trying to phrase an illegal suggestion with discretion: "But you know where EZ is. And you know what he is. Maybe you could use his drugs against him."

That attractive grin flashed across Ross's dark face again. "Why, Alex! Are you insinuating that I should use something as nasty as entrapment to scare EZ into talking? Should I let the poor boy think I can put him behind bars?"

"Yep," said Alex, crunching into her toast. "Then you could generously offer him a deal if he admits to framing Mark."

"Tsk. Tsk. Alex. That's hardly a kosher suggestion, as your boss would say."

"True. Maybe I'm too used to my ex-husband. Charlie is an attorney who always told me no honest lawyer was worth a damn." She looked at Ross appraisingly. "And I'll bet you're an excellent lawyer."

The grin became an outright laugh. "You've been in bad company." Ross's voice grew serious. "What I'd like to do is to take your idea a little farther and catch the kid dealing.

149

That would put him in danger of being arrested on a felony charge, while possession might only be a misdemeanor. I have a friend in vice who wouldn't mind a tip. How long do you think EZ will stay in Manzanita?"

Alex chewed, swallowed, and calculated. "EZ was frightened that I was the law. For all his boasting, I think that he's already regretting stuffing bloody clothes in Mark's Plymouth. He realizes on some level that it was an impulsive mistake. I wouldn't be surprised if he tried to get as much mileage between himself and the Santa Linda County sheriff's office as quickly as possible. That's the reason I came over. I want you to find him while he's still hanging out at the Bluebeard Bar driving a red, late-seventies-model Porsche with a license place that reads: 'KOOL 15'." Alex would not lose sleep if EZ had to face the police. It was the humane and kindly librarian facing a murder charge who held her interest. "If EZ talks, will the charges against Mark be dropped?" she asked.

"Possibly. But even if Mark goes to trial you've just shot holes in the strongest part of the prosecution's case." Ross took a deep breath and let it out slowly. "My God, when did I hire you, Alex? Saturday? It's only Monday morning and you've delivered the best news I've had since this nightmare began!"

Alex heard something she hadn't heard before from the arrogant Mr. Coulter, a compliment. Touched and a little embarrassed, she looked away from Ross and reached for jam although she no longer had any toast to spread it on.

But Ross had jumped up as if his emotions would no longer enable him to stay seated. His sudden movement upset the jam jar as well as the file on the table. Papers slid onto Ross's dish of scrambled eggs, but he didn't seem to notice. Crossing to Alex's chair, he took her hand in his, enclosing it firmly. "I'll never be able to thank you enough for what you've done for Mark."

Alex knew she hadn't had much sleep, but she must have been even more tired than she thought. Surely it couldn't be the touch of this distant, frigid man that made her palm tingle and sent a feverish jolt of heat right through her. But then, Ross was holding her hand as if he didn't wish to let go. Was it a trick of the firelight that made those icy gray eyes seem so ... so intense and burning?

She gently pulled her hand away as she stood up. She was more than a bit flustered by Ross's admiration. She preferred his disapproval. At least that didn't weaken her knees and set the pulse pounding in her throat. A sudden attack of nerves made her blurt out, "It was amazing how well Ms. Watson did with EZ. He was hostile and uncommunicative until he saw that cat. Somehow Watson managed to hold EZ in the palm of her ... er, paw." Alex heard the inanity of her words and felt her cheeks flushing. Damn. She walked behind her chair and tried to sound more sensible. "I was very lucky. You heard, of course, on the tape how EZ felt about black cats."

She waited for Ross to stare down at her with his old severe frown, but instead he repeated her description of Watson's behavior. "Amazing," Ross murmured as he moved toward Alex.

He was a very tall man and she had to look up to see if he was being sarcastic again. But what she saw in his dark, unsmiling face caught her entirely by surprise. Her heart began to beat in a very unusual way—it seemed to be jumping rope.

Ross came very near. Strong fingers grazed her arm and moved to clasp her wrist. "Bless you, Alex," he whispered in her ear while his other hand lightly tilted up her chin. He smiled into her eyes. "You're the one who's amazing, absolutely amazing!"

Alex didn't answer. She found that her throat had gone dry, and her legs felt as sturdy as whipped cream. Somehow the few inches between the two of them disappeared. Somehow their lips met. Her arms circled around his neck, and she was clinging to him, feeling his hands move up under her sweater, feeling his heart beating against her chest.

You've been alone too long, Alex's mind protested logically. One kiss, one sweet touch from a handsome man who cooks you a lousy dish of eggs, and you melt into a puddle—like Hamlisch's rum-raisin ice cream.

But now Ross was repeating her name in a husky voice while his lips brushed her throat. He lifted Alex up into his arms even as he moved to kiss her with a slow thoroughness, lighting up a heat that spread like sweet wildfire. Logic, such as it was, went up in the flames of passion. The disapproving voice still spoke in Alex's head, but it made as little impression as a second crash from the back of the house where Cyrano was attacking the kitchen counter again. Preoccupied with the comforting warmth of Ross's arms, Alex even forgot to ask about the photos of the slinky brunette above the fireplace. The outside world faded as the pair shed their clothes and made their slow, entangled way to the bedroom.

Tuesday morning, at nine, Grace Ghiringhelli was in her kitchen taking a platter from the cupboard for a guest who was drinking coffee in the dining room. She heard the wind howl as rain began to pummel the small window above the sink. The fierce sound suited Grace. It emphasized the furious thoughts that swirled in her head.

Yesterday, supervisors Yaeger and Smith had appeared on Cindy Fayne's KPXX local news talk show. They'd whined about "the two-million-dollar county shortfall of funds." Then those morons had come up with the brilliant idea of closing the Castle "as a means of extricating the county from its financial crisis."

Grace opened the oven door and took out the heated coffee cake. "I'll just be a moment," she called to her visitor. "And if the phone rings, don't answer it. I've already called in and left a message that I'm not coming into the library today and that I'm not to be disturbed."

Desiring to impress her company, Grace rushed through the kitchen preparing a tray of fruit before she eased the coffee cake onto a serving platter. Its warm, cinnamon scent did not soothe her. Webb was dead, but the library was still in trouble. It was a hell of a good thing she'd made contingency plans.

"We're going to have a terrible day today at the Castle," Grace told her guest when she entered the dining alcove with the tray. "Curiosity seekers will all want to see the room where Webb died."

She served the cake, poured herself a cup of coffee from the carafe on the table, and looked around with satisfaction. She'd used her best china cups and plates from a Lennox service inherited from her grandmother. She said, "I'll be quite relieved to work for you. With the scandal that's surrounding the library, and the budget deficit facing the county, the supervisors have already begun to talk of shutting the Castle down. They'll have some firm set up a book rental system to replace it."

Grace inhaled her exceptionally bitter coffee and wolfed down her cake, agitated with the injustice of it all. "Even if the public insists that the library be kept open, the county will slash funds, and it will only be a matter of time before I'm replaced by a temporary worker without seniority, sick-leave benefits, or an expensive pension coming due in five years. Those supervisors will fire me all right. I won't even get a tin watch for all the years of service I put in."

Her guest nodded sympathetically and nibbled on cake.

Grace poured herself more coffee, and she took another gulp. "I'll give all the energy I've wasted on an inconsiderate public to you. And you'll never have to worry that I'll say a word about—".

"Excuse me, Grace, but the handsome bookcase in your living room has caught my eye."

Puzzled, Grace stood up as her guest left for the bookcase. The pain hit her immediately, and she doubled over.

"This is a first edition of *Famous Flowers for Famous Folks*, isn't it?"

Grace opened her mouth to scream for help rather than to answer, but she lost her breakfast on the carpet instead.

"Why, Grace, you have a fine first edition of *A Child's Garden*, too," her guest called out while still absorbed in the books. "I had no idea you were interested in gardening. It's so odd. You don't have a yard, or even indoor plants."

With an enormous effort of will, Grace struggled up to her knees. She'd grasped the table leg to pull herself to her feet when the convulsions began. She fell back to the soiled carpet, her arms and legs flailing.

Her guest stuffed both books under an arm, and began to hum "Where Have All the Flowers Gone."

Walking slowly over to where Grace lay, retching blood in spasms that shook her entire body, the visitor stared into bulging, desperate eyes with calm curiosity. "Perhaps I'd better tidy up for you. You seem indisposed." Handiwipes were pulled out. Careful strokes removed fingerprints from dishes, the silverware, and the coffee carafe.

With a powerful effort of will Grace strained her uncooperative, spasming body toward the table and the cloth that was draped over its sides. Her shaking fingers reached up to yank the cloth.

"No, no, Grace. That won't do at all."

The library assistant screamed when a kick sharply smacked her elbow. She dropped again to the floor, her legs jackknifing out in uncontrollable convulsions. Now she could not seem to find enough breath to fill her aching lungs.

"Thank you for the lovely breakfast, Grace. Oh, and don't bother to walk me to the door. I'll let myself out. Though I will have another delicious strawberry, and a piece of your delicious cake. I only poisoned the coffee. By the way, blackmail isn't a nice occupation."

The last sounds Grace heard in a gray world going black were continued, cheerful humming and the slam of the front door.

Chapter 17

THE CASTLE GLOWED through a swirling bank of mist off the lake. Viewed from the vantage of the steep, winding road, the building was almost ghostly, its high white towers giving off a faint shine as pale and ethereal as ectoplasm.

It was late afternoon now. Alex had spent quite a bit of time at number thirteen, doing one thing and another. The work helped her forget the events of the early morning. From the moment she'd awakened in Ross's bed, she'd been thoroughly disturbed. Not Ross's affectionate note with a promise to see her tonight, nor Cyrano's sweet, silly face, and thumping tail (he'd somehow opened the back door and come through the house to jump on the bed) had cheered her.

Back at the Blue Flamingo under the curiously knowing gaze of Ms. Watson, Alex had refused to think about the needs that had propelled her into Ross's arms. Instead, she'd pulled her copy of EZ's tape out from under Watson's litter box and played it over again, checking on something that had nearly passed her by. EZ claimed to have seen the murderer climb back up the fire escape into the library. Why? Perhaps the murderer worked in the library and needed to return? Or, being frightened by EZ's sudden appearance, had the killer panicked, dumped the disguise in the bushes, bolted up the fire escape into the Castle, and then simply walked out of the building before Webb's body was discovered?

Alex had pondered the possibilities as she tidied up the apartment, then phoned Luke Bishop's social security and driver's license number into the Abromowitz and Stewart Investigative Agency. Gloria, the agency's secretary, was there to take down the numbers with her usual efficiency.

"Find out what Data Search can dig up. He might have left a credit trail. See if he's made any train or airline ticket purchases, will you? Also, he might have applied for driver's licenses in another state, though it's a little early for that. I also want to know if either Eden Selby or Luke Bishop have made any recent passport applications. That's all, Gloria, except for the tape that I'm mailing to the agency. It's important to Mark Salinger, and I'd appreciate it if you put it in the safe."

"Got it," Gloria said. "And Alex . . ." Gloria launched into a long story about George bringing a young girl up to the office as a file clerk. "This dimwit doesn't know the first thing about data entry. In fact, she doesn't even like to enter data because it might break her shining, red claws. So how am I supposed to train this gem to use the main computer? I'll bet George is angling to get his girlfriend into the office so that she can take my job and he can pay her next to nothing. I've heard Sam might be back in the next day or two, and believe me Sam's going to get an earful! George is becoming impossible!"

Alex assured Gloria that she agreed. But for once, George's behavior troubled Alex less than her own. She'd campaigned against being pushed into bed on bimbo cases, and then she'd tumbled into bed on a murder case. And with Ross Coulter of all people. Didn't she know better than to fall for another lawyer? The last time she'd found herself involved with an attorney, she'd come out of a divorce settlement lucky to have a T-shirt on her back. Where was her common sense? Where was her willpower? And where, for that matter, were her car keys, so that she could bury herself in work and forget about last night's temporary lapse of sanity?

Alex pulled the car keys out from under Ms. Watson, who was sitting on the kitchen counter listening to the radio play Mozart. Then she set off for the post office, and then the Castle.

Normally, the library was quiet on a Monday afternoon, but today the parking lot held enough cars to resemble rush-hour gridlock. Despite the damp, windy weather that threatened to break any moment into another rainstorm, two sets of pickets marched before the broad steps to the building. One picket line flashed signs that read: CLOSE THE CASTLE and NO MONEY FOR MURDER! The other line jeered at the first and held signs demanding: KEEP THE CASTLE OPEN and SAVE OUR LIBRARY.

Both groups were shouting at each other for the benefit of KPXX and Cindy Fayne, who kept withdrawing from the fray to comb and spray her windblown coiffure. Alex stepped through the marching crowd just as Cindy took the arm of a frail, stylish woman beside her.

"Now, Ms. Bigelow." Cindy flashed her rather large, pearly teeth to the camera. "Will you explain why you think the Santa Linda County supervisors would be right in voting to close the Castle immediately?"

While Ms. Bigelow squared her slender shoulders and demanded that the Castle never open its doors again, Alex shook her head in dismay and hurried into the building.

Inside the library, only one small woman held back a wave of emotion and confusion. *"Yes,"* Laurel told a large, noisy group. *Yes,* they could still check out books. *Yes,* they could have them for a full three weeks. *Yes,* if the library closed, books could be still be returned to the night slot.

But Laurel assured everyone that even if the supervisors voted to close the library, "It won't happen overnight."

Alex hovered in the background. It was more than fifteen minutes before the space near the front desk cleared and the woman gave her a harried, "May I help you?"

"I hope so," Alex said, introducing herself. "I've come to ask some questions on behalf of Mark Salinger."

"I remember you from that terrible evening," Laurel admitted. "And, I'd love to talk . . . but you can see I'm just swamped." She brushed her dark hair from her face, then took off her glasses and wearily rubbed at the red marks they'd made on her nose. "Saturday, hardly a soul came by. Today, herds of people are stomping in telling me they want to "take back their library.""

"Can I fit in a couple of quick questions?"

Laurel eyed a wobbling stack of recently returned books that cluttered one edge of the large front counter and sighed, "If it's for Mr. Salinger, go ahead."

"I'm trying to locate Luke Bishop and Eden Selby."

"I'm sorry. I didn't know either of them very well."

"Okay, second question: why were you out of the library during the time that Webb was murdered?"

Laurel shrugged. "I got a call saying Todd Hanson was in trouble, and he needed to meet me at the Castle Coffee Shop, in town. I rushed out to find him, but all the time Todd was here, working in his office on the tower floor. We rent rooms in the Castle tower to people with book contracts and Todd is one of them—"

"So the call was a trick to get you out of the building? Who called?"

"I don't know." Laurel busied herself with the returned books. She acted as though the interview were over.

"Let me ask you again," Alex persisted. "Who called?"

The round eyes behind the glasses blinked owlish in surprise. "What do you mean? I told you. I don't know."

159

"You don't know too much. You haven't told me whether the caller was male or female. Was the voice deep or shrill? I think you have a suspicion that you don't want to admit to."

Laurel hesitated. "It seems wrong for me to accuse anyone when I'm not sure of my facts."

"Isn't it wrong for Mark Salinger to be convicted of murder without every opportunity to demonstrate his innocence?"

Laurel stared at the counter, rubbing at the surface with her finger. "When you put it that way, I suppose I'm not thinking straight. I guess I've been rattled, but this is the second death we've had in the Castle in less than a month! First, it was that girl, Claire Fraiser. Then it was Perry Webb. It's enough to make anyone disturbed. Mr. Gilbert, our security guard, has quit. Grace Ghiringhelli seems to be on strike and won't answer her phone." Laurel paused, then said in a rush, "That call on Monday night? I thought it was a woman trying to sound like a man. You asked about Eden? Well, Eden has a gruff, blunt way of speaking, and the voice sounded like hers."

"Why would the caller think you'd go running off to find Todd Hanson?"

"He's my ex-husband for one thing. And Todd had a theory that a young woman named Claire Fraiser was murdered outside the Castle. He felt sure that Perry Webb had been involved in her death. When Todd has a theory about Mark Twain, or the history of Santa Linda, or anything from aardvarks to zinnias, he investigates it, publicizes it to the world, then fights to defend it. The call made it sound like this time someone had fought back."

"So you rushed out of the library to protect him?"

"Yes. I guess I've been worried about that brilliant idiot for so long that I just can't break the habit. Why don't you

160

talk to him about Webb's murder? He's bound to have a theory."

Todd Hanson came to the door of his study in the tower room wearing blue jeans and a frayed T-shirt. He held a yellow legal pad and pen in ham-fisted, callused hands that seemed more comfortable with picks or sledgehammers.

Alex introduced herself with a quick handshake.

"It's about time somebody defended Mark!" Todd roared at her. "Salinger's arrest is a goddamn crime! He's a saint, and if the supervisors had any brains they'd tear down that jail and drag him back to the Castle where we need him.

"Unfortunately, I can't tell you too much about what went on the night of the murder. I was working on my book the entire time. I'm finishing my manuscript to collect the rest of my advance and frankly, Ms. Winter, I need money."

"What's the book about?"

"It's the story of Twain's brief sojourn in Santa Linda County. I believe it's going to break new ground!" He motioned Alex into his office, which was cluttered with cardboard boxes filled with neatly coded files. "I'm sure Twain came to Santa Linda in the early 1860s, just before he accepted a job as a reporter for the *Enterprise* in Nevada." Todd offered Alex the only chair, an old vinyl-covered recliner that looked as if it had popped a few springs.

"Of course, the great Twain was still Sam Clemens then, but it's one of the few times in his life for which there's no absolute data. And I think I know the reason for that gap. I believe Twain had a brief but intense romance in Santa Linda, with a woman he'd met in Nevada." Todd pushed back his red-brown hair. "Twain's was a tragic romance, one that haunted his conscience but could never be revealed to his wife and daughters. Yet, it influenced all his work,

161

especially his protective, Victorian attitude toward women and—"

"It sounds like a wonderful book." Alex wished she'd never started Todd on his pet topic. "But about Monday night—"

"I sure wasn't at the Castle Coffee Shop. I don't have extra money for a glass of water, let alone doughnuts and coffee."

Todd did indeed look like he needed money. Despite his height he seemed unnaturally thin, his clothes bagging at the waist, his jeans hanging loosely on his long legs. Alex looked around at his box-filled room. "If you were working here on Monday night, weren't you disturbed by the fight between Pamela and Luke?"

"You mean the one where she called him the 'bastard who fucked my daughter'?" Todd tossed his head and laughed. "That did make me pick my head up, I admit. But I've worked through bar brawls and street fights . . . raised voices don't bother me much. This book is too important to me. It could become Mark Twain's definition of a classic: 'Something that everybody wants to have read and nobody wants to read.' "

He snatched a small sheaf of papers from his desk. "These are copies from my collection of letters that are from a married woman to a young prospector named Samuel. She thanks him for his help in extricating her from a brutal marriage and helping her escape from Nevada. In the next set of letters she talks of how much his visit to Santa Linda meant to her and how much she loves him. Finally there are letters apologizing because she knows he doesn't return her strong feelings, and at last she bids Samuel good luck and good-bye in a final suicide note." Todd flapped the papers in Alex's face, his eyes bright with enthusiasm. "If I can prove that these letters were written to Mark Twain, what do you think they'd be worth, Ms. Winter?"

Alex wasn't sure. She also wasn't sure how they'd gotten back to Twain again. She began to understand why Laurel worried about Todd's overwhelming enthusiasms.

"We're talking six figures." He waved the letters joyfully. "Because these letters also contain a copy of a short, comic melodrama that Twain apparently wrote to cheer and entertain her."

"About Monday night—" Alex began

"Twain knew the value of a dollar, Ms. Winter, and so do I! My ex-wife Laurel will tell you that I've lived on the street because I'm an impractical fool. But I've been roughing it, just like Twain. And like him, I'm searching for my own form of California gold. Twain wasn't a miner for long. He thought panning for gold was too damn hard so he made his money using his wit. So will I, Ms. Winter."

"Let's get back to the events in this library a moment, Mr. Hanson."

"Right. And thank God for this library! Mark Salinger made an attempt to preserve all the original letters and diaries, as well as any books that pertained to the history of this county. Ms. Winter, if I make my mark, so to speak, in the world of letters, it'll be because of Mark Twain and also Mark Salinger."

"Maybe you can help our librarian," Alex tugged the subject back to murder again. "Who do you think killed Perry Webb?"

Todd put his six-figure file reluctantly aside and prowled the room, dodging boxes. "You're beginning in the wrong place. Find Claire Fraiser's killer and you'll find Webb's. Oh, yes, Claire was murdered. There was no drug overdose. Claire was a tireless campaigner for God. She never touched drugs or alcohol. How could she have died of a drug overdose? Scott Wilson, the man you probably know as the mumbler . . . poor Scott would try to get Claire's attention by getting drunk. He loved to watch her pray for him."

Alex got out of her uncomfortable chair and went to stand beside Todd at the large tower window. Outside it had begun to drizzle. From here she could see the tiny drops slanting in the afternoon wind. "So Scott was in love with Claire?"

"Head over heels! And on Media Day, Webb and Scott nearly killed each other. Then, only hours later, Claire was found dead."

"But Webb was in the hospital that night because he'd been stabbed by the mumbler," Alex reminded Todd.

"No, he wasn't! He stayed at the emergency room an hour or two and left! I checked that out with Eden Selby, who had just started cleaning for Webb. She drove him from the hospital back to his office."

"Eden Selby," Alex mused. "I hear a lot about Eden, Mr. Hanson, but no one knows where she is. All I do know is that she was last seen driving off with Luke Bishop."

"Luke Bishop?" Todd scratched the new red-brown beard that was sprouting on his stubbled chin. "That's a puzzle. Luke wouldn't be interested in the places that Eden frequented. She knows a lot of the old-timers in Santa Linda and every inch of the county landscape, especially the sacred caves of the Indians. Eden was one of the first people to show me Rosalia Island in the Santa Linda River near Manzanita Springs. That's where I believe Twain's romance was carried out, and if I hadn't known that *Tom Sawyer* was based on sites in Hannibal, Missouri, I'd have sworn that the island where Huck Finn hid from his 'Pappy' was Rosalia. Eden also showed me the cave across from the island. It's a lot like the one where Tom and Huck found Injun Joe's hidden treasure."

"Could Eden be in Rosalia?"

"Not in a winter like this. And even in summer the

164

island's not posh enough for Luke Bishop! You know it's odd that a money-hungry leech like Bishop can write with such moral conviction. His novel is about a World War II European military hero who just happened to be a homosexual. The hero saved a town, only to be killed by the same town's homophobic prejudice—the book is a masterpiece. But the author is a jerk, totally preoccupied with big bucks. Not that I look down on money, but Luke is ruthless and amoral. He doesn't give a damn who he destroys. So where would Luke take Eden? Start looking for him among the rich and infamous. Lately he's talked a lot about buying an Italian villa. But one thing is sure, Eden will have to pay the great author's way."

Alex turned from the window and walked toward the door. Todd had plenty of theories but not much hard evidence. This conversation had merely added another suspect to Alex's long list. If Perry Webb had lived, his plans to privatize the Castle could have ruined Hanson's chances to publish his book. They would have also ruined Hanson's ability to research and prove the value of his "six-figure" letters. Hanson had gained a lot of opportunity the night Webb died.

But the interview had established her next move, the need to find Eden Selby. Eden kept cropping up in this investigation like the gophers in Alex's herb garden.

"Thanks for your time, Mr. Hanson. If you think of other information to help Mark, please let me know." She penned the address and phone number of the Blue Flamingo onto her card and left the card on his cluttered desk.

Chapter 18

"Ms. Winter, how good to see you! Have you heard the news?" As soon as Alex entered the Children's Room, Zoe Latham rushed up to her. Looking around at the crowded library, she pulled Alex back into the empty hallway. "I've been sneaking snatches of news from a radio I brought in. Judge Lipton set bail at one hundred thousand dollars. Mark has paid the bail and is already out of prison! I'm expecting to hear from him at any time."

"That's wonderful!" Alex smiled at the lively, cheerful woman. Zoe had always been beautiful, but her good looks had held a remote, princess-in-the-tower quality. Now Zoe's reserved face was glowing and her graceful limbs could barely keep still. She seemed almost giddy with excitement and emotion.

"How's the investigation going?" Zoe asked. "Ross sounded very optimistic. He told me you'd found valuable evidence to help Mark."

Alex frowned. Ross shouldn't have mentioned that. In Alex's mind, Zoe was a prominent suspect. She had the brains to carry out the murder and the important motive of her inheritance.

"Please tell me what you know, Ms. Winter." Zoe twisted her slim hands together. "You can't imagine what it's been like for me, worrying about Mark." The glow faded from her face, leaving her very pale. "I haven't had a message from Mark since he was arrested. He seems embarrassed to speak to me. You can't imagine how terrible it is not to know what's going to happen to him."

It was an admission of pain, and Alex answered it gently. "I'm sorry, I'm not in the position to offer much information. I can tell you that at this point in my investigation I'm trying to find Eden Selby and Luke Bishop. If you know anything that would help me—"

"I don't know if it's related to your investigation, but a week before the murder, Eden asked me about *A Child's Garden*. It's a valuable first-edition book written by her grandmother, Kate Selby, the famous landscaper. It's missing from the Children's Room special collection. Oh, and on the night Webb died, Eden's children were in this room. They told me that Webb was going to help their mother get a lot of money. Of course, they're very young, and, as Mark pointed out, the idea doesn't seem very likely."

The mention of Mark seemed to remind Zoe that she still hadn't learned enough about this case to satisfy her. "Ms. Winter," she began.

They were interrupted as Professor Clive Truesdell hurried down the stairs.

"My God, murder is inconvenient, Zoe, dear. I've had to give up my day off to help your shorthanded staff. It appears that old Webb has managed to obtain with his death what he was never able to achieve in life. He always was planning to discredit our wonderful librarian and close the Castle, but he never got to first base. As soon as the old troublemaker is dead, look what happens. We lose staff. Mark is imprisoned, and those moronic supervisors want to close the library. Next they'll sell the place to Webb's development partners, and our precious Castle will be a rich man's country club. Webb must be laughing in Hell!"

Truesdell came toward them clad in his usual tattered

jeans and Henley shirt. It was odd, Alex thought, that the distinguished professor was determinedly casual while the bigamist, Herbert Hamlisch, made such a studied attempt at dignity.

"Perhaps I'll sell my house and buy Salinger's brilliant collection of books on California history. The county of Santa Linda certainly doesn't seem to appreciate it. It's a shame but this great state of California, for all its natural and artistic wonders, doesn't seem to know how to preserve either one. Though I suppose someone made a stab at it (pardon the pun) when they killed Perry Webb."

He coughed and reddened when he noticed that Zoe wasn't smiling at his humor. Then he turned to Alex. "You're that detective, aren't you?" Truesdell gave Alex a sharp stare. "I suppose no one's privacy is safe now. Is the library bugged? Are secret cameras being installed?"

"Not as far as I know. Are you worried, Mr. Truesdell?"

"I was only joking, my dear, actually I'm glad to see you. Someone *must* ask Pamela Dysart whether valuable books from the library were sold to her friends via the used-book table. She ran those sales, you know, for the Friends of the Library."

"Oh, shut up, Clive," Zoe snapped. Worries over Mark had obviously tried her patience. "Why in the world would a successful businesswoman like Pamela bother to steal library books to sell on the used-book table? She never even handles any of the money. It all goes to Laurel or Grace at the front desk for the Castle slush fund. Do you have any proof that Pamela was robbing the library other than the fact that you've been squabbling with her for years?"

"Well, no, but . . ." The professor seemed deflated. Pam Dysart would have called him a scarecrow without straw.

"I'm so tired of accusations without proof!" Zoe whirled on him as the turmoil inside her found a voice. "Just like

I'm tired of the fools who accuse me of urging Mark to kill Perry so that I could inherit that evil man's money!"

In anger, Alex found the librarian a compelling woman. Her flaxen hair was braided, and pinned crownlike around her head. Her dress was silken, and its liquid lines and cinched-in waist contributed to the softness of her appearance. But there was heat in her baby blue eyes, and Alex didn't doubt that there was plenty of steel beneath her serene, story-book beauty.

Truesdell said apologetically, "I only came down here so that you could take a break. I know you've been on duty since ten without your lunch."

Zoe sighed and her delicate hand touched Truesdell's in apology for her temper. "That's very considerate. I'll just get my purse and take twenty minutes."

A small boy in blue sweats and a red cap came out of the library and tugged at Zoe's arm. "I want to read *The Little Engine That Could*."

"That's a fine idea. Mr. Truesdell here, will help you find it," Zoe told the boy. "Er . . . good-bye for now, Ms. Winter."

Alex barely heard the farewell. *"Engine,"* she was muttering, *"Injun!"* Of course that was it! She'd been so blind! The clue to finding Eden was here! Right here in the children's library.

"Ms. Latham, wait!" Alex exclaimed. "Where are your books by Mark Twain?"

Zoe, who'd been opening the glass doors to the Children's Room, stopped short. Clive Truesdell's heavy head bobbed on his thin neck in surprise.

"Why, they're in this section here." Zoe led Alex to the bookcase facing the bright muraled wall. She stopped at the spot where a pink pig, wearing a plaid cap, stood on his hind legs and peered at a chicken.

169

Alex went to the book shelf and pulled out a copy of *Tom Sawyer*.

"And do you have any good county guide books?"

"If we do, they'd be upstairs in nonfiction section 917."

"Terrific!" Alex beamed at her. "You've been a great help."

Zoe gave Alex an almost dazed look of confusion. "You mean *this* will help your investigation?"

"It sure will." Alex left Zoe Latham and Clive Truesdell behind her, staring at each other with open mouths. She sped upstairs and picked up a guidebook as well as a casette tape on growing irises that caught her eye just as she was dashing to the front desk. It was time to rush home and read a good book.

Ross scowled as he started up the Lincoln. "You can't protect that boy forever!"

"That's just it!" Mark exclaimed. "I haven't protected him at all! If I had, Virgil would never have come under EZ's thumb. I've let Trish take over the mothering *and* the fathering. I've let her separate me from my son. There was so much fuss when I disagreed with Trish about Virgil that I just backed off. I thought the kid needed peace from our bickering. Even when Trish said that Virgil couldn't see me on weekends because he was sick, or had some special project or event, I often let her have her way. My God, what a fool I was!"

"I know Patricia has a temper, but—" Ross began.

"I haven't fought back hard enough for Virge." Mark's eyes held a stubborn light that Ross was all too familiar with. "I know it's no excuse, but the boy's been under such pressure that I'm not surprised that he's involved in drugs. I should have seen it coming. Trish is determined that he go to Stanford on athletic scholarship. Virgil feels like a failure if he brings home anything less than perfect grades. At the same time, he trains to break school records so that he can win a scholarship as a marathon runner. Between studying and training it's no wonder he felt he needed Benzedrine. And he can't make enough money to buy pills without working for that hoodlum, EZ."

"Now wait, Mark—"

"Damn it, Ross! Trish wanted control, and unconsciously she tried to convince Virge that I don't care about him. If he's arrested because of me, and I do nothing to stop it, he'll believe that his mother is right. He'll think that I don't care, and I'll lose my son forever!"

"You'll lose him anyway if you're convicted of Webb's murder and imprisoned for life or put on death row," Ross countered with his usual blunt impatience. "And maybe the truth will open Trish's eyes to the fact that Virgil needs help. Besides, how could Virgil think that you don't care about him? You drive around in a car that has a trunk held together with a bungee cord so that you can afford to fix your son's teeth, hire a special track coach, and buy him a Civic."

"He needed that car to get to his—"

"Now listen to me, Mark!" Ross interrupted. "This time *your* problems come first! I'll talk to Trish and explain things to her, and I'll talk to Virgil, too, but if you're going to worry about someone, for Christ's sake worry about yourself! You're to stay home and stay out of the limelight. Don't give any interviews. Don't even go out unless you have to. . . ."

Ross heard himself giving unsympathetic, bullying orders. He paused to tone down his harsh style and stared through the rain-flecked windshield trying to find words of solace. But everything optimistic that he tried to say, even the fact that Zoe had helped put up bail and was looking forward to seeing Mark soon, seemed to agitate his friend more.

Finally, Ross decided on the strategy of distraction. He switched on the radio which, unfortunately, featured a news story about the turmoil at the Castle. Thinking that this, too, would likely add to Mark's distress, Ross reached to change the station, but the librarian's long arm stopped him. Mark was frowning and listened intently to the broadcast until they reached Ross's town house. There the librarian finally seemed cheered. His old Plymouth was parked in the drive. Police had temporarily impounded it to collect forensic evidence, and Mark appeared glad to see that his vehicle too was out of prison.

Mark shook Ross's hand and said in a resigned voice, "I suppose there was never any way to keep Virgil out of all this. He's not only using drugs, he's selling, and it's got to stop. I should have accepted that from the beginning. I'll think about all you said. Don't worry."

So why was Ross still worried as Mark drove off? Why did he feel as though he'd been dismissed?

Mark drove off from Ross's town house with detecting on his mind. When he'd heard Professor Truesdell on the radio complaining that the absence of a crucial front-desk person had sent the busy library into turmoil, he'd known immediately that Grace was very likely fuming at home about the supervisor's plans to close the Castle. It would be like Grace to show her displeasure with the county by going on a one-woman strike. He also knew that Ross would object to an impromptu visit with Grace, but Mark was determined to find out if *A Child's Garden* had been sold on the used-book table under a different cover.

Rain fell as he climbed the steps to the condominium complex. Someone else was hurrying into the building, and Mark turned to see Lucy Bigelow. She was holding some sort of protest sign like an umbrella above her head as she drifted vaguely up the front steps. He'd forgotten that she lived in the same building as Grace Ghiringhelli. "Hello, Lucy," he said.

Instead of answering, the slender woman gave a moan of horror and raced inside the main entrance. Mark shook his bare head and stood a moment on the steps, despite the rain. It was fine to be wanted, but not so hot to be "most wanted." He guessed that Lucy's reaction was one of the things that Ross was trying to protect him from by keeping him at home.

Mark climbed the stairs to Grace's condominium and knocked on the door. The last time he'd been here was in December. There'd been a small party for people who were opposed to Measure B and the closure of the Castle. December . . . it seemed like a hundred years ago. There was no answer to his knock on the door and he tried again, harder this time. He waited a moment, then turned the knob. To his surprise the door opened a crack. He leaned his head into the apartment, and smelled a strong, sour odor. "Grace," he called.

Then he saw her, her thick body sprawled on the stained carpet, her eyes open and staring, her mouth pulled wide in a terrible grimace. Mark walked toward her in a kind of daze, kneeling down beside her outflung arm. "Oh, Grace," he said, touching her inert, unresisting palm. "What's happened to you?" He shook his head in sorrow. "What's happened to us all?"

The hairs stood up on the back of his neck when screams answered his question. Shrieks streamed in from the doorway behind him.

"Murderer!" Lucy Bigelow screeched, with her thin hand on her heart. "Murderer!"

Chapter 19

RAIN DRIPPED FROM the glowing yellow beak and the gaudy, turquoise feathers of the Blue Flamingo as Alex was hurried to number thirteen. She was surprised by a shout from Mr. Rudnick, the owner of the motel-apartment complex. A cigarette glowed between his fingers, and his concave chest heaved with exertion as he lumbered toward her. It wasn't often that Rudnick left the entertainment center that sat behind the desk in the front office of the motel. What calamity had occurred to bring him out into the rain?

"Do you see that damage to my motel, Ms. Winter?" Rudnick thrust the cigarette in the direction of the doorway. Alex had no trouble perceiving what he meant as they stepped out of the rain into the relative shelter of the front alcove. The timed porch light was already on, and it gleamed down on the doorway of number thirteen, where a large cut and slivers of wood poked through the thick paint.

Mr. Rudnick's face was red, accentuating the deep web of lines around his mouth and eyes. "A knife," he bellowed angrily. "A knife slit that door. Some crazy person came through here in a black Eldorado, got out, and stuck a knife in this door, and that's not the worst!" Mr. Rudnick clasped his free hand to his head.

"Was anyone hurt?"

"A rat was hanging from that knife! A dead rat with a

174

noose around his neck!" Rudnick dropped his cigarette and clutched his throat. After a suitably dramatic pause, he took his hands from his throat to fish in his pants pocket. "And there was this note!" He handed Alex a folded piece of copy paper with words crayoned in red. *"Leave Santa Linda or Die!"*

"Talk, Miss Winter," Rudnick demanded. "Just what is going on in my motel?"

Alex stared at the paper. "I honestly don't know," she lied. She wasn't about to discuss her suspicions of Barron Dysart, who drove a black Eldorado and had already warned her to abandon the investigation of Webb's murder. Instead she asked: "Did you get the license number of the car? Did you see what the man looked like?"

"Naw, the screwball wore a big hat, and all I could see was the back of the hat when the bum drove away. I should have written down the license number, but who knew the guy was a psycho? I can tell you this: the Cadillac is the only car that's come through here today that didn't belong to our tenants."

"I see," Alex said. She'd become accustomed to the routine of the Blue Flamingo. Mr. Rudnick was a fan of C-Span and rarely left his reclining chair when "those turd-brained politicians" were holding forth on television. But his set was placed near the window so that Rudnick could keep an eye on cars coming to the motel. And he knew his tenants' vehicles by heart. "I keep track of who goes in and out," he'd told Alex. "I don't want these rooms reserved for wild parties. I give my tenants privacy and quiet."

Alex put the paper into her handbag, shifted her library books under her arm, and pulled out the motel key. "What time did you see the car?"

"Hmm." Rudnick screwed up his face in thought. "It happened when I was watching those bums in the House of Representatives gassing about the crime bill . . . at about

175

one-thirty or so." He added, "Fifteen minutes later Sabrina
went out to clean room eight and noticed the message on
your door. How could she help it? She was worried that
when you saw the rat and the knife, you'd get the holy ter-
rors. So, she threw them into the trash, which, thank God,
was just being hauled away. I had to give the poor kid the
day off. She was that upset."

"Did you call the police?"

"I didn't want to scare my other tenants. Now, I've been
good to you, Ms. Winter, letting you keep a cat because
you were quiet, and you seemed like a nice girl. But any
more trouble and . . ." he let the warning trail off. The
bright orange door to number fourteen was opening and a
colorful figure had emerged. Despite the rain, the man wore
Bermuda shorts, a Hawaiian shirt, and thongs.

"Hey," he yelled at Alex. "Is that your cat in number
thirteen?"

"Why?" Alex asked with trepidation.

"She sings along with the radio and the sound comes
right through the wall furnace. That cat's voice makes an
ambulance siren sound good."

Rudnick turned to Alex, his thick gray brows beetled into
a scowl. He opened his mouth to launch into another lec-
ture when Alex excused herself to "make sure the poor cat
is still alive." She then put her key in the door, opened it,
popped inside the studio and slammed the door behind her
in what was surely a short enough time to make the
Guiness Book of Records.

Inside the room, she leaned back against the door and
braced herself to find the results of a burglary. But a quick
search revealed the same tidy apartment she'd left behind.
It was peaceful and quiet except for Watson's machine-gun
snore, which was sawing into the radio's splendid rendition
of *Beethoven's Fifth.* Alex let out a slow breath of relief.

176

For now, the violence emanating from the library had remained outside the motel door.

She took her robe from her suitcase, hung it on the bathroom doorknob, brought her library books into the bathroom, and set them down near the tub. Alex poured in Natural Harmony Bubble Bath and turned on the hot water. She moved the cat box out of the bathroom and into the kitchen alcove where she also washed her hands, lit the pilot light on the old gas stove, and placed a wild mushroom quiche in the oven to bake.

Miss Watson awoke at the sound of the refrigerator door opening and the oven door closing. The cat padded after Alex and stalked pointedly around her bowl of kibble to indicate that it wasn't really adequate.

Alex made a face at Watson before she returned to the bathroom where steam swirled like the mist that often surrounded the beautiful Santa Linda Library . . . a library suddenly filling the local mortuary with corpses. If the Castle killer had indeed sent Alex a gruesome warning, it had been a very gentle admonition compared to the treatment dished out to Perry Webb and Claire Fraiser.

Pulling off her rain-damp clothing, Alex reflected that she'd cut her investigative teeth on Sam's teaching and advice, and the old man had rarely carried a gun. "Good cover and common sense keep a detective out of trouble," Sam had always told her. "You won't read a good operative's name in the paper, hear her voice on the radio, or see her interviewed on television. Anonymity is better protection than an Uzi—you can't shoot off your foot with it."

Sam was cautious, of course. He'd been careful to teach Alex to watch for the short-legged gait and shielding hand that indicated a suspect was protecting a weapon concealed in the waistband. She'd learned when an inappropriately heavy coat or sweater was being used to conceal the bulge of a shoulder holster, and he'd also pointed out that a quick exit was often a good defense. But Sam, in the main, had stressed that a quick mind, along with the ability to wheedle, cajole, or intimidate information out of people were the basis of an operative's success. And Sam's own success had set the pattern for an admiring Alex to follow—until now.

Now, Alex was faced with a death threat. Anonymity hadn't been an option in her quest to help Mark. And a bit of judo and karate combined with hot broccoli soup, a squirt gun full of cayenne pepper, and a perfume cap just didn't make it in terms of protection. Mark Salinger had asked Alex to help him prove his innocence, and she had no wish to be intimidated out of the job. She'd already come too far.

Alex was testing the bath water with her toe when the phone rang. It was her landlady, Kerry, on the line, with a warning that Pluto was retrograde. "You always seem to get into trouble when that happens, Alex. So be especially careful. By the way, be nice to that lover of yours."

"What lover?"

"Come on, Alex! Ross Coulter, of course. I totally approve of him. As soon as I saw you together I knew your auras would mingle. They seemed so compatible. You're both rather blue with tinges of gold."

"No kidding? You mean we're color-coordinated?" Alex was not in the mood for the omens of stars, planets, or invisible auras. But it was remarkable how Kerry often seemed to know more than she had any right to. "Kerry, when you saw Ross at my house, you said you were sorry about his wife. What was that all about?"

"Oh, he's had a terrible time. I looked in his eyes and recognized him from the television news. It was several years ago, but he has the kind of handsome face that sticks in your mind, and his wife was so lovely . . . something happened to her, I can't remember what, but I have this feeling it was awful."

"I see," Alex said, though she didn't. She began to long for the bath water. "Well, is that it? Is anything else new besides Pluto?"

"I have a hunch that Sam is flying in tonight, because he called and said so."

"Great. Please have him call me as soon as he's in, will you, Kerry?" Alex felt a bit exasperated with her landlady, but the exasperation was touched with fondness. When Alex had moved from Boston to California, escaping her memories of Charlie, it had been Kerry who'd introduced Alex to "my dear friend Sam Abromowitz." Then Alex's landlady had encouraged Sam to let Alex have a try at detective work. "Her mental planets are all in the snoopy sign of Sagittarius. And she's a bullheaded Taurus. . . . Alex will stick to a case."

By now, Ms. Watson had realized that she wouldn't get better food without a fuss. Alex tried to ignore the cat as she and Kerry said their good-byes, and this, of course, made Watson furious. She hopped onto the heater and howled for a snack until the man in the motel room next door began banging on his wall furnace. Alex swore at both of them but returned to the kitchen where she fed Watson an entire tin of sardines to purchase some peace and quiet while she sank into hot water. Like Kerry, Alex also had a hunch—a feeling that her case was about to break. She wanted time to think and relax. These few moments of calm might be her last for a while. She suspected she was coming close to Webb's murderer, and this latest threat had only underscored that suspicion.

Alex leaned over the side of the tub and picked up *Tom Sawyer*. Holding it high above the bubbles, she searched through it for a clue to Eden's whereabouts. "Listen to this," Alex called to Ms. Watson through the open bathroom door. And though Watson (apparently nose deep in fish) gave no signs of paying any attention to literature,

179

Alex read to her anyway. In an exciting passage near the end of the book, Tom Sawyer and his companion Huck Finn entered a secret passage from the river, into a huge cave. There, under a cross marked on the cave wall with candle smoke, the two boys discovered a treasure left behind by *Injun Joe*!

Alex gave a loud whoop of joy and ignored the banging on the heater that came from next door. "I knew it, Watson!" Alex exclaimed to her cat, who, having finished her fish, had come into the bathroom to bat at bubbles. "When Herbert Hamlisch was in the grocery store, he said that Eden had gone to 'Injun Joe's country ... into the bowels of the earth.' Hamlisch must have been talking about the cave across from Rosalia Island. Eden showed that cavern to Todd Hanson, because she thought it was just like the cave in this book. She and Todd called it the cave of Injun Joe!"

Alex put down *Tom Sawyer* and picked up *Exploring Santa Linda County*. "Ah ha! Not only that, Watson," Alex added in delight. "It says here that Manzanita Springs is the town closest to the state campground on Rosalia Island. And Mr. Hamlisch, bless his dear, inebriated heart, was terrified when I mentioned Manzanita. Watson, I'll bet you a fishstick that Manzanita Springs is where Eden is hiding. I don't imagine that she would be camped on Rosalia Island in the winter snow with two kids. Nope, she's likely holed up in some private, luxurious cabin with Luke Hanson, making love and making plans to leave the county—maybe even leave the country. Drat! Who could be knocking just when I'm starting to figure this all out?" Grumbling, Alex stepped out of the tub and shrugged on her robe.

"Ms. Winter? I've got to see you. I'm desperate!"

Alex recognized the voice coming through the mauve

door. "Herbie?" She opened the door and Herbert Hamlisch, his right eye blackened, the right side of his face patterned with yellow and purple bruises, fell into the room.

Chapter 20

STAGGERING PAST THE sofa bed to the kitchen, Herbert Hamlisch sank into a chair and laid his arms on the kitchen table. Alex picked up his paper bag from her doorstep, closed the door, and followed him.

"Alex," Hamlisch croaked. "I need your help."

"What happened?"

"I was attacked when I walked into my apartment." Hamlisch groaned with his head on his arms. "I kept saying I didn't know where Eden was, but those punk kids from the park wouldn't listen. They said they'd been paid to find her. By the time they gave up on me, my apartment had been torn apart, and the manuscript of my autobiography had been thrown everywhere. I know someone is looking for Eden's treasure."

"Treasure?"

The old man looked up slyly. "There's rum-raisin ice cream and cognac in the bag, dear. Could you pour us both a drink?"

"Herbie, you don't need a drink. You need a doctor."

"No!" His head came up and his eyes rolled in agitation. "Please! Just cognac and perhaps something to eat. Whatever you're cooking smells delicious."

Alex had forgotten the quiche, and she hurried to the oven. With frequent glances over her shoulder to make sure that Hamlisch wouldn't fall out of the kitchen chair, she busied herself with preparing him a meal.

The success of her effort was measured by Hamlisch's satisfied silence as he chewed carefully with the left, undamaged side of his face. Alex sat across from him, her own appetite dulled by concern—which was just as well because Herbert finished off all the food. He also drank most of the cognac.

"I do think quiche is heavy with a whole wheat crust. But this one wasn't half bad," he told Alex after a contented burp.

"Thanks." Alex was on her feet, searching through the meager store of silverware for a spoon. "What's this about Eden's treasure?"

"You must help Eden. She's in terrible danger." The old man straightened his shoulders, patted down his thin hair, and launched into a story-telling mode again. "On the night of Perry Webb's death, someone left a bottle of cognac outside my door. I went to the library like I always do, but I was very drunk and very bitter. Eden had suddenly announced that she was leaving Santa Linda, and it broke my heart, though I should have suspected it. She'd been acting strangely for weeks, ranting on about some great change in her damned fate or karma or whatever. But I was horrified when she told me she was going away with Luke Bishop! I knew that gigolo would ruin Eden and break the hearts of her children!" Hamlisch shook his head in dismay.

"What about Eden's treasure?" Alex persisted.

"I saw it when I returned to the apartment from the library, where I'd gone to do some research on my memoirs." Hamlisch offered Alex ice cream with generous flourishes. When she shook her head, he filled Watson's dish instead. "I was too sad and drunk to get much work done. Eden and I had been a team. She gave me a place to stay. She helped me with my memoirs and kept me on the wagon. I took care of the children when she was at work."

"I'm sure she was good to you, but tell me about that treasure. . . ."

There was a long pause while Hamlisch tried to gather his thoughts, gulp ice cream, and swallow cognac. At last he said, "I've always had a way with the ladies. I married two women in three months . . . wealthy, wonderful girls. Ah, those were happy times. I wined and dined them both, each on the other's money." He leered at Alex through bleared, blackened eyes.

"You mean those were happy times until you were arrested for bigamy," Alex snapped. "Let's get back to Eden and her treasure because 'she's in terrible danger.' Remember?"

"You're right, you're right! I must help Eden for the sake of her dear children. I was like their grandfather!" He paced the room in distress, then stopped near the radio and gave it a vague glance. "Did I promise you dancing lessons, Alex?"

"Mr. Hamlisch, what the hell *was* that treasure?" Alex was beginning to feel like a dog nipping at the heels of a woolly minded sheep. It certainly was hard to keep Herbie on the path of his narrative. He'd downed a good deal of cognac by now, and Alex knew from experience that it was strong stuff. She'd been fond enough of cognac in the days after Charlie left her.

"I call it treasure, but, my dear, it was junk, old books, and a painting of flowers."

"Any papers?" Alex asked, thinking of Webb's mortgage on Barron's estate.

"I don't remember papers, but I wasn't very clear-headed. I went to pieces seeing the apartment with most of Eden's things gone. I tried to talk sense to her, but she was furious with me. Not because I was drunk, but because I'd

184

seen some of the things she was stuffing into her backpack. I knew then she'd forgotten our friendship. I knew I'd never see the children again." He wiped at his eyes with a paper napkin.

"I'm sorry she's gone," Alex soothed. "But she may return from Manzanita Springs."

Hamlisch didn't seem to hear. He fiddled with the radio dials, lost in his memories. "At least she kissed me goodbye. And she said something very strange. Not to me, really, but to herself. She said she was off to bury her treasure in Injun Joe's cave and be as free as Huck Finn." Suddenly Hamlisch looked up, drunk and befuddled, his voice slurring. "But Alexandra, how did you know Eden went to Manzanita Springs, to some isolated cabin that Luke had already rented? I heard about it, but it wasn't Eden who told me. It was her little boy, Forest. Forest said his mother and Luke would live happily ever after on buried treasure. But how can Eden live on treasure that is buried?"

Alex felt a jolt of new understanding. Blackmail was the way to bury a treasure and make it pay. All you had to do was find someone who'd reimburse you to keep the treasure buried and out of sight. Was Eden blackmailing someone? Was she blackmailing Webb's killer?

Herbie's mind had wandered from his grief, distracted by the radio that was playing a lively salsa tune. "Come on, dear, I'll give you free dancing lessons. All beautiful women must learn to dance." He weaved toward her with his thin arms extended, half leaning half guiding her around with hiccupped cha cha cha's. He pushed Alex backward trying to spin her around.

Alex caught his arms and tried to dissuade him. "You've been through a terrible experience, Herbie. Why don't you rest?"

"Rest? Nonsense, Alexandra, you have to loosen up."

Hamlisch put his hand on his middle and wiggled his backside as he tried to dance backward. "Watcha me cha cha," he sang, but his voice quavered and his legs sagged. He'd danced backward into the small corner at the end of the kitchen, where he banged his head on a shelf and slumped into the same space of floor occupied by Watson's litter box.

Chapter 21

IT WAS AN exhausting process cleaning Herbert Hamlisch, not to mention the kitchen floor. Alex hauled his long limp body (clad only in boxer shorts) on to the opened sofa bed and put a blanket over him. She prepared another bath, put a frozen homemade three-cheese-and-olive pizza in the oven, and went to finish her research.

Stretched out under a new set of bubbles, she thought about what she'd learned from Hamlisch. Someone had indeed helped Hamlisch to get drunk so that he would help disrupt the library. And if Hamlisch was correct, Eden Selby had robbed Webb's office. Not only that, but she was probably using the stolen items as a form of blackmail. Finding Eden was more important than ever. Alex picked up the guidebook to read about Manzanita Springs. The resort had once been a religious center for California Indians, then a mining center for the gold seekers. These days the tiny town catered to tourists who came to ski, explore the caves, or sit in the hot springs and hot tubs. Alex made a note of resorts that featured private cabins before she turned back to *Tom Sawyer*.

She found the passages that concerned her near the end of the book, and she was engrossed in the adventures of Tom and Becky Thatcher, who were lost in Injun Joe's cave, when there was a furious rapping on the door again. "I'm coming!" Alex yelled in frustration. She dried off the bubbles and pulled and tied the robe around her. Ms. Watson scampered ahead of her, scratching at the door.

"Who is it?"

"It's Ross."

"Damn!" Alex exclaimed, looking at the nearly naked Hamlisch, who'd kicked off the blanket and lay sprawled across the bed.

"What?" came the offended voice. "You know it's raining out here."

"Okay. Okay." Alex said. "Come on in."

Opening the door, she stepped back and Ross stomped in, pulling off a wet overcoat. He patted Watson, who was so delighted that she rolled over like a dog. "Do you have anything to drink, Alex? This has been one shitty day!" He paused and looked at her robe, "Did I wake you? I'm sorry."

"I was working," Alex answered quickly. "And I'm making great progress. Now about that drink . . . I think there's a smidgen of cognac left." Her voice trailed off as Ross's gaze flicked to the man on her sofa bed. Mr. Hamlisch, active in sleep, was now lying on his back with open arms and open legs and an open mouth sputtering cognac scented snores. Ross's eyes took on their usual icy quality. His nostrils seemed to flare at the scent of spilled cognac. The sarcasm came back in spades.

"You were *working*?" Ross repeated. "Just like you were *working* with Barron? What kind of work were you doing, and how much did you charge?"

Alex's face warmed as her temper caught fire. "If it weren't for Mark Salinger, I'd throw you right out that door. Clean up your filthy mind, Ross Coulter! I was working for you. This man is—"

"Is in your be," Ross finished for her. "I don't recall that I hired you to take men to bed. So why is he there?"

188

"Because, Goddamn it, I couldn't leave a poor, old drunk passed out in Watson's litter box!"

"The litter box?" Ross turned his face away and shook his head slowly in apparent disbelief.

"Yes, I know you don't believe me but—"

"Oh, but I do believe you, Alex." Ross leaned against the heater and she realized he was trying to choke back laughter. "I'm sure you pulled this man out of . . . out of the litter box." To his credit he kept a straight face for all of five seconds. Then Hamlisch let out a huge snore causing Watson to leap from the sofa bed with a startled yowl, which, in turn, encouraged the man in number fourteen to begin banging on the heater again. Watson jumped on the heater to howl at the banging, but that only made it louder. At that point Ross could no longer contain his laughter, which raised the general decibel level even further. Alex was forced to open another can of sardines.

Ross wiped away tears of laughter. "As a defense attorney, I meet a lot of detectives in my work. But Alex . . . you are unique!"

Alex glared at him through narrowed eyes. She wasn't sure "unique" was a compliment. "I'll get you that drink," she said stiffly.

Fighting back his smile, Ross apologized, "I'm sorry. I meant to take you out to a champagne dinner and sweep you off your feet. Instead, I came here and—"

"And laughed at me."

"And laughed at you." Ross went into a sudden spasm of coughing and Alex knew he was trying hard not to laugh again. "But I brought you something . . . a present."

Alex, straining on tiptoe to reach the third and last clean glass from the cupboard above the sink, turned her head to see the glint of metal. Ross had laid a revolver, a small box of ammo, and what looked like an official document on the speckled tile of the counter. She put the glass down and picked up the gun. "A Smith and Wesson," she breathed.

"A thirty-eight," Ross concurred. "I've been worried about your squirt gun for days. When I first talked to George Stewart he assured me that you can shoot . . . is he right?"

"I've practiced at the Culver City firing range." Alex felt the substantial weight and heft of the weapon.

"Good. I've pulled a lot of strings for a special use permit within county limits."

"I'll take good care of this." Alex felt absurdly touched, the way another woman might feel receiving flowers, jewelry, or (God forbid) one of those disgusting fur coats.

Ross poured his own cognac, while Alex put the gun in her purse. "My undercover friend arrested Mr. Moore today," he said. "EZ's sitting in the police station in Manzanita right now, telling officers his story. He's admitted that he found blood-stained clothes in the bushes near the Castle and that he cut them up and planted them in Mark's car."

"That sounds like good news to me. Let me get the pizza out of the oven and get dressed. Over dinner, I'll tell you my own good news. Are you hungry? I am." It was odd, she realized suddenly, how comfortable she felt with Ross. He was overbearing and sarcastic, but so far he'd also been a great ally. And a good lover too . . . a mischievous part of her mind whispered. Alex shut up that part of her mind and put on oven mitts.

"I'll have to skip dinner." Ross sat down at the table. "I haven't had much of an appetite since Mark discovered Grace Ghiringhelli's body."

"What?" Alex almost dropped her pizza. She shoved it onto a hot pad on the table. "What are you talking about?"

The dark head shot up in surprise. "You didn't know? It's big news. Mark went to ask Grace about stolen library books. He found her dead. She'd been poisoned. A neighbor saw Mark enter the building and discovered him beside the corpse."

Alex pulled out a kitchen chair and sank into it.

Ross took another slug of cognac. "And now our innocent friend Mark is the center of a second murder investigation. Thank goodness, this time it's the Santa Linda City police who are in charge of the investigation and not that vindictive Sheriff Brody." Ross tossed off the rest of his cognac. "Thanks, I needed that drink, believe me."

"Has the post mortem been done yet?" Alex asked. "Do they know when Grace died?"

"One of the detectives told me that judging from the rigor symptoms it's likely she died this morning while Mark was still in prison. So this time the physical evidence is probably in Mark's favor. Still I don't like having him involved with another murder. It just gives the district attorney, Jenkins, more ammunition to keep his case going. And I've had more bad news today. The library page, Jamaica Polonsky, who discovered Webb's body? She's going to testify for the prosecution and repeat what she first told Sheriff Brody. When the murderer emerged into the connecting passageway of the Castle, Jamaica was sure that the person she saw was Mark Salinger. She was about to call out to him when she heard him speak in a voice that sounded like the mumbler's. Remembering the mumbler's earlier knife attack on Perry Webb, Jamaica was terrified. And in that dark, close tunnel, she fainted from fright."

"If the tunnel was dark, Jamaica couldn't be sure she saw Mark."

"You're too logical, Alex. Think of that cute, honest kid facing the jury and telling what she fully believes to be the truth. I'll tell you something. She's a much more credible witness than EZ, who is so far gone that it'll take him weeks to dry out. If the prosecution claims that EZ is lying, if they tell the jury that we made up the story about those

191

slashed clothes and paid EZ to say the words . . . Well, the jury may very well believe them. EZ's not a young man you'd associate with the truth."

"How is Mark taking all this?"

"He's more shaken than he lets on. First of all, he's known Grace for years. She was a difficult woman, he says, but always reliable. He regarded her as a close colleague, if not a friend. And he's depressed about Jamaica's testimony. Not to mention the fact that the county supervisors issued an emergency closure of the library as of tomorrow. Grace's murder was apparently the last straw."

Alex found that she'd bolted down slices of pizza without really noticing. She was upset, too. She pushed the platter aside. With unaccustomed tidiness, Alex picked up Ross's empty glass and took it to the sink. She felt restless with anger and frustration. Another murder! Why?

"Those stolen library books!" she said suddenly.

"What in the world are you talking about?" Ross came up beside her.

"Mark Salinger is a smart man." Alex began compulsively washing the quiche plates and ice-cream bowl. "I mean, think about it. Webb's office is robbed and old library books are stolen. Why in the world would any burglar—no matter how stoned or stupid—steal a bunch of discarded library books? Zoe told me today that a valuable edition of *A Child's Garden* had been stolen. Maybe that was one of the books in Webb's office."

Ross picked up a striped dish towel and began to dry a glass. "What's a valuable first-edition worth? Five hundred dollars? And they're worth a lot less with a library stamp on them. You're hardly talking about big-time crime."

"Maybe there was something hidden in the bindings—drugs, or an important paper. Maybe Webb died because he discovered some kind of scam at the used-book table.

Grace worked near that book table and took in the money. Did she die for the same reason?"

"Actually Mark had those same ideas, but I was too busy yelling at him to pay much attention. He was out investigating murder when I'd practically commanded him to stay home and avoid trouble." Ross sighed and put down the glass and towel. "I haven't been at my best today. But I did follow up Mark's suggestion to check the used-book stores, and I discovered that Scott Wilson of all people had bought up every copy of *A Child's Garden* that was available." Ross shrugged his broad shoulders. "I couldn't make any sense of it. The only thing that kept me going was my promise to myself that I'd see you tonight." His hand lightly grazed Alex's cheek. "When I found you weren't alone here, I was disappointed and jealous."

Alex began to wash dishes that were already clean. This was not the time to be so satisfied that Ross had been jealous of Hamlisch. And this was not the time to feel her skin tingle with awareness of the man beside her. She began speaking rapidly, trying to keep her mind focused on her case and not Ross's physical presence. "I've actually made several exciting discoveries, one, oddly enough, in a book by Mark Twain. Have you ever read *Tom Sawyer*? A lot of it takes place in a huge cave off the Mississippi River, which is very like a cave on the Santa Linda River, just across the island of Rosalia. And do you remember a character named Injun Joe?"

Ross didn't seem interested in Twain, Tom, or injuns. He'd turned off the water, and while he dried Alex's hands, he kissed her gently, his warm lips moving toward her ear. . . .

"And besides, what about that brunette above your fireplace?" Alex blurted in a voice that was far more cracked and wavering than a detective's should be.

Ross stiffened. He stepped back from Alex as if she'd

slapped him. "That's Niki. My wife. She was murdered over two years ago."

"Ross!" Alex touched his cold, clenched hands.

"It was when we lived in a cottage on Black Creek Road. Niki argued with a neighbor of ours. She'd decided he was abusing his dog . . . chaining the puppy to the front porch in the sun without water, beating the animal. My wife won the argument. She usually did. She even walked away with the puppy—Cyrano—though I tried to convince her that was hardly a triumph. Unfortunately, the neighbor stewed over the incident and came back to our house two weeks later. There was another argument, and this time the neighbor shot and killed Niki."

Ross was staring at Alex, but from his grim expression she knew he saw something else in his mind's eye. A wave of compassion shook her, and her arms went around him, easing the knotted tension in his muscles.

"You must miss her so terribly."

He nodded and began to talk rapidly while Alex listened, reaching up to stroke his face. The world seemed to narrow down to this harsh-voiced man who spoke about a life built and shared and lost. After awhile there was less talking.

Then Ross whispered her name against her throat, half in pain, half in passion. "Alex, I need you too damn much."

They clung together in the ugly little kitchen alcove. Watson circled around them, purring. From the sofa bed, Hamlisch's snores occasionally erupted with volcanic strength that in turn led to an angry banging on the heater from number fourteen.

Alex, her head resting on Ross's shoulder, her heart quickening to the touch of his hands beneath her robe, noticed none of it. She and Ross might have been alone in a honeymoon cottage at the ends of an enchanted earth.

Then, for the third time that night, a pounding on the door told Alex that she had yet another visitor. Flushed and startled, she pulled her loosened robe around her. Rudnick was outside demanding to know how many men she was entertaining in her motel room.

"You've got to help me," Alex whispered to the equally startled Ross. "Go to the door and tell Mr. Rudnick . . . oh, tell him anything! Wait, I've got it! Tell him that you're here to investigate the threats against me that occurred this afternoon. Keep Rudnick on the defensive—if such a thing is possible. Whatever you do don't let him see Mr. Hamlisch. I'll get dressed and help you."

Ross grabbed her shoulders. "Who threatened you?"

"It's nothing, except for the poor rat of course," Alex explained it briefly while she pushed the attorney toward the door.

"I don't call that 'nothing.' That's damn serious." But he went to cope with the increasingly boisterous Rudnick while Alex dove into her suitcase to pull out a long-sleeved shirt, black pants, and sweats. Then she fled into the bathroom.

Alex dressed quickly and tugged a brush through her tangled curls. Rudnick's voice, loud and quarrelsome, grew milder after some stern comments from Ross. Soon it sounded as if Rudnick was indeed on the defensive. By the time Alex emerged from the bathroom, the owner of the motel was sullenly defending himself for destroying "evidence."

Alex hastily searched through the studio for money and her pendant watch. She stooped to yell into the heater at her next door neighbor, telling him to "quit that damn banging." Then she grabbed the library books from the bathroom. By the time she was ready to leave, Rudnick was promising that the next time a suspicious incident occurred involving Alex's safety he would call the police immediately, and Ross was turning down an offer for a free stay at the Blue Flamingo.

"I think the hint of liability and a lawsuit may have subdued him . . . say for five minutes," Ross came back in and shut the door.

"You were terrific. Next time Mr. Rudnick comes around see if you can get him to provide me with a microwave." Alex shrugged on her quilted jacket, and pulled her prepacked overnight bag over her shoulder. "Please take care of Mr. Hamlisch for me. I can't leave him alone. Someone may try to hurt him again. And if you wouldn't mind keeping an eye on Ms. Watson for the next day or so, I'm off to do some important kibitzing."

Ross frowned at the watch around her neck. "What's all this? I'm supposed to take care of your cat and your drunk?"

Alex could hear it easily now, the intense emotions that Ross covered over with sarcasm. She'd like to stay here with him and share a little of that intensity. To fight her strong, sudden longing Alex anxiously launched into words, "Mr. Hamlisch came here after some kids broke into his apartment and beat him up. The attackers wanted information about Eden Selby and the items she stole from Webb's office. So you see, those items *are* valuable . . . maybe even valuable enough to kill for. Anyway, from what Hamlisch said, it sounds as if Eden is hiding the stolen items in that cave near Rosalia Island. And after what I read in *Tom Sawyer*—"

Ross grasped her shoulders as soon as she paused for breath. "Don't start spouting your long, nonsensical explanations at me, Alex. I know when you're trying to confuse the issue. You don't have to rush out into danger—I don't care what you read in *Tom Sawyer*, or *Huck Finn* or . . . or the *Cincinnati Telephone Directory*."

Alex took Ross's hand from her shoulder. She brushed the inside of his wrist with her lips before she let it go. "I have to get to Manzanita Springs. I have to find Eden while she's still hiding there with Luke Bishop." She watched the dark, vulnerable face, feeling presumptuous in her belief that she understood loneliness. Ross knew more about the emotion than she ever would. The love of his life was lost, and he was fiercely protective of any friendships (like Mark's) or any newer, lesser loves like Alex.

"I always knew you were trouble," Ross grumbled. "I should have run the other way when you appeared out of the mist . . . a beautiful screwball trying to save the world with the aid of a one-eyed black cat. Damn it, Alex, you're just like Niki, rushing in to rescue the lambs and never giving a thought for the wolves."

"The wolves had better watch out." Alex patted the heavy gun as she picked up her shoulder bag.

"I'm sure they're shaking with fear." Ross's sarcasm was thick again. "Look. At least take my car. And call me as soon as you're in Manzanita Springs."

"I can't take your car!"

"Yes, you can. I don't want you stuck on a damn mountain road in that ancient rattletrap of yours. So take these keys and shut up!"

She stood on tiptoe to kiss him one more time. "This case may be about to break, Ross. If I leave tonight, maybe I'll solve it before anyone else is murdered."

Chapter 22

As a speech the idea had sounded quite plausible, with a touch of the heroic. Inside the Lincoln, headed up a mountain toward God knew what kind of trouble, the idea seemed less than sane. Alex probably wouldn't arrive in Manzanita Springs till midnight, and in her hurry she hadn't taken along any coffee. A huge mistake.

The storm had died down, but everything about the empty roadway that cut its way into the silent, snow-frosted mountains was conducive to sleep. Alex longed for the irritating chain-saw snore of Ms. Watson to break up the deep, white peace and quiet. It was a good thing that the Lincoln had a tape player. Inside her shoulder bag, along with the gun, was the cassette from the library: *Gardening with Irises*. A friendly, cultured voice was soon explaining to Alex all about the propagation and identification of the Iridace floral family. She hoped the voice could keep her awake until she found a place to pull off the road for coffee.

"Irises were originally named for the Rainbow Goddess of Greece. In its wild state this flower delighted our ancestors," the friendly voice began.

The Lincoln corkscrewed steadily around the bends of the highway while the friendly voice taught Alex that "irises are grouped according to the presence or absence of their beards. Wild irises, like those found in California, and the Gulf Coast areas, are most often the star-shaped flowers of the beardless, or Apogon, variety. Most man-made hybrids with their majestic size, and their combination of upright and arched falling petals," the voice explained, "are bearded or Pogon irises. They are named for the golden upright fuzz growing along the haftlines of the flowers, across the center of their arched, falling petals."

Alex had pushed aside the idea of growing flowers for a living as soon as the Salinger case had come her way. And she realized now that calm, tranquil gardens could never satisfy her the way a tangled, messy case did. Yet, Alex still loved the irises that bloomed year after year, pushing their way toward sunshine every spring regardless of human admiration or neglect.

The voice was soon listing the best varieties in both the Apogon and Pogon groups of irises, but by now, despite her interest, the detective could barely pay attention. Even when the tape began to praise that glamorous hybrid, Eden's Legacy, better known as the Rainbow Iris, Alex didn't feel her usual, overwhelming enthusiasm. Her hands kept slipping on the wheel, and her head nodded forward. She sighed in relief when she glimpsed the neon flash of a coffee shop on the highway turn off.

On automatic pilot, Alex parked the car and grabbed her bag and the county guidebook. Then she honed in straight for the coffee counter visible through the plate-glass windows. She was so intent on a quick chemical fix that she missed the sight of the big, black car that pulled in only seconds later.

Inside the coffee shop it took two cups of coffee before Alex felt alert enough to read her county guidebook, searching for information on the caves near Rosalia Island. She'd decided to look for "Eden's treasure" even before she looked for Eden Selby. She wanted to find the cave and the heist from Webb's robbery before Eden moved it.

"Do you know anything about the caves near Rosalia Island?" she asked the waitress who was pouring her a fourth cup of coffee.

The woman had the name Leah typed on a card pinned to her dress. Her hair was dyed a wild purple-red that matched her lipstick and her long nails. She leaned forward with curiosity. "Are you a spelunker, honey? One of those people that explores caves for fun? Better you than me. This is a bad time to try your hobby. Most of the caverns are along the river. What with all the snow and rain we've had this year, the river's so high that most of those caves are full of water. By the way . . . you could get sick to the stomach just drinking black coffee. Now soup is really healthy."

To make Leah happy, Alex ordered the soup of the day. She was still strung up from the death threat on her door, the news of Grace's murder, and most of all Ross's personal revelations about his shattered life. Her emotional turmoil made it difficult for her to eat—a rare occurrence. But a contented waitress was often a talkative one, and Alex wanted Leah to talk.

When the waitress returned with the soup, a sickly looking concoction that featured strings of tough asparagus, Alex fibbed: "My friend scouted out a cave up here several days ago. She said the cave was dry and fun to explore."

Leah pursed her painted lips in thought. "You mean Joe's Cavern. But you'd have to hike in a couple of miles from Orlando Road, and the trails could be full of melting snow. Honey, you'd better see Freddy Mullen, who runs the Claim Jumper Motel." Leah wrote out the name of the motel on a page of her order pad and handed it to Alex. "Freddy has a boat, and it's easy enough to find Joe's Cavern from the water—it's straight across from the channel at

200

the southern tip of Rosalia Island with a madrone tree fallen across the entrance just like a welcome sign." Leah chuckled. "Freddy was telling me just last week that he'd taken some goofy lady to the cavern. She'd brought in all kinds of supplies and wood so she could have a big fire and practice some wacky ceremonies to placate the Indian spirits."

Alex nearly chuckled, too. Leah must be describing Eden, who was such a devotee of Indian lore. The detective was sure she was on the right track.

"See, there's a crevice in the rock near the entrance that leads through the roof of the cave up to open air," the waitress explained. "It makes for a natural chimney. The Indians built fires in that cavern and used it for ceremonies. Then there was old Miner Joe, a half-breed who lived in that cave while he panned for gold on the mountain. Even today, a person could practically move in if the NSS allowed it."

"The NSS?" Alex asked.

"The National Speleological Society," Leah said eagerly. "Oh, I know it sounds like a dirty word, but it's a nice group. They keep a trunk of emergency supplies in Joe's Cavern 'cause of all the rescuing they do. This is earthquake country, and cave passages can collapse at any time. But tourists don't want to hear about that, and we've had swarms of tourists ever since the mayor commissioned a statue of Miner Joe and put it in Joe's Cavern as an attraction. City folk go caving without hard hats, lug-soled boots, gloves, or even a good light source. Then they panic down in the dark when the rocks start to rumble, and it's the NSS that has to come to the rescue." Leah gave Alex a motherly glance. "Dear, are you prepared for caving?"

"Oh, totally!" Alex lied with enthusiasm. "How far is it to the Claim Jumper Motel, and this Freddy?"

"Take the highway north. It's just past the Rosalia turn-off on Orlando Road."

Alex left a large tip for Leah, paid for her untouched meal, and hurried to the car. She felt high on more than caffeine as the Lincoln sped toward the Claim Jumper Motel. She felt sure she was getting close to Eden's treasure. Rain began to drill the roof. The road dipped closer to the Santa Linda River, and Alex could hear the wild rush of water. Cars passed or fell behind, but Alex barely noticed any of it. Her imagination played with the treasure that Eden might have buried in Joe's Cavern. Would there be evidence against one of her many suspects, proving that one of them had killed Perry Webb? Then rain turned to wet sleet, and Alex was forced to concentrate on the icy road.

Suddenly, on a one-lane mountain-pass road twisting along a cliff face above the wild river, a car roared up behind the Lincoln. It tailed too closely, failing to pass when Alex slowed and edged to the road shoulder.

Alex pulled out and picked up speed but couldn't lose the other driver, who abruptly switched on the high beams, flooding her car with blinding light. Several dazzling seconds later, the pursuing car shot forward and moved up beside her, crowding her off the road.

Alex wrenched the wheel and rode the screeching breaks as the Lincoln slithered over the wet asphalt crowded toward the road's edge. There was an ugly squeal as the Lincoln scraped against a flimsy wooden barrier, a barrier that was all that kept the car from plunging over the side of the mountain to a deep ravine where an engorged Santa Linda River boiled up over its banks.

The car lurched out to the road again as Alex's foot slammed the gas pedal, screeching over tight corners at dangerously high speeds, but though the Lincoln was powerful, Alex couldn't shake the driver on her tail. The dazzle of the high beams still blazed in her mirror. Then, abruptly, they disappeared. Alex felt a sudden rocking. Her pursuer had pulled alongside to sideswipe her car with a crash that sent the Lincoln skidding toward the thick, looming trunk of a stocky oak.

"That bastard means to kill me!" Alex jerked the wheel over, hit the brake, and missed the trunk by inches. She sped around the curves again trying to outpace the car behind her. Sweat ran down her forehead, and her left hand was moist, sliding on the wheel as she swerved out toward the center divider to avoid being shoved off the high mountain road. Her lip bled where she'd bitten it. Approaching headlights blinded her, and she was forced back into her own lane again. She'd barely missed a head-on collision.

Muttering curses she hadn't even realized she knew, Alex steered with her left hand as her right hand hunted through her purse. Her hands touched but discarded the cellular phone. She was searching for the reassuring metal of the Smith and Wesson. She pulled off her seat belt to wrench the door open, and a slam of cold air caught her as she leaned out and fired at the lights behind her. She heard the explosion of the shot, and then the sharp, sweet sound of glass breaking.

Alex gave a sigh of relief as she fell back into the deep, cushioned seat and eased the Lincoln around a blind curve. In the rearview mirror one of the tailing headlamps was blank and dark. She leaned against the open door, preparing to shoot again, crippling the car for good.

Before she could set her aim, a flame erupted from the driver's window of the car behind her. With a tremendous thump that tossed Alex up to the padded ceiling, the Lincoln wobbled forward, dragging a flat back tire. There was a tearing, splintering smash as the car lurched through the road barrier and over the side of the cliff. Alex was hurtled forward with terrific force. She flew straight toward the flying glass of the imploding windshield ... crashing into the cushion of a billowing, inflated air bag.

The car shuddered and lurched downhill. Alex fell out the open door while the Lincoln's heavy body slid down the embankment. It plunged into the river, while Alex landed in the stinging cold of a melting snow bank. She lay there a moment, panting, spitting snow, and cursing the fact that her gun had gone down with the car. Another shot cracked through the darkness, and Alex jumped to her feet, running and sliding downhill in the path made by the car. Near the base of the ravine she tripped over a small log and took a steep, snow-buffered slide, before she turned a neat somersault to land in icy water.

Alex came to the surface of the Santa Linda River choking and sputtering. She squinted upward toward the road where the highway lamps burned with a brightness that shut out the stars. In their light, she saw the gleam of a shining black car, and she heard the sharp snap of a bullet ricocheting off water.

Alex began to remember all the prayers of childhood as she took off frantically for the opposite shore, chopping through the water with all her strength. She accomplished little besides swallowing half the river and losing her shoes and pendant watch. But the brief distance that she'd traversed placed her directly in the water's power, and she was pushed into the current that tossed her downstream.

From then on it was a constant struggle to stay atop the surface of the swiftly moving water. Alex paddled frantically, her eyes wet and stinging, her body rapidly losing feeling. She knew that she was safe from the owner of the black car, but it seemed a poor sort of safety that left her shooting through the darkness doomed to either drown or die of this bone-numbing cold.

She fought her way across the current, trying to reach the rough snags of the rocks that cropped out from the shoreline farthest from the highway. The Santa Linda River couldn't have been much more than twenty yards wide. But the drag of the current and the icy chill that stiffened her arms made the shoreline that was so tantalizingly close just about impossible to reach.

Still she flailed with determination through the whirling water. Her thrashing arms and legs pumped with all the pistonlike strength of a soggy rag doll. She went down into the swirling eddies, fought her way up, and went down again. "If I ever see you again, Ms. Watson," Alex vowed, "I'll never, ever force you to take another bath."

It wasn't long before she realized that the faster she swam toward that black line of land the farther it seemed to recede. The river was widening. But instead of despair, the realization brought hope. Her mind cleared a little. Sweet God, could she be drifting toward the channel, toward Rosalia Island?

Yes, that must be it, that hulking shape within the darkness, a finger of high rock and forested land jutting out of the water. And somewhere opposite Rosalia lay a fallen tree, the madrone that hid the entrance to a cavern. In that cave there was shelter and perhaps even warmth. *Warmth!* The dream of it propelled Alex through the water.

She flopped forward, her limbs as tough as wet paper. She swallowed more of the river. But the rush of water had eased a bit. The long spit of island broke the current into two narrow channels. The black ridge of land that formed the spit must have also run along the river bed, for abruptly the land rose and Alex found herself wallowing through shallows.

She half staggered, half crawled toward the bank across from the island. She began to let herself imagine with quite unladylike viciousness the ways she could finish off her attempted murderer—beginning with disemboweling and ending with decapitation—if she could only survive. Those thoughts kept her going until her numb fingers scraped through sandy gravel. Finally, she was standing, or rather crouching, clutching her stomach, and heaving up river water. At last she came floundering out of the river, to collapse on an outcropping of rock with all the grace of a beached whale.

She must have blacked out. There was no snow or rain when, with a soft moan, Alex returned to painful consciousness. The clouds had parted to reveal a waning moon that hung like a lamp in the dark sky. There was a gentle breeze, too, with a warm hint of spring in it. Yet, it hit the detective's shivering body with the sharpness of a razor. "It's die out on this rock or find shelter," she decided. Stiffly she came to her feet, wincing with pain.

The cuts and bruises from her descent into the river were much more evident now that she was out of the water. She tasted the warmth of blood. A gash on her cheek near her mouth was bleeding freely. But Alex kept inching forward. Soaked, frozen, and exhausted, she clambered through snow-camouflaged blackberry brambles, scrub oak, poison oak, and God knew what else.

If it had been any further, she never could have made it. But the tree was just ahead. Its twisting branches were dusted with rain-spattered snow and were clearly visible in the moonlight. She limped the last yard to the madrone's papery red trunk, and with a whoop of joy, happily fell over it.

Inside the cave, she leaned heavily against the arched rough walls, trying to control her tears of relief. She'd never have thought that an entrance down into the earth's darkness could be so miraculous, but Alex limped into Miner Joe's Cavern with all the joy of a newborn returning to the comfort of the womb.

Chapter 23

THE MOONLIGHT, STRAGGLING in through the cave's entrance, barely lit the darkness. Alex stumbled forward, shivering, one hand on the wall of the cave, the other stretched in front of her. From somewhere there came a steady dripping, the constant sound of water trickling through rock. Aside from that, there was silence, and Alex's every halting step seemed to echo into tunnels of shadow. When she banged her shin and cried out, the sound shattered, pulsing all around her.

Dropping to her knees, Alex fearfully touched the object she'd nearly tripped over. Her thumb ran lightly over a rough surface then jerked back from a pinprick of pain. A splinter! She felt a surge of energy fueled by excitement. This must be the wood pile that Leah had spoken of. Sniffing the air, she happily inhaled the fragrance of wood that had been burned to charcoal.

She inched forward, her teeth chattering. In minutes, judging from the pain, this time in her knee, she knew she'd been lucky enough to stumble into a metal trunk. Kneeling beside it, her cold, stiff fingers fumbled for the latch, only to find that the top simply lifted up and back. Alex stuck her shaking hand gingerly into the trunk and immediately closed her trembling hands around a smooth, cylindrical treasure that had been conveniently placed near the top. With the aid of the flashlight, Alex discovered that she'd found the emergency supplies left behind by the NSS. The trunk contained a first-aid kit, food, blankets, and maps describing the cave. Alex shed her wet clothes and wrapped herself in thermal blankets. Then she grasped the precious item that was just under a package of trail mix. Triumphant, she pulled out a box of matches.

Still shivering, Alex haltingly prepared a fire inside a stone-lined pit that already existed near the river wall of the cave. Kindling had been piled near the stones, and red, tinder-dry pine needles caught instantly. The flame crept up the brittle branches, and Alex sat back on her heels in relief as the fire flickered then held. She piled wood on and then just sat motionless—baking like one of her frozen dinners.

The lick of flames illuminated the cave, a deep, curved space where shining cones of stalactites dripped from the ceiling. Dark walls of stone glittered with brilliant bits of metal that Alex thought might be fool's gold. The rough walls curved into alcoves that very likely tunneled deeper into the earth. Alex reached over to throw yet another dry piece of oak on the roaring blaze. The flames shot high, extending their flickering light . . . and she gasped in shock. The light had revealed a man coming out of one of the alcoves. Ghostly silent in the firelight, he stared at Alex and into her fire with blank, dead eyes.

"Who the hell are you?" Alex snatched the piece of wood back out of the fire. She jumped painfully to her feet and shoved the burning log out toward the stranger. But he didn't flinch. He didn't even blink an eye. The man and the detective stared at one another for an entire minute before Alex's ragged breathing began to ease. She threw the wood back on the blaze, collapsing down beside it.

"Sorry if I scared you, Miner Joe," Alex apologized. "I'm glad you've been properly honored with a statue." She turned on the flashlight to examine him more closely. No wonder he'd looked so real. Some wag had fitted him out with a red jacket and an old hat and had flung a pair of chaps over his legs. Frayed leather boots had been left beside the statue—it must have been impossible to put them on Miner Joe's large feet, which were fused to a metal base.

Alex waved to Joe while munching trail mix and making a bed of the blankets she'd found in the trunk. Joe wasn't much of a conversationalist compared to the personable Watson, but then, Alex didn't have the energy to talk much. She cuddled into her blankets and continued to enjoy the lick of the flames and the heat reflecting off the rough rock walls.

Even as physical relief settled over Alex, her mind felt free to worry again. "I wonder, Miner Joe, was it Barron Dysart who forced me off the highway? Whoever it was, has he given me up for dead, or is he still looking for me? And now that I've survived, will Ross kill me once he finds out that his gorgeous car is at the bottom of the river? What about the gun, the cellular phone, my pendant watch, and the tapes and books that belonged to the library?" Worries, important and unimportant, flooded through her mind and then receded. Speculations faded. The exhausted detective slept.

Alex dreamed of the Castle, as Scott Wilson had painted it, and as she'd imagined but never seen it—surrounded by a multitude of flowers. *Ms. Watson wandered through the heavenly scene, being, as usual, an absolute nuisance. The black cat chased squirrels through a field of Marilyn's Roses, scattering full, white petals everywhere. She knocked them about, forming a perfect blizzard so that Alex could barely find her way through the garden.*

The garden became the inside of the Castle, where instead of books, Barron Dysart was stocking the shelves with pots and pots of brilliant Rainbow Irises. Ms. Watson kept batting at the yellow beards of the irises with her black velvet paws. The batted irises turned red ... blood red. Curiously this did not bother Alex as much as the fact that she kept hunting for ice cream in a refrigerator that contained only cat kibble. And she was so hungry. ...

It was hunger that woke Alex. Hunger and cold, for the fire had died. Outside it was already morning and thin echoes of the daylight filtered into the cave through the entrance. Rising stiffly to her sore feet, she checked her clothing only to find that her sweatshirt was still damp. Alex remained in her blankets, and over a leisurely breakfast of trail mix and bottled water, she mulled over the best ways to find Eden's treasure.

Sometime later, an odd figure descended the deep sloping passageway of Joe's Cavern. Clad in black sweat pants, a red jacket, bright curls tumbling from a hard hat, the figure moved clumsily in large leather boots.

"Damn!" the odd individual muttered, her eyes scanning the map she'd found in the trunk, a map that indicated miles of subterranean passages that honeycombed through earth and hollow rock. "Eden could have hidden her package of books and papers in any one of these tunnels. Joe's Cavern could easily swallow up her treasure and keep it safe from me forever."

Alex braced her flannel-clad shoulders, tilted her hat, and descended into the dank, still gloom. The flashlight feebly pierced the endless shadows of the main passageway. Dampness and the potent smell of river water grew stronger with every step forward. The tunnel undulated and narrowed but remained easy to follow until she reached a low-roofed recess where it branched out in a three-way fork.

"I'll take one path at a time, go down a ways and come back." Alex fought down the sense of searching for a needle in an abyss. She mustn't give up. She had extra batteries for the flashlight in her pocket. And surely Eden had left for herself some recognizable clue to where these items were buried.

But five minutes farther into the central passage, Alex sat down in a shell-shaped crevice and leaned her back against the rock to sigh in discouragement. The tunnel led into a circular "room," similar to the one she'd slept in last night. Stalactites glowed from the ceiling, and the dazzle of fool's gold brightened the walls. From this room, a labyrinth of thin tunnels stretched like strands from the center of a spider's web. And Alex felt like the trapped fly.

The silent, heavy air filled her with nervous fears. From somewhere close by, she could hear unstable rock clattering to the cave floor. She would give up. She would bolt from this deadly, stagnant place and head back toward the light. She would find her way to Eden and turn the woman over to the police, as a suspect in the robbery of Webb's office.

Her hat slipped off as Alex put her head in her hands. "I can't go cave crazy," she thought. "Without that treasure I've got nothing . . . not even enough proof to charge Eden with jaywalking. I'll finish exploring every inch of this room, then I'll search the other two main passages. After that, I'll let myself get discouraged." Jamming her hat back over her curls, Alex rose to her feet. She switched on the flashlight, and streaked, yellow-brown rock stared back at her. She slogged on to the next alcove before she halted in surprise.

"Holy Huck Finn!" she breathed.

There on the wall was a large cross written in candle smoke. Alex remembered reading *Tom Sawyer*, and in that famous story, the clue leading to Injun Joe's treasure had been a cross written in candle smoke. Had Eden used that same method to mark the location of *her* treasure?

Alex forced the flashlight beam down toward a heap of stones too carefully and evenly piled to have been placed there by nature. She dove into the pile, pulling up rocks like weeds, until the hollow cavern rang with the sound of stones thrown aside to strike the floor and walls. And then she felt a wonderful sensation—the smooth slick surface of a plastic bag! Hallelujah! The stones flew faster. Alex pulled out a heavily laden garbage bag and ripped that open to find yet another garbage bag and inside that an old backpack.

Then she was literally running back up the passage, tripping over her clumsy shoes, clutching the bulky backpack so tightly to her chest that it might have been filled with precious jewels.

Back in the cavern's entrance, Alex unzipped the knapsack. Her heart pounded with anticipation. A stranger might have thought that her eager fingers and bated breath were far more suited to a velvet box from Cartier than a frayed nylon backpack. But as its contents came into the glow of the flashlight, Alex gave a groan of disappointment. This was Eden's "treasure"? Why, it was only a framed watercolor and a pile of discarded library books!

Alex lit a fire and settled down to study her windfall. She propped the watercolor against several pieces of wood and examined a small portrait of irises, encased in a whitewashed frame. In the honey glow of the fire and the reflected glitter from the cave walls, the simple botanical was exquisite. Alex knew that the worth of the painting lay in Judy Garland's signature and the dated inscription on the back: "I'll think of these flowers whenever I sing about rainbows." But, iris-fancier that she was, Alex was more interested in the streams of color splashing over the arched petals and under the sunny beards of the Rainbow Iris. These flowers were Eden's "legacy," and the detective wasn't surprised that Eden had found this portrait of her legacy too beautiful to resist. Besides, according to Professor Truesdell, the painting was worth thousands.

Still, Alex was puzzled. She'd hoped for some clear clue

to Webb's murder. Instead, she'd risked her life for a damn painting and a few old books. There were three of them, and they ranged from worn volumes on public health and library management to outdated information of California agriculture.

Alex picked up each book, examining it. Unfortunately, there was nothing hidden in any of the bindings, but in a volume on public health that was a sure-fire cure for insomnia, Alex found various circled combinations of letters underlined in the Table of Contents. The "C" in Contents was circled. The "Chap" in Chapter 1 was circled, too. Page number nineteen was circled, as was page fifty-four and page five-hundred, which had a dollar sign doodled in front of it. It was followed by the number "59." These hieroglyphics, were they a code? Alex felt rather guilty asking Miner Joe about this theory, considering that he looked rather chilly without his clothing, but she had no one else to discuss her ideas with. In any case, Joe had no ideas of his own to offer.

Alex turned to the other two books. Inside a dust jacket describing an outdated work on public library management, Alex found an entirely different book. It was expensively bound in white leather and entitled *Famous Flowers for Famous Folks*. This was the history of Kate Selby and her celebrity flowers. It was the very book that Alex had been searching for in the Castle on the night that Perry Webb died. And here, inside a dust jacket entitled *Agricultural Diseases in California: Avocado Root Rot to Zucchini Brown Spot*, was actually a gilt-edged book entitled *A Child's Garden*. This was the children's book written by Kate Selby that Zoe had said was missing from the children's library. Perhaps Professor Truesdell had been right after all. "Perhaps valuable books were being stolen from the library via the used-book table. Was Webb killed because he'd discovered book thefts?" Alex asked Miner Joe.

Alex popped handfuls of trail mix and thumbed through the books. In *Famous Flowers*, she discovered a slim, ribbon bookmark and turned to it eagerly. It marked a chapter about Kate Selby's landscapes and a 1940s snapshot of a smiling teenage Judy Garland who stood next to a ramrod stiff Barron Dysart I. Behind them, a disorderly crowd of Rainbow Irises bloomed along the brick path that wound underneath a lemon arbor behind the Castle. Alex examined the photo carefully, though it was little more than a black-and-white snapshot. She was disappointed to see that those delightful rainbow flowers, so breathtaking in Garland's watercolor, here appeared blurred and muddy. Only their form, delicate and star-shaped, beardless and elegant made them memorable.

Alex slammed the book shut in frustration. She was searching for clues and proof of murder where very likely none existed. True, it was odd that these books had found their way to Webb's office, but there were valid, emotional reasons for Eden to have stolen them. Except for that agriculture book, these items were all sentimental items that involved Eden's famous grandmother and her horticultural accomplishments. This backpack probably had nothing to do with Webb's murder.

But were there more items back in the cave? After all, this pack hadn't even been deeply buried . . . just hidden under a shallow pile of rock as if Eden meant to go back for it. Perhaps the true clues to Webb's murder had been hidden separately in a safer place.

Alex stood up, shining the flashlight into a recess of the cave. The beam was steady. It didn't flicker, and she still had those extra batteries in her shirt pocket. It wouldn't hurt to take another look around. "What do you think, Miner Joe? Shall I give it another try?"

In the flicker of light, Joe seemed to give a Watsonlike wink of encouragement. The books and the painting went into the backpack and Alex slung it over one shoulder. Mark might find some meaning in all this, and she wasn't about to leave a possible clue behind.

She made much better progress down the passageway this second time. The cave had become more familiar, the map less of a challenge. She soon found the "room" where the backpack had been hidden, and without wasting much time she began exploring the tunnels that led away from it. While exploring the second tunnel which, according to the map, led up to another cave entrance in the woods, she heard voices echoing in anger.

Chapter 24

"IF YOU MISS her so much why didn't you crawl back to her, you stinking worm!" the gruff female voice shouted.

"I don't miss her, Eden, I only said she isn't—"

"A stupid bitch! Oh, I heard you, Luke! And by saying that Pamela isn't a stupid bitch, I know you mean that I am."

Turning off the flashlight, Alex stood perfectly still. She'd experienced enough arguments in her unhappy marriage to recognize a lovers' quarrel. And these two lovers at the moment meant more to her than Romeo and Juliet. These were the lovers she'd been searching for . . . Luke Bishop and Eden Selby.

"Come on, Eden, if you're going to piss in your bikini pants every time something unexpected happens, then you were fucking stupid to take up robbery and blackmail in the first place!"

"You didn't say that when I picked you up that night in the library after Pamela had kicked your ass into the dirt. Oh no, that night I was an angel, and my kids were little cherubs. . . . As for robbing Webb and using his books and paintings for blackmail, that was your idea, remember?"

"Yes, and it will make you rich as well as me. It's still the clue to Webb's murder."

Alex's mind started spinning with excitement. She had to force herself to remain still when she felt like doing a triumphant jig, or at the least, a Hamlisch-type cha cha. These books and paintings were indeed a clue to Webb's murder. She must get them safely back to Santa Linda. . . . Alex remembered that the passage she stood in led to an exit from the cave; she began edging blindly through the black shadows, down the narrowing tunnel and away from the bickering voices that echoed through the cavern.

"Doesn't it bother you to see those blankets and those smoldering coals? You know that someone's obviously been staying in here?"

"Eden, don't be such a fucking paranoid. Joe's Cavern is a way station for people on the river."

"Yes, but not in weather like this!"

The pair were arguing down the main passageway, coming into what Alex had come to think of as the treasure room. They were making better progress than Alex, who moved by inches through the darkness, trying not to disturb loose rocks in the cave walls, or on the floor at her feet.

"Luke, I'm scared we've been found out. We've got to get the kids and get away. I never should have hidden blood-tainted books in this holy place."

There was a pause in the bickering and Alex's straining ears heard the sound of a shovel, clanking into loose rocks. "They're searching for the pack," she realized. She eased herself further from them.

"Shit, it's gone! Look at the way these rocks have been tossed around! It's been stolen! I can't believe it! Couldn't you take more time to hide our meal ticket? Or were you stupid enough to think that your fucking Indian spirits would protect it?" It was Luke who was hollering now.

"Don't you dare blaspheme against the spirits. You couldn't possibly understand their power. The only stupid thing I ever did was bring you here with me. . . ." Her angry words trailed off. "Luke! Did you hear that?"

"That," of course, was Alex, who'd been slowly creeping

down the tunnel. Her tentative, exploring hands had loosened a small rain of boulders from an unstable section of the passage. A rock hit her hard hat, and another cut her cheek, but she barely noticed. She was more concerned with the rattle of the stones exploding like gunfire in the underground silence.

She held her breath, and she could feel perspiration beading her face. The loud argument had ceased. Bare, unintelligible threads of whispers reached her. These were followed by footsteps, soft but unmistakable. The lovers had patched up their quarrels to come after her. The choice was to stay still and hope she wasn't found, or to risk the noise of flight. Could she lose the bickering couple in this maze of tunnels?

Alex ran. Switching on the light, she darted down a path that grew increasingly narrow, hemming her in with protruding slabs of rock. Hearing the pair searching behind her, she plunged through the darkness, following the crazily moving beam of her own flashlight. She was hampered by her ill-fitting boots and by the unstable earth, which, when she hurtled through the passage, sometimes sent showers of rock and dirt down around her. But she raced forward, and over the echoes of her heavy tread she could hear approaching steps.

Eden and Luke had found the passageway. The clumsiness of her movements in the oversized shoes had caused enough commotion to betray her. The pair ran toward Alex with a frightening competence. In a long, fairly straight stretch, she lost ground, and their footsteps pounded closer. Ever time unstable stones tumbled to the cave floor, she could hear Eden's cries of fear and Luke's curses.

Moments later, the beam from a powerful flashlight that was not her own lit the darkness ahead of her. Alex saw it pick up the fire in a gleaming stalactite that lay in a pile of rubble at the side of the passage. A quick glance over her shoulder took in the pair behind her, with Luke ahead and Eden following with the flashlight. They were nearly upon her. Flight was hopeless. She'd have to deal with them somehow.

Then, between the pursuing footsteps, Alex heard the click. It wasn't loud, but it began a slamming in her heart. She knew she'd heard the release of the safety catch on a revolver.

Her own light revealed that the corridor stretched straight for a yard or two, then took a steep upward turn that would take her out of sight. But though safety might be only yards away, Alex knew it was impossible to reach. I can't hope to outrun a gun, she thought. I'm not faster than a speeding bullet.

Trapped, Alex whirled to face her pursuers. She flashed the beam of light in Luke's face in the desperate attempt to temporarily blind him and gain some small advantage. Luke had been lunging toward her, but the light slowed him. His handsome face was no longer cool and amused as it had been when Alex viewed him making love in the library studio. Luke's sensual mouth was pulled back tightly so that his white teeth were actually bared. He blinked fiercely into the light while his left hand went up automatically to shield his eyes.

"Give me that backpack!" he bellowed. "Give it to me or I'll shoot!" His right hand lifted, metal gleamed, and Alex saw that Luke did indeed have a weapon. Its muzzle was pointed straight at her.

A desperate scream jarred the narrow space in which Alex and Luke stood. The shriek tore around them, and Luke jumped back, startled. Alex, her eye on his gun hand, shuddered. In the horror and confusion of the moment, she thought that it had been she herself who'd screamed.

But it was Eden who was howling a protest, bolting toward Luke with her dark braids flying, her eyes narrowed and fierce. Her strong fists came up as she dropped her flashlight and pummeled Luke from behind. "Don't shoot!" she cried. "Haven't I warned you this cave is sacred? The spirits of the Indians are all around us. If you steal their peace and sanctity, they'll put a curse on us forever!"

"Get off me, you psychotic bitch! Or you'll join your damn spirits!"

Eden's hands reached him from behind, scratching, clawing, and grabbing for his revolver. "You're the one who's insane!" she shouted back. "How could you bring a gun into a holy place that people have worshipped in for centuries?"

Luke gave a frustrated, furious snarl and spun back toward her.

"Give it to me," she was shouting. "Give me that gun, before they bury us all!"

A crack echoed through the corridor as Luke's fist smacked into Eden's cheekbone. She lurched backward with a cry and fell against the side of the tunnel, sinking to the cave floor under a spattering of dirt and rock.

Luke picked up the flashlight with his left hand and flicked its light over his fallen partner, who was slowly struggling up. "Stay still," he ordered and turned to go after the hard-hatted thief, but it seemed that the passage in front of him was empty. The arc of light picked up only dull rock and the occasional glitter of fool's gold.

He stepped forward slowly, his light carefully raking the corridor. His right hand was sweaty and shaking with tension, but he kept the gun high and aimed ahead of him. A few steps forward he barked out a furious demand, "for that friggin' pack!" But his shouts returned to him, hollow in the echoing emptiness. How had the thief vanished like that?

Only two steps farther, Luke saw the clue—the path

sloped sharply down six yards or so before it swirled up a steep, twisting chimney that would have taken his quarry out of sight. He hurried toward the escape route, his heavy steps rumbling through the passageway.

Then a boulder crashed and rolled down from somewhere behind him. He heard its clatter and felt the smash of impact as the huge rock bowled into his legs, almost toppling him backward. Luke flailed his arms, crying out in pain and frustration. Then he cried out in fear. He saw the second blow coming from a sparkling, gleaming stalactite that was swung like a bludgeon to crack across his forehead. The big blond man staggered and went down. His light shone momentarily on the damn, redheaded nut with the big feet and the yellow hard hat, who'd jumped out from behind a jutting ledge of rock.

But even as Luke fell and his flashlight clattered and rolled away, the gun was still in his quaking hand. An accidental shot burst and went wild, boring into the tunnel wall. The very sound of it seemed to burst the cave apart, splitting through the still air and hollow rock with a fierce, echoing explosion.

Alex's ears rang with pain. The air vibrated around her. Parts of the unstable wall of the passage began to collapse, first in a trickle and then in a flood that seemed to shake the very floors of the cave passage. The roar of rocks became unbearable, and clouds of dirt and waves of dust choked the air. Coughing and gasping, Alex dodged through the beginning of a blinding waterfall of stones and earth cascading down to fill the passage. She shot up the twisting spiral tunnel and put a wall of rock between herself and the shifting, crumbling earth. She thought for a moment that she heard a scream filter through the crash of boulders, but she couldn't be sure. Then, after what seemed like forever, there was silence.

She moved cautiously back to the spot where the cave-in had occurred. The air was still thick with dirt and dust, and the passage was shuttered off with rock and stone. Alex feared she was looking at a grave site. Then, with relief, faintly through the rubble, she heard the two lovers screaming at each other again.

"Jesus, Eden, quit your bawling. This cave isn't safe, and we've got to get out of here. Okay, I know you've been hurt, but I'm not crying and my head was nearly bashed in!" Luke gave a loud groan.

"Of course I'm hurt, you bastard! You slammed me into those rocks! I thought you were like the loving, sensitive heroes in your books. I thought I'd finally met a real man. But it really was just fiction, wasn't it? You're just another greedy asshole who can string a bunch of words together. And you think you're so damn clever. I told you the spirits would harm anyone who shot a gun!"

"Yeah, yeah. Well, let's get away from these spirits and get the hell out of this country. Then you can spend your time in Italy helping me research my next book in the old abbeys and monasteries, where you can meet and make friends with a whole new set of ghosts."

"And what about my backpack? My grandmother's legacy? That was our ticket to Tuscany, Mr. Smartass!"

"Don't you understand? Your Indian friends took care of it for us, better than we ever could have. It's perfectly safe. Nobody knows you don't have it. And no one else will ever find it. It's buried forever. Along with that damn redhead. God, my head hurts!"

Buried forever. The words seemed to reverberate through the gritty air. Alex thought she could hear the phrase long after the cave was silent. She picked up her flashlight and hurried away on trembling legs. She knew that Luke was wrong. This passage led to the outside world. The map said so. Besides, it just had to.

She ran uphill, through the narrow passage, until a stitch bit into her side and her breath came in punishing gasps. Forced to a halting walk, she pushed on through the sliver of tunnel between the rough rock. She ducked under low archways and pulled herself up through narrow crevices of rock at a slow pace. She was tired, and she was frightened. "Pull yourself together," she warned herself. "Somewhere at the end of this rabbit hole is an exit into trees and flowers, fresh air, and above all, light."

But every time a loose rock rattled, she shuddered in fear of a landslide. With every new curve in the tunnel, she feared that she'd misread the map and that this passage led to blank walls of stone.

To distract herself from her growing phobias and the dread knotting up in her stomach, she concentrated on the load on her back. "Blood-tainted books," Eden had called them. Alex reviewed every conversation she'd had with suspects and every aspect of the paintings and the books that might relate to Perry Webb. But she came to no new knowledge.

Then the flashlight beam began to grow fainter, and Alex's heart fluttered in her chest. She had extra batteries in her pocket. She'd tested them and she knew they worked. But for how long? She turned the flashlight off to conserve its power, and struggled along in darkness. It was better to be in the dark, she told herself. That way she could easily spot any pinprick of daylight that indicated a cave exit. But her hands scraped against sharp rock. Fear dried her throat and trembled in her legs. "Take it easy, Alex, spelunkers explore these sort of passages for fun ... the half-wits." The earth, the silence, and the shadows engulfed her in the close, still air. Visions of being buried alone in blackness were beginning to overwhelm her.

Try to think of something else, anything else. Think about the Castle, the way that Scott painted it—surrounded with

arches and spillways of blossoms. Think about those Rain-
bow Irises, flowing with streaks of color.

Alex stopped in her tracks. She clapped a hand to her hard hat in excitement, then sucked at the stinging pain in her fingers. Of course . . . it was the irises! The Rainbow Irises!

The chimney of rock wound on in a series of twisting levels, and Alex clambered along it with new energy. As the passage grew steeper and twisted in on itself, Alex struggled through the jelly roll of a corridor, still frightened, but mentally finding meaning where there had only been confusion before. "I should have paid attention to how easy it was for Ms. Watson to disturb that grouch in number fourteen by yowling through the heater," Alex murmured. "Watson, why don't I listen to you more carefully?" The detective was piecing together the code in the discarded library book when she nearly walked right past the pinprick of daylight to her left.

She rushed back and jumped toward the brightness. Dropping to her knees, she scrabbled in the dirt, pulling out gravel, branches, and small stones. These were all that separated her from the cave's exit onto a wood side trail. Alex stuck her head out of the cave, blinking and brushing dirt from her eyes. She heard highway noises, a sound more enchanting than music, and she wiggled her way out of the hole and scrambled over a windfall of tangled branches. She collapsed on a fallen log and simply drank in the breeze and the damp, drizzly air. Slowly, she let her eyes adjust to the bright dazzle of the gray, cloudy day.

Chapter 25

MARK WALKED THROUGH the closed, empty Castle, though he had no business being there. He paused at the front desk where Grace had always presided. She'd had a "Shh" that was as soothing as a castor oil nightcap and a tremendous knack for striking fear in the hearts of any library patron whose books were more than a week overdue. Who had reduced the formidable Grace to a . . . a thing . . . silent, inanimate, and uncomplaining?

With a mental shake, Mark marched with determination to his office, ignoring the ghostly whispers that seemed to follow him through the building.

He would concentrate on the mysteries behind the murders plaguing the Castle. That was all he could do for poor Grace now. Somewhere in the piles of books that he had pulled for rebinding he might find *A Child's Garden*.

But a search of his office revealed no such volume, and Mark sat down in his chair, tired and temporarily stymied. He rested his hands on his chin and gazed at the wall. But the photographs and the paintings of the Castle failed to soothe him as they once had. And then Mark noticed something odd. He stared at the photos of the Castle and at Scott's painting. He took them down to compare them more closely.

"Mark, didn't you hear what I said?"

The librarian looked up to see Pamela and her son

Barron staring at him with worried gazes. "We're so happy to see you back in your office. We hope you'll be back here running things again." Pamela smiled at Mark over the top of a box of paintings. "In the meantime, we've come in to get my few things from Luke's studio in the tower."

"It seems that closing the library can't stop Mother." Barron's laugh was high and nervous. "She has her own keys. Maybe we'd better return them to you."

"If you like, you can turn them in at the Civic Center." Mark nodded vaguely then went back to examining the flowers that lined the brick path in Scott's beautiful painting.

"He's gone all absentminded," Barron whispered to his mother.

"Who can blame him, with all that's happened?" Pamela whispered back. She said, "I hope you don't mind, Mark, that we let Mr. Hanson into the library. He seemed eager to get some of his papers. He didn't want to wait for the special hours tomorrow that the county set aside for those of us with belongings in the library. I didn't want to wait either."

Mark nodded in a preoccupied fashion. It was as if he'd noticed the sparkling Rainbow Irises for the first time. He wanted to study them more carefully, but it seemed that the Dysarts were slow to say good-bye, and Todd Hanson stepped into the office to say hello.

"Mark, it's good to see you here! Have you heard what's happened?" Todd boomed in the librarian's ear. "The supervisors want to sell off part of our California history collection to Ian Yardly!"

"Hmmm," Mark replied, his attention still on the photo and painting.

"Haven't you heard of Yardly, the owner of *Books by the Yard*?" Hanson asked in disgust. "He buys books to decorate what the builders call upscale homes. Of course, the

227

rich can't have just any book in their million-dollar monstrosities. They have to have authentic antiques, and old books are the latest gimmick." Hanson's big face turned an angry red under his new beard. "He's buying our collection of the diaries of California governors for their *bindings*."

But Mark, who seemed oddly unconcerned, was dreamily quoting Thomas Hardy: "Why should this flower delay so long/To show its tremulous plumes?/Now is the time of plaintive robin-song/When flowers are in their tombs."

Todd Hanson and the Dysarts stared at one another dismayed as the strangely abstracted librarian muttered something about flowers and excused himself to head off to the microfilm room.

Alex had set off to find the highway. But on a steep upward grade her weary body rebelled. So it was some time later before she awoke in a sheltered overhang of cliff hidden by high, spreading pines. Immediately she sat up and rubbed her eyes, clutching the now precious backpack. A noise had awoken her, and she stared at the strange figure turning a bend of the trail. Alex's mouth fell open and she rubbed her eyes again.

The detective now realized she hadn't escaped from the cave unscathed. Her mind had obviously been affected by the experience. Why else would she see a willowy woman in a hot-pink jacket wafting this way, her hair pushed up under a Day-Glo turban that, in turn, was covered with a waterproof, plastic rain scarf?

"I've reached the last strand of my mental and physical rope," Alex muttered in dismay. "That can't be my landlady walking toward me in sensible hiking shoes? Kerry doesn't hike. She never even walks when she can ride, and the only travel that Kerry knows about is astral travel. I'm seeing a mirage."

"Don't worry," the mirage called out to someone behind

her. "It's all downhill from here. And I can feel the cave growing closer. It has powerful vibrations."

"It better not be far. . . ." said a man who hadn't yet emerged from the copse of bay trees. "That Alex! She's a good kid, but why can't she do her investigating in a bar, or a coffee shop, or fishing around in wastebaskets and garbage cans like other decent detectives? What's she doing in some meshuggah cave?" The second voice belonged to a man who had yet to round the bend of the trail.

But Alex recognized the dry, gravelly tone, and the considered hesitation between words was unmistakable. She couldn't have imagined that voice. "Sam?" she cried out, waving her hands. "Sam and Kerry, hello! Over here!"

"Alex!" Kerry gasped. "I can hardly believe what you look like. And those shoes! I barely recognized you!" She pecked Alex quickly on the cheek and looked her over. "Goodness, when you disguise yourself on a case you certainly are thorough. But there's blood on your face. Darling, is that a *boulder* in your hair?" Reaching into Alex's curls, Kerry pulled out a marble-sized stone.

"You found Alex? Thank God! Believe me, I can't take any more of this nature nonsense." A man picked his way around the corner of a trail, stepping gingerly over the puddles. He wore a yellow slicker, its hood just covering his distinguished silver hair. A cigar protruded from the tight-lipped, mustached mouth and jutted out beyond a grizzled square jaw. "Alex!" Sam exclaimed when he saw her. "Why are you out here, schlepping a backpack through all this unhealthy fresh air?"

"What on earth are both of you doing here?" Alex countered.

"Damn good question." Sam gazed around at the snow-dusted canopy of evergreens and gave a slight shudder. "We came up to Santa Linda this morning because Kerry was worried when you didn't answer any calls. Then that attorney, Coulter, said you were missing and put Kerry in a damned panic."

"I had visions of you buried alive under the earth." Kerry frowned at Alex's dirt-streaked face and clothing.

Sam was still staring suspiciously at the greenery. "Coulter was frantic because he had a court appointment and couldn't come to find you himself. Between his paranoia and Kerry's psychic premonitions, I was stuck. They recruited me to trail you to Manzanita Springs immediately. I flashed your photo in quite a few places. In the Gold Rush Café, a waitress remembered you and said that you'd planned to find Joe's Place, or whatever the silly cave is called. Anyway, here we are."

"I see," Alex said. Here she was with her private rescue service because Ross had been worried about her. He'd sent Kerry and Sam to find her . . . bless his overbearing, overprotective heart.

Kerry was still examining Alex critically. "I wish you would have more respect for the metaphysical, Alex. You can laugh all you want, but you look terrible. I warned you that Pluto had gone into retrograde. You know you always get in a mess when that happens. How *could* you travel at a time like that?"

"Let's talk while we get back to the Buick," Sam interjected. "This place gives me the creeps. . . . I'd take a back alley or a smoke-filled room over these gloomy woods any day." He looked down at the mud spots on his wing-tipped shoes and sighed.

Once they were settled inside the car, the detective reclined her seat and rested her weary muscles, while in the backseat, Kerry fished through her large embroidered bag for crackers, cheese, and wine.

Sam started up the Buick and sucked on his unlit cigar until Alex had finished her small meal. "Okay, Alex," he rasped. "You told Ross you were going off to solve the

Salinger case, so give me the dope on this Webb mishegoss. And I hope you're not going to waste my time with some theory. Theories in a murder case come in swarms like flies. They're as irritating as flies, too."

Alex smiled at this diatribe, which she'd heard many times before. "I'll give you facts, but I warn you, I have quite a few. Katherine Selby was a brilliant woman who did the landscaping for the Castle at Santa Linda. People come from all over the world to see her work, the lemon arbors, the arches of climbing roses, the snowy walls of clematis. . . . Kate created a paradise. She even created her own flowers. One of the most famous varieties was an iris called 'Eden's Legacy,' a flower that Barron Dysart I presented to Judy Garland. This iris was so colorful and so spectacular that it quickly became famous under the nickname Rainbow Iris. The flower's lower, dew-lapped petals were striped with bright rainbow variegations of crimson, gold, peach, cream, lavender blue, and deep purple. . . ."

Kerry piped up, "When you get through with these facts, remind me to tell you how tired I am of all the potted irises I've watered since you were gone."

Sam, irritated, sped into a curve and spun the wheel around to avoid a scenic trip over a canyon. "I ask about murder and you tell me about flowers."

"Famous flowers," Alex countered. "Beautiful flowers that caught the eye of Scott Wilson, a man with terrible mental problems and great gifts as a painter, a man who was easily exploited. Scott forged a portrait of the Rainbow Irises for Pamela Dysart and then forged the signature of Judy Garland. To make the painting even more valuable, Pamela dated it 1939. This was the year that the star played Dorothy in *The Wizard of Oz,* and the date implied that when the talented child sang 'Somewhere over the Rainbow,' she was thinking of her watercolor and its Rainbow

Irises." Alex paused a moment. "Then Pamela sold the forgery to Perry Webb."

"Aaah," Kerry and Sam exhaled the knowing sigh together as they made the connections. "Webb found out his painting was a fake, confronted Pamela, and she killed him to protect her business," Kerry mused.

"Wait a minute." Sam chomped on his cigar. "This is just conjecture. You don't actually know that the watercolor is a forgery. Right?"

"It has to be a forgery. The Rainbow Irises that Kate developed have arched, falling petals and a lovely golden fuzz called beards. In one of the library books in this backpack here, there's a vintage forties photo of Judy Garland standing near the iris blossoms at the Castle. The photo is black-and-white, but the irises in the forties photo aren't Rainbow Irises. They have an open star shape, and they sure don't have beards. Not only that, but the official name for the Rainbow Irises is 'Eden's Legacy.' I'm willing to bet that the flowers were actually named for Kate's granddaughter, Eden Selby, who wasn't even alive in 1939."

Sam chewed the facts over. "So Webb's painting was dated 1939, but there were no Rainbow Irises around in 1939 for Judy Garland to reproduce in watercolor. I'd say you're right, the Garland watercolor is a fake. So how did Webb find out that his painting was forged?"

"Kate's granddaughter, Eden Selby, went to work for Perry Webb just about the time that Webb began to complain about crimes in the library. If she saw the painting on Webb's office wall, she'd know immediately that it was forged. After all, she knew when her grandmother developed the flower."

"So Eden told Webb the truth about his forged painting. Webb confronted Pamela Dysart and threatened to expose her. Then Webb was stabbed." Sam led Alex back to her story. His dry, considered voice was now loud with enthusiasm and he zipped the Buick around the tight bends of the mountain with gusto.

Sam enjoys a good theory after all, Alex decided. She added, "There was a complication."

"Complications? Life is full of those," Kerry muttered. "Otherwise the psychic business wouldn't be booming."

"Eden wanted revenge for the way her family had been treated by the Dysarts, but she also wanted a young, handsome author named Luke Bishop. Eden simply told Webb about his forgery and told him how to obtain the library books that proved her point. But she also told Luke. He suspected that Webb's days were numbered, and he convinced Eden to steal the watercolor and books. He wanted to use them to blackmail Pamela."

Sam nodded and began to drive less erratically. "Blackmail and murder go together like scotch and water, or like chickens and soup," he agreed.

But this time it was Kerry, with her surprising shrewdness, who was the skeptic. "If Celebrity Art paintings sold for big-ticket prices, some expert must have examined them. Why weren't the forgeries discovered?"

"Professor Truesdell was an essential part of the scam. Scott forged the paintings, Pam Dysart sold them, and Clive Truesdell authenticated them."

"Now you're really off into theories," Sam protested and nearly rear-ended a Corvette in his dismay.

"Think of the money Pamela and Clive made together," Alex pointed out. "That's what this murder was about, money. Of course, the two claimed they hated each other, but that was pretense. Truesdell couldn't let anyone know that he was sharing profits with Pamela, or that he was falsely appraising paintings for the benefit of Celebrity Art. Pamela was consistently in the library on Monday nights, supposedly to be with Luke Bishop. Actually she was there to communicate with the professor who taught classes that same night. She probably talked to him on the sly, and she also wrote notes to him in discarded library books that she put on the used-book table."

Alex began explaining the markings on the public health book in her pack. It was clear to her now that the "C" and the "Chap" had been circled because they stood for the name of a painting that Celebrity Art was selling . . . the Charlie Chaplin portrait painted by Picasso in 1954. The numbers that had been circled in the book could read as 1954 and $559,000. This particular book told the professor of the supposed artist of the painting, the date that he was supposed to verify, and the price that Pamela hoped to get.

"Once they realized that they'd goofed on the Garland painting, Pamela also got rid of books that might help date the Rainbow Irises," Alex mused. "She hid them at the back of the used-book table where Truesdell could buy them. But Eden had been watching the way Pamela operated. She tipped Webb off to the stolen books, and he picked them up first." Alex's voice trailed off a moment as she thought of Grace Ghiringhelli, whose observations of the discard table had cost her her life.

Sam said, "Pamela and Clive sound like some team. Did they think they were in a spy movie, with their secret codes and this business of hiding books on the book table? They could have just used the telephone and walked out with books under their arm."

"Truesdell made some comments to me about wire taps and surveillance systems in the library. He *was* a bit paranoid. But I think that the very absurdity of anyone communicating in code via the book table also made the method attractive. Who'd have guessed it? If the pair was ever accused, who would even believe it?"

"I understand it," Kerry said. "In business, appearances are crucial. Why else would I wear this crazy turban, which is only good as a rain hat?"

"Pam and Clive were good at business," Alex agreed. "Celebrity Art was heading toward stratospheric profits. All at once, everything blew up. The bombshell was Claire Fraiser, a religious young woman who honestly tried to live a moral life. Scott was in love with her, and to capture Claire's heart, or just her attention, he confessed that he was forging paintings. Claire convinced him to quit, and to expose Celebrity Art. At the same time Webb discovered that his painting was forged, and to save their skins, the pair took to killing with the same finesse they used in business. First they killed Claire; then they framed Scott for Webb's stabbing. Finally they found they had to kill Grace, who'd seen too much from the front desk and was intelligent enough to figure out the scam." Alex could feel Sam and Kerry's full attention. Her friends understood the tragedy of murder.

She went on. "Pamela used to be an actress and she was wonderful as the betrayed lover. On the night of Webb's death, the pair set up the library for chaos. They made a fake call, for example, to get Laurel, an assistant librarian, out of the building. Then Pamela made a scene at the front desk and ran up to the study tower holding a large leather carryall, which, I imagine, held the disguise that she and Clive would need to carry out their plan. In the tower she got rid of Luke Bishop with threats. She didn't know that Luke was quite happy to go because he planned to meet Eden. They would rob Webb of his painting and of his proof that the painting was a forgery. Then they'd use the painting to blackmail Pamela.

"After Bishop left, Pamela cried and carried on until, as arranged, Clive Truesdell knocked on the door and forced his way in. Then Pamela played a tape recorded argument featuring herself and the professor. All she had to do was make sure that the quarrel was heard on the first floor of the library through the heating ducts. She knew that the argument would be a distraction—and a sensation. I was on the first floor, and I remember that the voice of Professor Truesdell was far more audible than Luke's had been when Pam threw him out of the study. I think Pamela just aimed the speaker right down the register at full blast. While the tape was running as an alibi, either one of the pair could have dressed up as the mumbler, and hurried downstairs to the microfilm room where Webb was waiting to discuss the Garland painting. The killer knocked Webb out, stabbed him, and ran through the library so witnesses 'saw' the mumbler. Then the murderer ran out the door and hid the bloody costume in the bushes. Those clothes probably belonged to Scott and were meant to be found as further evidence against him. Finally, the killer went back up the fire escape to the study tower to wait for the hue and cry."

There was a pause while all three pondered Alex's story. Then Sam broke the silence. "Mazeltov!" he said softly. "You've left only a few questions, with one of them most important. Did Pamela or Clive go down and do the dirty deed?"

Alex blushed, "I don't know," she said.

"You don't know?" Sam threw up his hands in dismay and only at a screech from Kerry did he remember he should be gripping the leather-covered steering wheel. "How could a theory-maven like you figure so much out and not know who the killer is?"

"I don't have X-ray vision and I figure one of them did it, but I don't know which one."

"Surely you have a hunch!" Kerry put in. "Or at least an eensy-weensy psychic suspicion."

"Well . . . Barron Dysart tried to keep me off the case, probably because he suspected his mother, and he feared she would disgrace the Dysart family if she was caught. Still, I suspect Truesdell. He was the knowledgeable expert, and, I'm sure, the brains behind Celebrity Art."

"Oh, Alex, women mustn't always blame men," Kerry said primly. "Though I always do," she added thoughtfully.

"Men are usually the killers in our society," Sam growled. "But in this case I'd bet on the woman."

Both the women in the car turned to stare at him. Kerry leaned forward to put her hands on the back of Alex's seat. "And why is that?"

"Where's your car, Alex?" Sam demanded. "I mean, there you were, on a muddy trail in the middle of nowhere, wearing clothes that don't fit—not to mention your shoes, kid. Ross told me you left in his car and that you were packing a Smith and Wesson service revolver. He was also surprised that you didn't call on your cellular phone. Where is everything, Alex? In the Santa Linda River?"

Her boss's power as an interrogator caught Alex by surprise. His sharp reasoning embarrassed her. She saw everything suddenly from Sam's point of view. He'd come back to L.A. only to be hauled up to Manzanita Springs to search for a missing operative named Alex. Then he'd realized that a borrowed car she'd driven on official business, had plunged into the river, along with a gun and cellular phone. Things wouldn't get better when he found out about the bugged pendant watch.

"I . . . I'm so sorry. I should have told you that I was driven off the road."

"You see?" Sam exclaimed in triumph. "Pamela is the killer. Whenever I'm run off the road, it is always by a woman!" He slammed on the brakes as he came down off the mountain and screeched to a halt before nearly hitting a stop sign.

Chapter 26

MARK EXAMINED THE Santa Linda Courier article he'd found on the microfilm. It was the article that described the painting stolen from Perry Webb's office. There it was. Judy Garland's painting was dated 1939. But that was impossible! There were no such irises in 1939. The photograph in his office was from March 1947. *There were no Rainbow Irises in that photo.* Mark tugged at his hair, trying to prick his memory. When had those lovely blossoms entered the horticultural world? As far as he could remember, the irises had been one of the last flowers that Kate had developed for the owner of the Castle, Barron Dysart I.

Continuing his search through microfilmed newspaper, the librarian came at last to a 1955 Courier article hidden in the society pages, and a grainy, microfilmed photograph showing a mature Judy Garland with a frail, elderly Kate Selby. They were smiling together over a group of irises. The article explained that these flowers had officially been named Eden's Legacy in honor of Kate's new-born granddaughter. But they'd also been presented to Judy Garland, in honor of her talent, and Garland was nicknaming them the Rainbow Irises.

Mark read the article aloud slowly. Then he suddenly turned to God with the same heartfelt words that Sherlock Holmes had used with Dr. Watson. "Ah, me!" Mark turned his eyes to heaven. "It's a wicked world, and when a clever man turns his brains to crime, it is the worst of all."

Sometime later the librarian was jotting down notes from the microfilm when a figure behind him cast a shadow over the screen. Mark turned to see the murderer staring down at him.

Alex dropped Sam and Kerry and her backpack off at their hotel. She borrowed the least exotic pair of pants and sweater that she could find in Kerry's closet, and she borrowed Sam's Buick to drive back to the library. When Sam had driven past the Castle on his way to the hotel, the sun was just breaking through the mist. Through the car window, Alex had noticed a golden shine on the dented bumper of an aged vehicle, a familiar, battered Plymouth that she knew belonged to Mark Salinger. Alex had plenty of news for her client, and she wanted to talk to him, even before she talked to Ross or Ms. Watson.

It was nearly sunset when she returned to the Castle. She parked Sam's car near the Plymouth and hurried to the staff entrance of the library. The late afternoon was chilly as always, but there was a hint of spring in the breeze. Alex knelt near a spot of ground near a clump of heavenly bamboo. A thick stem of green poked through the sodden leaves. A hyacinth would be sweetening the air soon. Alex fingered the green stem, imagining the spring that would grace the Castle.

And Mark would be there to see it. She'd make sure that the killers would be convicted and Mark would be back at his job, fighting to maintain the integrity of the library as well as the building and the grounds. The Castle would be available for people to enjoy this coming year and even the year after that. Alex straightened up, her heart light, her step quick. Then the clatter came from above, and she jumped in terror.

Damn, I'd better get over my experiences in the cave. I can't keep imagining landslides every time something falls, she thought.

She knelt to pick up a section of tile that had dropped from the roof, shattering on the edges of a balcony railing before it dropped to the path below. This was another black mark on the county supervisors who had allowed the decline of the property. So was the loose brick that Alex tripped over a second later. Swearing under her breath, she picked herself up and dusted off her slacks. Yet another tile came crashing to the walk, only inches from her head. The building seemed to be crumbling to pieces before her eyes. Alex stared up at the Castle, its rounded towers gleaming against the shadows of the fading afternoon.

Her eyes scanned the curving rooftop. It was a separate world, a dizzying confusion of tiles spiraling into ornamental turrets, stacked into towers, layered into pointed gables. Into this twisting landscape, Mark Salinger had emerged from a tower door. He walked reluctantly, his tall frame bent and stiff, and behind him came the nervous, fluttering figure of Clive Truesdell, who prodded Mark Salinger along with a gun.

Alex scrambled frantically for the shards of tile that had hit the ground moments before. She dug at the loose brick in the walkway, ignoring the stinging bite of her knuckles as they scraped against the mortar. Her hands were bleeding by the time she had the brick in her jacket pocket. Then she tore through the damp grass around from the staff entrance to the back of the Children's Room. She took a short cut over the roped-off, rotting deck near the picnic area and nearly turned her ankle on a splintering board.

She went up the metal steps of the fire escape, as quickly and quietly as she could, fearing that at any moment she'd hear a fatal shot. At the top of the steps, Alex put her sore hands around the unsteady balcony railing and made the mistake of looking down at the steep, far drop to the brick walk. She had to fight back dizziness, gritting her teeth as she clambered to the rooftop.

She came out onto a crazy red sea of tiles, turrets, and gables. Beyond the roof, the sky, too, was beginning to take on the first red tinges of sunset. Clive was some yards away, with his stoop-shouldered back to her, facing the north edge of the roof. His usually deep, rolling voice was whining. He was complaining, or "kvetching," as Sam would call it. Sam had always said that murderers were primarily "kvetchers," so immersed in their own needs that even someone else's death barely touched them. Now, it appeared that Clive's current cause for self-pity was Pamela.

"Lady Pamela has a great desire for lucre but no stomach for the type of work the filthy stuff requires." Clive grouched. "Lady Dysart wouldn't dirty her hands with Claire's blood or Perry Webb's. Oh, no, that was my job. All she would do was serve a little poison to Grace. I suppose that fit in with her grand hostess role."

Alex picked her way carefully and quietly over the brittle, deteriorating roof. She kept behind a wide, flaring gable that hid her from view.

"Even the date on the iris watercolor was Pamela's mistake! I wanted to research a proper date for a so-called Judy Garland painting, but Pamela was in a hurry to make money to keep up that estate of hers. She never really gave Luke much, you know ... just enough to keep him on a string and to keep her son worried so that he'd trade control of the estate for her funds. Pammy has wonderful head for business. She made me wealthy, but she drove me crazy."

Alex was sure that Mark had seen her. His face was beaded with sweat and locked in a frozen lack of expression. But for just an instant his dark eyes had narrowed in recognition, though he gave no other sign.

"They're a nutty family anyway," Truesdell was still

complaining. "It was Pammy's father-in-law, Barron Dysart I, who started the rumor that Garland was thinking of the Rainbow Irises when she sang in that twaddling Oz movie of hers. The idea was impossible, of course, but by then the old boy was senile or he'd never have let his conniving daughter-in-law, Pamela, cheat Katherine Selby out of her property. . . ."

Crouched under the cover of the soaring gable, Alex edged closer to the professor, taking the brick from her pocket as she eased her way toward the north end of the roof.

"Ah well, Mark," the professor sighed. "Once you've committed suicide off this roof, my bloody work will be done."

Alex was sneaking past a turret when the poorly maintained Castle betrayed her. She nearly lost her footing on an old weakened tile that broke underfoot with a loud crack.

Clive Truesdell spun around at the noise and made an exclamation of shock. Clearly, he thought he'd already finished Alex off. In an erratic, shaking movement that froze all time in the steep, red world of the rooftop, the professor raised his gun hand and took aim.

There was a hideous, breathless silence before the shot. Time crawled and shuddered to a stop. Then there was chaos. With a fluid grace and speed that Alex would never have expected, Mark Salinger dove at Clive's gun hand, trying to save both Alex and himself. Clive screamed out a warning and turned the gun toward Mark. In the same second, Alex lobbed her brick straight at the professor's head. A red gash opened up above Clive's right eyebrow. He swayed and stumbled against a winding, tiled turret. His gun wavered, and fire flashed against the darkening sky.

Smoke and cordite stung the air. Alex heard a terrible moan. Mark, his long arms flailing, his pant leg stained

242

with a spreading patch of red, collapsed and staggered backward, nearly falling over the side of the roof.

"No!" Alex screamed.

Clive wiped blood from his eyes with the back of his arm. He advanced to the edge of the roof, his trembling hand shivered upward and aimed again at Mark. As Truesdell's gun came up, Alex struck the professor with the loose tiles from the roof. The heavy missile went straight to Clive's eye, and he let out a roar of pain even as the gun exploded and Mark cried out, falling to his side, clutching his wounded leg with a bloody left hand.

Blood blinded Truesdell's right eye as he aimed the gun again, this time at Alex, who in desperate fury was throwing the smaller missiles that had filled her pockets. One must have stung Clive's battered face. The gun wobbled for an instant, and the professor staggered backward onto a crumbling stretch of rooftop. There was a frustrated shout as his feet slipped from under him. Alex saw her chance and dashed forward. She thrust her foot into his chest, putting all her remaining strength and anger into the savage kick.

Clive let out a surprised groan that sounded like a collapsing balloon. He stuck his arms out, flailing backward in a futile attempt to regain his balance. The gun clattered as it fell to the very edge of the rooftop. At the last moment Clive stretched out his long strong arms imploringly toward Alex, and his thin mouth twisted into a horrified scream as the steep, unstable tiles aided his fall off the roof.

Alex hadn't forgotten her fear of heights, but as she crouched on her knees to grab at the gun, she did risk a look over the Castle's edge. That was how she saw the gangling body of the professor tumbling downward to the picnic deck. Rotten wood splintered and cracked as the thin boards moaned and shuddered under the impact of his fall.

For an instant, the planks split apart, thrown open briefly like the covers of a man-eating book. Then they collapsed, burying Clive Truesdell beneath them.

Chapter 27

Dear Alexandra:

I read your letter, and I'm happy to know that you solved some big case and that you're being promoted to a partner. I certainly hope that's more than an empty title and actually means more money. I just can't understand why you don't go to the television studios and apply for a job doing the weather report. I know they'd take you in a second! If you came back to Boston you could take the place of our weather lady. She can't speak half as well as you, and she has a very spotty complexion!

I know I haven't written in a long while, but something happened that has upset me greatly. People have been whispering that you posed for a magazine this winter. . . . I can barely write the name of it—Playboy! Everyone is talking about it. Roberta Gimble found her husband searching for you in his old February edition. (Roberta always did have trouble with Dexter; I told you about the time he tried to lure me into the backyard at Cecily's wedding reception.)

Honestly, Alexandra, did you do it, and if you did, how could you? Couldn't you think of me for a change? I didn't even go to Bunny's funeral. Well of course I never could stand Bunny, but we were cousins, and I'd have liked to have made an appearance. Anyway, I just couldn't go and face the sly looks and the whispers about you. Can you please get a decent job so I can lead a normal life like other mothers?

Now, to speak of good news and the reason I'm writing.

Charles came by, and the dear boy told me that he'll be stopping in Malibu on his way to a Club Med vacation in Mazatlan. I know he still misses you, Alexandra. There's a catch in his voice when he speaks of you, and he as much as told me he regrets the divorce. I hope that for my sake, you'll give Charles a warm welcome. Listen to your mother, Alex, there are worse things than being a wealthy lawyer's wife—like being photographed without your clothing.

Love, Mother

Dear Alex:

Hi, doll. Did Momma Winter tell you I'd be in town April 5? Maybe we could go out and get to know each other again. I've got a great girl with me who'd just love to meet you. And there's plenty to talk about. For one thing, Babe, I have this suspicion that you're the gorgeous bod in the February issue of Playboy! Am I right? Isn't that you on the left in a brown wig and brown contact lenses? I've told this story to quite a few people, but we can't decide if it's you or not. I asked your mom, but she didn't know.

Secondly, there's that emerald broach and earrings that I gave you for our first anniversary. You know, the ones that originally belonged to my grandmother? Well, since Aunt Lois has been kind of nagging me about family heirlooms, I know you wouldn't mind returning them to the family vault. Hey, those gaudy, old-fashioned emeralds aren't the California rage, anyway. Crystals are in, aren't they? Anyway, think about it, I'm sure we can settle this, and any other matter between us, amicably. Lawsuits are so expensive and time-consuming. Catch ya later . . . as they say on the coast.

Love ya always, Charlie

Dear Charlie:

I'm devastated that I won't be able to see you on the fifth. Perhaps we can get together some other time. I'm sure you'd be proud of me, though. Having been married to you, I've learned to save my records, including the judgment that let me keep the emeralds in lieu of two house payments from you. How is my old house, by the way? I've heard it's worth a fortune by now. And I'm still waiting for the last payments that I'm owed for signing the deed over to you. So Charlie, if you're as anxious to avoid litigation as you claim, you'll quit spreading lies. I'll bet you had fun telling everyone that I posed for *Playboy*, and I'm sure you knew it wasn't true. What you probably don't know is that this time I'll fight back if I have to. So watch your ass, Charlie . . . as we say here on the coast.

By the way. I hope your dear Aunt Lois won't mind that I'm wearing those "heirloom" jewels on the fifth. Ms. Watson and I have been invited to quite a formal occasion—in a castle.

Ta Ta, Alex

The night of April 5 was unseasonably warm. The mild air was sweet with the scent of spring bulbs. Soft, white clematis cascaded in early blooms over the curved, eccentric walls of the Castle like a shower of moonlight. Far in the distance, the stars shimmered close to the top of Manzanita mountain. Alex stood at the entrance to a voluminous tent that had been set up along the brick walk, fifty yards or so from the Castle. Inside she could hear music and laughter, but it was almost a shame to step inside and leave the enchanted night behind.

A young, volunteer doorman checked her off the guest list and breathed in admiration, "You're *Alex Winter*? And this is *Watson*?"

"That's us," Alex replied. She held tightly to Watson's leash. "Could you point us in the direction of the caviar?"

The young man pumped Alex's hand before he stabbed a finger to the left. Alex saw that the tent was divided into two sections, one for the buffet, the other for dancing. Alex, knowing which section her date would prefer, resignedly headed for the buffet. Across from her, wearing tuxedos and fancy gowns, glamorous couples whirled to the sounds of a live dance band.

Alex herself wore a satiny, emerald dress with long sleeves to keep a girl warm. This, Alex supposed, was some compensation for a neckline and hemline that guaranteed pneumonia. It was quite a change from that afternoon on Media Day when she'd come to the castle in a ratty old coat and a secondhand wig. Or was it? Of course, George hadn't changed. He was still trying to pimp her seductive charms to clients. But Alex had decided that without literally holding a gun to her head, George couldn't force her into *Playboy* or into bed either. And even if he tried holding a gun, Alex just might shoot first. She was stronger now. Too strong to let George interfere with her career.

"I've been thinking about having a third partner to take over some of my L.A. jobs since I'm gone so much these days," Sam had told her. "And I like the way you handled most of the Salinger case ... except for the equipment that's still in the river. Start thinking about how you'd like to fight head to head with George as his equal."

Yes, she was a partner now. But she was still a lonely divorcée, though she'd never admit it to Mother. ... Alex turned to frown down at her date, Ms. Watson. No use trying to talk to a cat who was whisker deep in caviar. Then a tap on her bare shoulder interrupted Alex's fretting.

"What do you think of our library? We've really gone from rags to riches, haven't we?" Todd Hanson had grown a full, reddish-brown beard that nearly covered his speckled bow tie.

"Congratulations," Alex said. "I understand that you organized this affair."

"We have to do more to get money for the library than

just sell a bunch of old books! The supervisors still grumble about selling off some of our great collection to pay for repairs to the building. And I don't want Mark's fabulous collection to wind up with Ian Yardly!"

"Who is Ian Yardly?" Alex asked politely. Her question triggered Todd's description of the man, which included many words not normally printed in the books of the Santa Linda Library. Several guests who'd been shoveling fruit salad onto their plates, turned to glare at Todd with disapproval.

"Listen, Todd, maybe you'd better ease up on your comments about inferior decorators." Mark Salinger put his hand on Hanson's tuxedo-clad shoulder. Then the librarian leaned over to kiss Alex's cheek.

"You're right, of course." Todd lowered his voice to an enthusiastic shout. "I don't want to scare away money for the library roof. And as Sam Clemens would admonish me, 'Better to let people suspect you for a fool than to open your mouth and remove all doubt.' By the way, have you seen Laurel anywhere? She's used to my ranting and raving, poor woman."

"Laurel is taking dancing lessons from Herbert Hamlisch." Mark pointed to the unlikely couple.

"I'd ask you to dance," Mark told Alex when Todd had gone. "But this cane makes it difficult. Maybe I'll be dancing again in August when Todd plans to have another one of these affairs. How are you, Alex?"

"Just fine," Alex fibbed, slipping Watson a cocktail shrimp.

"I've been admiring those jewels of yours," Mark said. "But I'd be careful with them, or before you know it they'll show up in our silent auction. We've become quite shameless in our search for funds."

Alex touched her winking, glittering necklace. "I am rather grand tonight, aren't I?"

Alex felt the tap of a claw through her stocking. She knelt to the ground and put a spoonful of smoked salmon on the cat's paper plate.

There was a silence as Alex and Mark each tried to think of something cheerful to say. There were many topics that they avoided as painful. Alex didn't ask about Mark's son, who'd been arrested on drug-dealing charges. Luke Bishop and Eden Selby were two other nasty topics to avoid. They'd gone off to New York, expecting to blackmail more money from Pamela and Clive before they traveled on to Italy. It had taken awhile for the bad news to reach them that their source of funds had dried up, the professor being dead and Pamela under arrest on suspicion of murder. Stranded in New York, they'd sent a letter for help to various people, including Mark, the man they'd allowed to be charged for murder though they knew he was innocent. There was even a new scandal facing the Castle. Clive Truesdell had borrowed anatomy books from the Castle in order to discover how to properly, and quietly, stab Perry Webb. Lucy Bigelow was trying to have the books removed from circulation.

"What do you think of our new president of the Friends of the Library?" Mark suddenly broke the silence. He nodded in the direction of Stacy Dysart, who had cut in on Laurel to sweep across the room with Herbert Hamlisch. "I'm told Herbert's book received one of the largest advances in recent years. It's going to be a television miniseries. We're really quite lucky he's helping the library."

Alex smiled. "Well, it's not everyone who can prove that he was descended directly from Casanova. And when I helped Hamlisch with the manuscript, I learned that your new president had married the daughters of two Hollywood moguls. It's just a shame that he married them at the same time. I wonder if those powerful studio heads had Herbie arrested because of the bigamy or because of all the gossip their daughters told him. His wives must have talked all night and all day, judging by the number of Hollywood scandals Hamlisch reveals in his book."

"Celebrities, celebrities," murmured Mark. "What would we do without our celebrities? It seems that poor Scott Wilson is also becoming a posthumous celebrity. Apparently owning a Wilson forgery is that latest thing."

Mark and Alex were silent again, thinking of Claire and Scott. But for all the sadness surrounding Mark, Alex was glad to see the chief librarian back in his Castle. And there was good news, too. The library would stay open a good long while. Santa Linda County's budget deficit had reached a crisis, but the Castle itself had been a large beneficiary of Zoe Latham, who had donated her substantial inheritance from Perry Webb to the library. There were also rumors that she and Mark would soon announce their engagement.

Mark and Alex watched the dancers as Zoe herself swept by, in a golden gown and in the arms of Ross Coulter. Alex felt a pang that she was not entitled to feel. She and Ross had very sensibly cooled their relationship. He wasn't ready to love someone who was always going off drowning Lincolns and risking her life in crazy investigations. And Alex wasn't prepared to live under the shadow of Ross's fears that he might lose her. Yes, it had been logical to break things off.

To turn her pure, logical thoughts from Ross Coulter, Alex hurriedly spoke. "Have you ever thought of being a detective, Mark? If you ever experience a lack of moneyed celebrities and have to leave the Castle, please let me know. The pay is terrible, but you might get to pose for *Playboy* if you're lucky."

"A detective!" Mark tugged at his hair, and his eyes shone with the old enthusiasm. "Investigations! Mysteries!"

"Speaking of mysteries," Alex bent suddenly to look

under the buffet table. "Where did Watson go? Drat! Her leash must have slipped out of my hand. But she was just here a minute ago, eating salmon and shrimp and even caviar."

"Can't you keep an eye on your *amazing* cat?" Ross patted the rear end of Alex's bent form. Ms. Watson sat on his shoulder and as Alex came out from under the table, the cat gave her a knowing look. "You'll excuse us, won't you?" Ross said to Mark and to Zoe, who'd moved to stand beside the librarian. "I'd like Alex to come and investigate those Rainbow Irises that caused so much trouble."

But Alex was busy removing her emerald necklace and earrings, handing them to a surprised Mark Salinger. "These are my contribution to the Santa Linda Library. Maybe they'll help finance a new deck or roof." Alex turned again to look up at the grinning Ross. "You don't even know if the Rainbow Irises are in bloom tonight," she scolded.

"Love blooms tonight," Ross countered firmly. He linked his right arm with Alex's left elbow and forcefully escorted her toward the entrance door. With Watson following, Ross led Alex into perfumed moonlight, down the path of herringbone brick.